DEATH OF A SECOND WIFE

A DOTSY LAMB TRAVEL MYSTERY

DEATH OF A
SECOND WIFE

MARIA HUDGINS

FIVE STAR
A part of Gale, Cengage Learning

GALE
CENGAGE Learning®

Detroit • New York • San Francisco • New Haven, Conn • Waterville, Maine • London

LIBRARY OF CONGRESS CATALOGING-IN-PUBLICATION DATA

Hudgins, Maria.
  Death of a second wife / Maria Hudgins. — 1st ed.
    p. cm. — (A Dotsy Lamb travel mystery ; 4)
    ISBN 978-1-4328-2592-8 (hardcover) — ISBN 1-4328-2592-5
(hardcover) 1. Murder—Investigation—Switzerland—Fiction. I.
Title.
PS3608.U326D426 2012
813'.6—dc23   2011051004

First Edition. First Printing: June 2012.
Published in 2012 in conjunction with Tekno Books and Ed Gorman.

Printed in Mexico
1 2 3 4 5 6 7 16 15 14 13 12

For Brian and Marie Smith

CAST OF CHARACTERS (IN ORDER OF THEIR APPEARANCE)

Dotsy Lamb— College history professor from Virginia and mother of the groom.

Marco Quattrocchi— Carabinieri captain from Italy and a good friend of Dotsy.

Juergen Merz— Brother of Stephanie Lamb and owner of Chateau Merz.

Gisele Schlump— The cook.

Stephanie Lamb— Chet Lamb's wife and sister of Juergen Merz.

Babs Toomey— Mother of Erin.

Patrick Lamb— Erin's fiancé and third-born son of Dotsy and Chet Lamb.

Chet Lamb— Dotsy's ex-husband, currently married to Stephanie.

Erin Toomey— Patrick's fiancée.

Lettie Osgood— Dotsy's best friend and Patrick's godmother.

Kurt Kronenberg— Cantonal police detective in charge of the case.

Brian Lamb— First-born son of Dotsy and Chet Lamb. He works for his father.

Zoltan— Handyman who works part-time at Chateau Merz.

Sergeant Seifert— Kronenberg's assistant.

Odile Grunder— Newly hired cook.

Milo— Gisele's boyfriend.

Kelly Wheeler— Waitress at the Black Sheep Bar and at the

Edelweiss Restaurant.

Herr and Frau Eggenberger— Neighbors who share the elevator with Chateau Merz.

Anallese Gaudin— Dotsy's lawyer.

François Bolduc— Brian's spy, looking into the Merz businesses.

ONE

"Are you serious?" Marco turned his gaze from the sea to me. "You are leaving me, the Isle of Capri, this sun, this *paradise*"—he waved his arms in a big Italian gesture—"to freeze your ass off in the Alps with your *ex-husband?*"

I smiled and shrugged, maintaining my cool façade. "When you put it that way it does sound stupid." I let my feet drop from the extra chair at our table and drained the last bit of wine from my glass. From our vantage point at the top of Capri, we could see the mainland a short hydrofoil ride across the Bay of Naples. Behind us, bougainvillea cascaded over stone walls, and below us, a funicular train slid down through lemon trees to the Marina Grande at sea level. Over our heads, a yellow sun umbrella cast Marco's olive skin and graying beard in a warm glow. "I'm not going to the Alps to be with my ex-husband. I'm going for my son's wedding. The fact that I'll be staying in the same house as my ex-husband is, I'll admit, worrying me. My stomach is in knots."

"You need more wine," Marco said, signaling the waiter for two more.

"I've told myself a thousand times to relax, speak softly, and not take anything Chet or Stephanie says seriously." Chet Lamb is my ex-husband. Stephanie Lamb is the woman for whom Chet dumped me as soon as the last of our five children left the nest. Stephanie, originally from Switzerland, still had family there, and her brother owned a large chateau near LaMotte where the whole family was staying until the wedding on Thursday. My son Patrick and his fiancée had their hearts set on getting married within the shadow of the Matterhorn, where they first met. At one point in the planning of the wedding, it looked as if our whole family might be together for the first time since Brian, our oldest, left for college more than twenty years ago. In my fondest dream, we were together again: me, all five children, their three spouses, and my five grandchildren. Big turkey in the center of the table. One grandkid on my lap. Chet—or Chet and Stephanie—if there at all, were present only as shadow people. Grey outlines that couldn't talk unless you clicked on them or something. But number two son, Charlie, a high school principal, had to stay home to deal with a yellow bus accident. Anne cancelled at the last minute for no good reason, and Jeffrey, number four son, was on tour with his dance troupe. The dream, however, was still alive. Someday. I stopped talking while the waiter deposited new glasses of red wine in front of us. *Should I just ask?* Marco hadn't said so for sure, but I assumed he wanted me to come back to him for the few days I had between the wedding and my flight back to Virginia. Awkward. "I'll be free after Thursday." I peeked at him over the top of my sunglasses. "And I'll be in need of a little TLC."

"TLC?"

"Tender loving care." I couldn't break myself of the habit of using American acronyms and expressions that made no sense to this Italian man who still hadn't mastered the use of contractions.

"Aha. And you think you can come flying back to me for the TLC."

"I didn't mean . . ."

"I have to work next weekend," he cut me off. "There is no way I can leave Florence. We are having a big festival, and I will be putting extra men on duty, so I certainly must be there myself." Marco was a captain in the Carabinieri, Italy's military police. His headquarters were in Florence where we first met. Chewing a bit of lemon peel, he glanced at me and quickly away, as if to keep me from reading his mood. Was he angry or what? With Marco, I could only be sure that he intended to be enigmatic, but being enigmatic did not preclude his being angry as well. He could be both.

"Do you want me to come to Florence on Friday?"

"You may if you want, but I may not have a lot of free time."

"I'll call you Thursday night."

If you don't have a helicopter, traveling from Capri to this particular chateau in the Alps requires a minimum of five modes of transport. I'm counting the three trains as one, and I'm not counting the funicular train down to the harbor.

Early Sunday morning Marco walked as far as the pier with me and slipped a small gift-wrapped box into my hand. "This is from me to the bride and groom. Do not open it, Dotsy. I worked hard wrapping it up." *Why is Marco giving them a present?* I looked down at the small box in my hand, and the airport warning *Do not accept any parcel you have not personally packed yourself* flitted through my head. It took me a moment to recall that Marco had met Patrick in Florence last year when my son was there on spring break. They'd had lunch together, Patrick had told me.

"You didn't have to do that."

"I know. But this is something very special and rare, and I want Patrick to have it."

"My curiosity is going to kill me. Why do you always do things like this to me?"

Marco pressed his hands on either side of my face and gave me a kiss that I suspected was designed to show me what I'd be missing, ruffled my hair like he always does, and turned toward three young women sunbathing, topless, on the beach next to the marina.

The hydrofoil churned plumes of white water across the bay to Naples where I caught a cab to the train station. One train would take me to Milan, another to Visp, Switzerland, and the third to a station in LaMotte, which was as close to my destination as rail could deliver me.

On the first train, I slid into a window seat and pulled out the gift Marco had given me. It was nicely wrapped in Florentine paper and white ribbon. Tape secured both ends. I figured I could slide the ribbon off without disturbing the bow, but I'd never manage to peel off the tape without ripping the paper. *Something very special and rare.* What could it be? I hadn't expected Marco to give them a present. He wasn't invited to the wedding. I jammed the gift into my bag before temptation could get the better of me and pulled out my needlepoint.

The young woman in the aisle seat beside me said, in heavily accented English, "How beautiful! Is it in Latin?"

"Yes." I held the material, stretched in its plastic hoop, at arm's length and pointed to the phrase I had almost finished. *Amor est vitae essentia.* "It says, 'Love is the essence of life.' It's for my son and his bride. They're getting married this week." My main wedding gift to Patrick and Erin was the sterling silver flatware I inherited from my grandmother. I couldn't bring the entire silver chest with me so I planned to give them this needlepoint, suitable for framing, and a note telling them the silver was theirs. Of all my kids, Patrick was the one most likely to appreciate and use my silver. The Latin inscription, I thought, was suitable for a young couple founding a Catholic home. We raised our children in the Episcopal Church, and they had since drifted into lifestyles with varying degrees of involvement and non-involvement with the church. Patrick had shocked me when he announced his conversion to Catholicism and his intention to become a priest. He dropped that last idea after he met Erin.

In Milan I had five minutes to change trains amid a swarm of directional signs in Italian, jostling travelers and head-splitting noise. I'd never have made it without the help of the young woman who had been my seatmate. She pointed me to the train headed for Visp, and soon I was speeding toward the Swiss border and cooler climes.

From the train station in LaMotte, I tried to call the number I'd been given for Juergen Merz's chateau, several miles outside of and above the town. I checked my phone's screen and saw the signal was weak at that spot, so I grabbed my suitcase and headed for what looked like the main street of the little village. As I rounded the corner of the train station, a cold gust of Alpine air hit me head on. The jacket in my luggage, I decided, wouldn't be adequate for the time we would spend outdoors this week. I wanted a new jacket anyway. I could wait a while before I made that call and, in truth, preferred to wander this pretty little town a bit before starting my week-long marathon walking on egg shells around Chateau Merz.

I turned into the first clothing store I passed, mentally envisioning the ideal jacket that would work with the green dress I planned to wear to the wedding and with the other outfits I'd brought with me. This store sold only ski and hiking apparel, I deduced from a quick scan of the racks. Back to the street.

LaMotte had plenty of restaurants, bars, stores selling ski equipment, stores selling touristy things, but few regular clothing stores. I had almost despaired of finding one when I passed a window with female mannequins hawking designer clothes. One mannequin, silver and headless, sported a jacket with which I instantly bonded. Brown and green tweed with a cut-away collar, rounded hem, and fabric-covered buttons. I studied it, shifting this way and that until I knew for sure I wanted it and had decided on my top price. Folks passing on the street had to swerve around me, maneuvers that brought jangles from the bells on little electric cars. LaMotte allowed no petrol-burning vehicles.

A pair of Italian-made shoes paused at the next window. I recognized the shoes from a store I'd visited in Capri because they were most unusual. Cordovan leather with no visible seams but with patches of the same leather sewn haphazardly around, serving no purpose. Eighteen hundred Euros, they had wanted, for one pair of shoes! I glanced up to the face of the shoes' wearer, a nondescript man in a gabardine suit who wasn't moving along and didn't appear to be very interested in the display, either.

I entered the shop, holding the door open with my shoulder until I could muscle my wheeled suitcase through without banging the door facing. Forced to set my luggage and my purse near the wall while I tried on the jacket, I decided it was safe. This wasn't a pickpocket sort of store. Unfamiliar as I was with European sizing, the first jacket I tried was too small. An assistant located the right size for me. I would have balked at the price but the girl quickly announced this item was on sale. Half-price.

"I'll take it."

As she was ringing up the sale, I glanced around the store and steeled myself to leave as soon as she handed me the jacket. I couldn't afford anything else. But the gabardine pant legs and the Italian shoes I saw beneath and beyond a rack of blouses arrested my gaze—the shoes weren't moving and the blouses on the rack weren't shifting.

TWO

Forced to stand in the middle of the street for adequate cell phone reception, I got warning bells dinged at me twice by electric car drivers who seemed to think I should have intuited their presence. Stephanie, Chet's wife, answered with her butter-wouldn't-melt voice and I felt my stomach knot up. She told me to take a cab to a certain spot along the road where Juergen would be waiting for me. I was to tell the driver "Chateau Merz," and he would know where to go. This trip involved a lengthy climb around hairpin turns, switching back and forth as the boxy little cab whirred and whined upward and my ears popped with the changing altitude. No more than a few miles as the crow flies and, I imagined, less than a mile as the balloon rises, the trip seemed endless. How did they build houses up here? How did they lift building materials this far, and how could they work in air so thin?

The cab stopped on a curve at a spot that looked frighteningly vulnerable to oncoming traffic. A strange vehicle parked in the field to our right must have had suction cups on its wheels, I thought, given the slope. Rather like a golf cart but with extra-large wheels, it supported a seat big enough for two, a flat cargo space behind, and a canopy over all. Any little shift of the rocks under its wheels, and it would have tumbled down the slope and into the road.

A barrel-shaped man with thinning grey hair approached and introduced himself. "Juergen Merz," he said. "And you must be

15

Dotsy." He extended his hand and signaled my driver to tote
my luggage to the fence. This was Stephanie's brother. Late fifties, I'd have guessed, with a red face and heavy jaw line set on
a sagging neck. He reminded me of a former athlete now gone
to seed. I tried to imagine him in lederhosen and knee socks
rather than his current polar fleece jacket. Expecting him to
sound like an alphorn, I was startled to hear his high, reedy
voice.

Juergen waved off my attempt to pay the taxi driver and dug
into his own pocket for Swiss francs. He took my suitcase and
heaved it onto the back of his vehicle. I looked up the hill, tracing the tracks of Juergen's cart through patches of snow and
wet grass. We had a long trip ahead of us and I was glad I'd
bought that jacket. I had donned it as soon as I left the store.
Even in April, dirty ice and snow still lay under scrub conifers
and in the shade of exposed boulders. I climbed into the cart
and Juergen handed me a fur wrap for my legs.

"First trip to Switzerland?" he asked. When I nodded, he
smiled, then switched the machine on and threw it in gear. We
jerked up the hill at about three or four miles an hour, the mo-
tor of the little cart protesting as we bounced and swerved
around outcrops to the crest beyond which I couldn't see until
we were there. At that point we picked up speed alarmingly,
careening down and around, sliding on a patch of snow, up
another, even steeper slope and stopped. I gasped. As far as I
could tell, we were poised on the head of a pin with the invisible earth far below us. In every direction, nothing but blue sky.
I dared not turn my head too far because it seemed as if our
perch could be overbalanced by the slightest move.

"Beautiful, *ja?*" Juergen apparently thought I was enjoying
this. He threw out both arms in a gesture I feared would tip our
delicate balance. "This is the top of the world!"

"I'm scared." My fingers clamped on the fur leg wrap. I fixed my eyes on the floor of the cart. "Sorry, but I don't do well with heights."

Juergen chuckled and took his foot off the brake. We pitched forward and down but somehow didn't turn over. When my courage built to the point that I could look higher than my own knees, I found we had rolled into a broad sloping glen. Ahead of us, a slate roof marked the edge of another precipitous slope—assuming the roof had a house under it.

A woman popped up out of nowhere. Juergen slammed on his brake and called to her. One long blond braid hung down her back to the waist of her jeans. She carried a coil of rope over one shoulder and slung it onto the back of the cart as she approached us.

Juergen introduced us. "Dotsy Lamb, this is Gisele, our cook."

Gisele nodded and smiled. I estimated her age as mid-forties, her face somewhat weathered but her body robust and trim. "Cook, he says! Cook! And housekeeper and organizer and social planner and girl who fixes whatever is broken. I wish I had nothing to do but cook! Don't listen to him!" she glanced at Juergen and winked at me. Her accent sounded German.

"All you do is complain," Juergen chided her flirtatiously. "Shut up and hop on." He hooked his left wrist over the steering wheel and turned, waiting for Gisele to settle herself. Juergen's wristwatch seemed alive. So many wheels and things turning at the same time, it made me dizzy. Giddier than I already was.

Gisele plopped onto the back of the cart beside her rope and rode the rest of the way facing backward, her feet dangling. I wondered where she could possibly have been before she materialized, right beside us. I could have sworn there was no one around for miles.

Chateau Merz turned out to be not much smaller than a hotel. In natural wood and with porches all around, it hugged the slope in multiple levels. Flower boxes, not yet planted with summer flowers, underscored its windows and railings. The lowest level sat on a relatively flat space perhaps a half-acre deep. I was greatly relieved to see that a nocturnal ramble outside the house would not necessarily mean a plunge to one's death. Swiss mountain homes, with their gingerbread trim and natural wood, never look like mansions no matter how large they are. Instead, they tend to look like a collection of cottages, each of which might hold a cuckoo bird ready to pop from a window. Chateau Merz hugged its slope like a jumbo spill of Lincoln Logs. Inside, it smelled of cedar. Juergen ushered me in on one of the middle levels and to my first encounter with my favorite person, my replacement, the current Mrs. Lamb— Stephanie.

Stephanie had changed her hair. Now swept up and back in a clever counterpoint to the downward pull of gravity on an aging face, it made her look a bit like Cat Woman, I decided. Stephanie was only forty-eight but, like many redheads, had that thin skin that wrinkles early. She led me to a small room fitted out with twin beds and twin dressers. It was on the same level as a large, rustic dining room and an open landing that overlooked a living room strewn with cushy sofas and armchairs.

"I'm putting you next to the dining room so you won't have to worry about stairs. We do have a lot of stairs, I'm afraid."

Was Stephanie insinuating I'm too old to climb stairs? I can still dance backward in high heels. I can moonwalk, but it's been years since I was last called upon to do so. I felt the blood rush to my face in a torrent the likes of which I hadn't experienced since the last time I saw Stephanie. Hard as I tried not to take offense, Stephanie invariably peppered every comment with body slams to my ego. I was the matriarch, the dowager, the mother of everyone—including Chet. Chet, who had wisely upgraded to a newer model. I prayed for strength because I did not want anything to mar Patrick and Erin's wedding. If that meant gritting my teeth and smiling through a hailstorm of Stephanie's slings and arrows, so be it. I could do this.

"Lovely view," I said, referring to the window between the beds.

"You get first choice of beds because Lettie isn't here yet."

"I know. She'll be getting in late this evening."

Lettie Osgood, my dearest friend and Patrick's godmother, was flying from Washington to Geneva and hopping a train from there. So Lettie and I were to be roommates. That was good. I had a feeling I'd need to vent occasionally, and Lettie was a great ventee.

From below, a door slammed and Patrick's voice rose up from some obscure passage. "Is my mom here?"

I ran out to the landing and looked down. Patrick stood in the middle of the living room looking up, his arms spread wide like Romeo under Juliet's balcony. "Wait right there! Don't move!" He clattered up a flight of stairs hidden from my view, popped around a corner, and caught me up in a hug. His cheeks and hands were cold.

"Where have you been? You're freezing."

"Hiking. I walked down to the church to talk to Father Etienne, the priest who'll be marrying us. The hike back is five miles and all uphill." Patrick hugged me again, even more tightly this time. I leaned back and took a good look at his face. New glasses. His new glasses with black, squarish frames added something to his thin, pale face. Patrick's skin had always had a grey translucency that exposed every vein or the tiniest whisker. The new glasses gave his face a touch of boldness. "Let's go for a walk. Put on some better shoes first."

"Give me a minute to unpack a couple of things."

The first thing I did after Patrick left the room was pull out my now-finished needlepoint, tack it to the rectangular board

I'd brought with me, and weight it with a couple of books I found lurking under a night stand. I might need to use a steam iron on it, I thought, before I framed it. I flopped my suitcase onto one of the beds and opened it, pulling out the new dress I planned to wear to the wedding. Gossamer green wool that hung in soft folds. Protective layers of tissue paper floated to the floor as I shook it out. I slipped it onto an empty hanger and hung it from the closet door to air out.

From behind me, a soft contralto voice said, "Dotsy. You're here."

Babs Toomey, mother of the bride, stood in the doorway stating the obvious, as usual. Tall and thin with amber-red hair, Babs, like a champion Irish setter, was beautiful. None of us ever mentioned it, of course, but Babs had taken plastic surgery and collagen injections to the point of complete facial immobility. Lips with no creases, skin like wax. Add to that her habit of saying things like *you're here* to someone standing five feet away, and the result was a woman you could never feel you knew. Never offensive, never endearing either. A mannequin.

"How do you like the dress I bought for the wedding?" I asked, shaking the hem.

"It's green. Patrick told me you were wearing peach."

"The peach dress was too tight, so I bought this one." I waited for her to say something to indicate it wasn't the worst dress in the world. "You don't like it?"

"I do. It's just that my dress is green, too." Babs floated over and touched the sleeve. "But it's a small wedding in a town where nobody knows us anyway. It doesn't matter if we both wear the same color."

Wheels turned in my brain. Somewhere in my reading of the arcane literature on wedding etiquette, weighty tomes I had read before my eldest son's wedding and hadn't thought about since, there had been a suggestion (actually a sub-suggestion under the heading of Attire for Mothers of the Bride and Groom) that the matriarchs should choose dresses of a formality appropriate to the rest of the wedding. Pastels were nice, and the mothers should not wear the same color as the bridesmaids or *each other*. It was suggested that the mother of the bride had first dibs on color choice since she was the more important personage on this particular occasion.

"If you're worried about the wedding photos, there's always Photoshop. Patrick can make our dresses any color you want."

Babs gave me a blank look. "It's pretty—but with your coloring, something warmer, I'd think."

I peered around her and spotted Patrick in the doorway. I laced up my tennis shoes and headed for the hallway, pulling my son along with me. "I'm afraid I've committed a *faux pas*. Wrong color dress!"

"Don't worry about it, Mom," Patrick whispered as he pushed me down the cedar-scented hall. We exited by a door on the same level and climbed around the outside of the house, passing a porch and a small stoop. The door of the stoop led to a kitchen, I deduced, from the clatter of pans and smell of roast meat emanating from it.

"Ich sehe, was du tust! Du kannst mir nichts vormachen!"

I recognized Stephanie's voice. She sounded furious. A female voice, muffled, answered, also in German. Patrick saw the look on my face and offered a translation. "That's Stephanie. She said something like 'I know what you're up to.' "

"To whom, Gisele?"

"Probably. Pay no attention, Mom. It's not our problem."

Patrick led me along a trail eastward and around a hill where blue and yellow crocuses poked fresh heads through patches of lingering ice and snow. A cowbell clanked in the distance. On our left lay a valley peppered with spiky evergreens, and beyond, a half-dozen snow-capped peaks. The tallest one, glowing gold in the late afternoon sun, had that witch's hat tilt that could only be the Matterhorn. I gasped when I saw it. Patrick indicated a boulder on the inside of a bend in the trail and I sat, breathing in the clean Alpine air, filing this scene away in my mind to return to and savor again and again.

"Tell me about Babs," I said, taking Patrick's hand between both of mine.

"Babs will be my mother-in-law in a few days." He squinted up at a cloud and took a deep breath. I waited. "But I don't feel as if I know her. Erin's afraid of her."

"Afraid of her? Why?"

"What I mean is . . ."

I waited.

"Babs is into image. Hers and Erin's. Babs . . . has had plastic surgery . . . and other things done to her. More than once."

I laughed. "You think I don't know this?"

"Right." He grinned and clapped a hand on my shoulder. "Erin is a plain, simple girl. She's honest. Totally honest. That's what I love about her. She wears no makeup and she loves animals. She loves the outdoors. She'd rather be feeding elephants than redecorating the house." Patrick glanced at me as if to make sure I understood. Erin worked at a large Illinois zoo and spent most of her days in muddy boots. She had a master's degree in animal husbandry. "Babs says Erin is un-feminine. She's told her, more than once, she'll never get a man dressed the way she dresses."

"What does Erin say?"

"Nothing. Erin has lost her father. She's terrified of losing her mother."

"Oh, but surely she doesn't think Babs would disown her over a little thing like that."

"Erin doesn't know. How can you tell what Babs feels or thinks about anything?"

"I certainly can't. But Erin has lived her whole life with her! Surely . . ."

Patrick took his hand off my shoulder and leaned forward, his elbows digging into his knees. "Erin reminds me, sometimes, of that pathetic little monkey clinging to the wire surrogate mother. The one in all the psych books."

"That will be over soon. She can cling to you now. You're real."

"Yeah." Patrick turned to me, wrinkled his nose, and studied my face through his new glasses, as if he were seeing me clearly for the first time. "And I'm looking forward to that."

"How do you like this, Babs?" I employed one of Marco's Italian gestures to indicate contempt. "You *can* catch a man without makeup."

"So how have you been, Mom? School going okay?"

"Like everyone else, we've been slammed by the recession."

The college where I teach ancient and medieval history was on spring break until the end of the week. Patrick and Erin had scheduled their wedding to coincide with Patrick's and my own time off. "We have a hiring freeze in effect, so natural attrition has loaded up our classes to the exploding point. I've had to take on an extra section of European history and we've all been forced to take a week's unpaid sabbatical. That's why it was so easy for me to get next week off. I can go back to Florence for a few days, but my next paycheck will be microscopic."

"Sorry, Mom. This trip is a burden on you, isn't it?"

"No problem."

I diverted my eyes quickly, before Patrick had a chance to study them for clues as to whether that statement was true or not. I had already used a credit card to buy that jacket after vowing to limit myself on this trip to the cash in my wallet.

Across the meadow north of the boulder where we sat, the trail curved upward and vanished behind a pile of boulders. In the opposite direction, a dense stand of conifers cast the slope in shadow, darkening to black a few yards in, like Hansel and Gretel's forest. I glimpsed the corner of a brown structure, deep within the trees. "A gingerbread house?" I asked.

Patrick stood and shaded his eyes, peering in the direction I pointed. "Believe it or not, it's an elevator. Juergen and his neighbors have had an elevator shaft dug through the mountain. Down below, it comes out near LaMotte. On this end, it's disguised as a cutesy-poo little shack."

"So that's how you got up here from the church, you cheater! You didn't hike up, you took the lift."

"Uh-oh. Busted."

"Why didn't Stephanie tell me about this? I had to take a cab up the side of Sheer Terror Canyon."

"When we have time, I'll take you. But it's complicated the first time you do it. Finding the entrance down below without divulging where it is—you have to know where to look. They don't want just anybody using it."

I had heard the Swiss were clever, but an *elevator through a mountain?*

The landing outside my bedroom door overlooked the living room where everyone had gathered for drinks before dinner. I took in the scene from my lofty perch as I inserted and fastened my hoop earrings by feel. A real fire crackled in the stone fireplace. Upholstered furniture in a maroon plaid and a large leather armchair with a deep crater in the cushion sat angled toward big picture windows along the south side of the room.

Patrick and Babs stood at those windows with their backs to the rest of the room. They each held a wine glass. Patrick's free hand swept across the panorama outside. He pointed to something in the distance and Babs's head turned, following his finger. In profile, her face looked like a cameo.

At the fireplace, Stephanie was talking to Erin, my future daughter-in-law. Erin's slight figure, in a loose knit sweater and black slacks, stood facing the fire, her arms folded across her waist, her head down. Stephanie, by contrast, faced Erin directly, her hand on Erin's shoulder. I watched them for a minute. It seemed as if Stephanie was doing all the talking.

The third twosome in the room down below was Juergen and—who else—Chet Lamb. They each held glasses, but Chet's appeared to be an old fashioned glass with amber contents, undoubtedly his usual scotch and soda. Chet looked small from this angle. He had lost weight. His jacket hung awkwardly from drooping shoulders and his cheeks looked flabby. His eyes darted restlessly around, as if he wasn't paying attention to whatever Juergen was saying.

Ah, well. Deep breath.

It was hard not to make a grand entrance with the stairs from my little balcony leading down into the middle of the living room, and heads did turn toward me as I descended. I concentrated on not missing a step. Juergen asked what I wanted to drink and left the room to fetch it.

"Chet."

"Dotsy." He stepped forward and kissed me on the cheek. "How's school?"

I told him the same story I had told Patrick earlier and asked about his business. Chet owns a John Deere franchise in the western part of Virginia, in farming country. Our son, Brian, has now joined him in the business and, I've heard, works harder and does more actual managing than Chet does these days. Every Sunday, Brian leaves his own family and drives two hours up the Shenandoah Valley to have dinner with me. I see more of him than any of my other four children, and he's the one I imagine I'll depend on most if I live long enough to need help. Brian was to be Patrick's best man but he hadn't arrived yet.

"When will Brian get here?" I asked.

Chet took a mouthful of his drink including at least one ice cube and crunched a bit before answering. "I don't know. Stephanie probably knows." Crunch. "Tomorrow, I think."

"If only Anne and Jeffrey could be here." Anne is our youngest child and our only daughter, now living somewhere in the Bahamas on a boat or something. Anne rarely contacts me, and any address I manage to get for her is outdated by the time I get it. Jeffrey is our adopted son, now performing with a famous dance troupe. A biracial child trapped between two cultures and neglected by both dysfunctional parents, he came to us when he was seven. The day we adopted him was possibly the best day of my life. Unfortunately, Jeffrey's troupe was booked solid through the month of April so he couldn't be here.

Chet nodded in response to my comment but glanced toward the stairs as if he was distracted. His mind was on something else, I could tell.

Juergen sidled up and handed me a glass of red wine, his animated watch face dancing as his wrist turned. That's when I noticed the compass rose built into the watch's face, swiveling to keep track of north as he moved.

"I have to ask you something, Juergen," I said. "Today, when you were driving me here in that little—thing, Gisele popped up out of nowhere. It was so strange. One second, no one was around and the next second, there she was. How did she do that?"

Juergen grinned, glanced at Chet. "The bunker."

"The what?"

"The bunker. Air-raid shelter. Bomb-proof, weather-proof, impenetrable to nuclear radiation, biochemical attack, you name it." Juergen straightened his back, his chest expanding.

"They're all over Switzerland, Dotsy." Chet interjected. "The Swiss don't maintain a standing army because they are historically a neutral country."

I decided not to remind him I teach European history.

"But that doesn't mean we care to be vulnerable," Juergen said, waggling a finger at me. "With mountains protecting us all around, we're geographically insulated, but mountains don't protect you from an air attack, do they? No. So during World War II we built bunkers inside the mountains and disguised the entrances so they look like normal mountains." He gestured toward the vista beyond the room's picture windows. "But don't let that fool you. These peaks can open up in a moment and out will come more artillery—ground-to-air missiles, tanks, guns— than you could ever want to face!"

"We went through a phase in the United States," I said, "during the fifties, of building bomb shelters, stocking them with food, and putting school children through horrifying air-raid drills. We don't do that anymore."

"*Ja.* We don't either." Juergen ran a wrinkled hand through his grey hair. "After the Cold War, there didn't seem to be much point, but there they were. We had already built them and it seemed a shame not to use them for something." He tilted his head to one side. "We use ours to store ski equipment and wine."

"So that's where Gisele came from. I knew there was a simple explanation."

"But just because we keep our skis and the family silver in them now, don't get the idea that you can invade Switzerland and get away with it. We also keep artillery there."

"I wouldn't think of invading Switzerland."

"The family silver, eh?" Chet raised an eyebrow as if hinting that the bunker might be ripe pickings for theft.

"That reminds me." I set my glass down on the nearest

coaster. "I have a presentation to make." I tripped up the steps, grabbed the box I had gift-wrapped an hour ago, and returned, calling for everyone's attention.

"I think this is as good a time as any. Patrick and Erin?" They both left their conversations and moved toward me. Erin's sweater hung on her small bony frame, the sleeves covering most of her hands. Her black flats were too big for her feet, I noticed, forcing her to shuffle across the rug. "This is not exactly your wedding gift from me, but . . . well, open it. It's self-explanatory." I had intended to make a little speech welcoming Erin into the family, but I seemed to have skipped that part.

Erin, her big brown eyes wide, took the package, tore off the wrapping, looked at the needlepoint quizzically, and turned to Patrick. He lifted it and smiled. "Love is the essence of life," he said, translating from the Latin.

My face flushed, I know, for in that moment I was certain everyone in the room thought that was it. My entire gift to my son and his bride. They were all thinking, *What a piker!*

Erin read the enclosed note aloud. "The silver flatware service Grandmother Strait left to me is now yours. Sorry I couldn't bring it with me. I wish you a life of happiness. Love, Mom." Erin stepped forward and hugged me. Her body beneath the sweater felt like a little bird.

"You shouldn't have, Mom," Patrick grinned as if he, too, was glad I was to be spared the embarrassment of having presented an inadequate gift. "Wow. That's great."

I pulled the second gift from behind my back and handed it to Patrick. "This is from Marco Quattrocchi. You remember him, Patrick? From Florence?" I let my gaze sweep past Chet's face and noted the tiniest tightening of the jaw in response to that name.

Patrick slipped off the Florentine paper and handed it to Erin. He opened the box, looked in, pulled out a small note, and read it to himself. Tears welled up in Patrick's eyes and he dashed from the room.

We were all left standing awkwardly, speechless.

Erin and I looked at each other, jockeying for position. We were about to establish an important precedent. When Patrick needs a soft shoulder, whose shall it be? It had always been mine but now Erin, wife-to-be, appeared ready to throw down the gauntlet, shove me aside, and claim the spot for herself.

Incredibly, Stephanie stuck her pinched nose in before either Erin or I could react. "Since everyone else seems to be paralyzed, I'll go and see what's wrong with him."

I grabbed her by the elbow as she flew past me.

Stephanie whirled around, defiant. Her green eyes flashed.

"Patrick would prefer to be alone now, Stephanie. Trust me. I'm his mother."

Stephanie's gaze darted toward Chet, but she stayed put.

I considered this minor skirmish won by Yours Truly.

Like a long-established evening protocol, Gisele appeared on the landing above us, nodded to Juergen, then turned back toward the dining room.

"Dinner is served," Juergen announced in his high-pitched voice. "Dotsy? May I escort you to the table?" Very formal, but in this case very much appreciated. Good timing.

As I turned toward Juergen and his outstretched arm, I caught the briefest glimpse of a large shadow sweeping across the meadow beyond the living room windows.

Juergen and Stephanie sat at opposite ends of the rustic table with Chet and Erin on one side, Babs and me on the other. The dining room walls were of natural wood with big exposed beams overhead and a rough stone fireplace on one end. Casement windows along the two exterior walls looked onto a steep slope, now in shades of blue and pink with the setting of the sun.

We were all seated when Patrick slipped in and, with a self-conscious cough, seated himself between Babs and me. "Sorry I ran out like that, folks." He glanced around the table, and I noticed his nose was red. "I'm all right now."

"Super!" Juergen said, then raised his wine glass. "I'd like to propose a toast."

Gisele appeared at a door on the far end of the room. "Telephone, Steph. In the kitchen."

I happened to be looking straight at Erin at that moment, thinking about how innocent she seemed with her elfin face and big brown eyes that bulged a bit in their sockets. At Gisele's words, Erin froze. She looked across the table toward her mother and her eyes flashed cold fear.

I couldn't see Babs's face because Patrick sat between us, but I saw the wine glass in her hand shake. She quickly lowered it to the table.

Shifting my gaze to Juergen at the end of the table with his back to the crackling fire, I caught another strange reaction. His eyes darted swiftly left and right and his hands dropped to the arms of his chair. His body tense, he leaned slightly forward as if to stand up. *And follow Stephanie?* He watched his sister's retreating form as she stood and slipped past Gisele, then vanished through the doorway.

It felt as if an icy wind had blown through. I shivered. "Someone's walking on my grave," I said. All heads turned to me and I realized how that must have sounded. "Old country saying," I added.

After several seconds, Juergen repeated his last statement. "I'd like to propose a toast," he said, his voice quavering as he raised his own glass again.

"But first, I'd like to explain," Patrick interrupted.

Juergen nodded, his sparse grey hair framed by the glow from the fire behind him.

"The gift from Captain Quattrocchi overwhelmed me." He cleared his throat, reached over, and placed his hand on mine. He smiled at Erin. "I got choked up, and I do hate to cry in front of the girl I've tried to convince I'm her knight in shining armor."

We all laughed, and Erin said, a bit too loudly, "Well? What was it?"

He pulled the box from his pocket. "It's a rosary. Blessed by Pope John Paul the Second shortly before his death. Captain Quattrocchi knows how much I loved the Holy Father, and although the rosaries he blessed are now all gone—all in private hands—he gave Erin and me this one. He's had it since two thousand five and he knows he'll never be able to get another one. But he wanted me to have it." He pulled a silver and crystal rosary from the box. Some of the beads, I noticed, were emerald green; most were clear.

I couldn't wait to tell Marco how much Patrick loved his gift.

Gisele brought in a tray and lowered it onto the sideboard. On it sat seven small plates of melon slivers wrapped in thinly sliced prosciutto. I wondered about Gisele's position here. She had called Stephanie "Steph," and her interactions with Juergen seemed to range from the flirtatious to the formal. She called Chet, Babs, and me by our last names. She called me Mrs. Lamb, but Stephanie, also a Mrs. Lamb, was Steph. She served us at the table and didn't eat with us. An employee, albeit a casual one, I decided.

After we drank Juergen's toast to the new couple, Chet turned to Gisele, holding up his empty wine glass and asked for a refill.

"Oh, I forgot. I took the bottle back to the kitchen." Gisele, both hands full of starters, hesitated as if she didn't know which way to turn.

31

"I'll get it." Erin popped up and headed for the door to the stairs.

Gisele whispered, "You will need to open another bottle. It's the Chardonnay. Do you know where is the opener?" I noted her odd placement of the verb. Otherwise, Gisele's English seemed flawless.

Apparently, it's considered okay for guests to help out. Erin had been here longer than I, so I supposed she knew better than I how the Chateau Merz functioned. I couldn't help thinking Erin had another motive for volunteering and dashing off like that. Stephanie was on the phone in the kitchen.

During the main course, a lovely filet of sole poached in wine with red potatoes, Chet asked, in Juergen's general direction but in a tone that indicated anyone could answer, "With the American and European economies both in a state of flux, is this a good time to invest in U.S. interests or is Switzerland a better bet?"

Juergen lowered his fork. "Any time is a good time to invest in Switzerland. We are solid as a rock in spite of the current state of affairs. Our problem here is that we are land poor. In America you think an acre of land is nothing. Here, well! You can see! We are using every half-acre that can be tilled and have been doing so for a thousand years."

"Even your mountains," I said. "You hollow them out and put bunkers in them."

Juergen laughed, his brown eyes sparkling. "Dotsy has great curiosity, *ja?* She wants to know all about our bunkers. Where we keep our artillery."

"Mom's a spy," Patrick said, deadpan.

"In World War II, we were forced to arm ourselves in order to maintain our neutrality. Here we were. Germany to the north, Austria to the east," Juergen's hands described an imaginary map of Europe. "Italy to our south and poor old France to the west. But nobody invaded us. They would have been crazy to try it."

"The Allies would've appreciated a little help, though," Chet said.

I thought Chet's remark inappropriately argumentative for the dinner table, but Juergen ignored it. He flipped a finger past his vein-red nose. "That's why we have a law. Be prepared. Every Swiss household has a gun and ammunition. Did you know that? Our government gives every adult man between twenty-one and thirty-two years of age an M Fifty-Seven assault rifle."

Stephanie came back in and took her seat.

"Strange, isn't it?" I said. "In some countries private gun ownership is forbidden. In others, like here, it's mandatory. In the U.S., it's a perennial topic for debate. But where is the relationship between gun laws and the murder rate?"

Stephanie said, "The murder rate in Switzerland is practically non-existent if you subtract the ones committed by immigrants and foreign nationals who—let's go ahead and say it—come here for the express purpose of committing crimes." She cocked her head to one side, looked straight toward Juergen as if he were in charge of Switzerland's immigration rate.

Chet opened his mouth, then shut it.

Juergen pushed back from the table and nodded toward Gisele, stationed in the doorway. Gisele began clearing plates. "Before the Great War, they say, the German Kaiser asked us, 'What will your quarter-million Swiss do when they have to face a half-million German soldiers?' and a Swiss answered him, 'Shoot twice and go home!' "

THREE

The house phone rang again after we finished our meal. It was Lettie Osgood calling from the village below as I had done earlier in the day. Patrick volunteered to go and pick her up, and Juergen tossed him the keys to the little cart.

Chet, heading for the living room with a rather unsteady gait, caught Patrick on his way out. "You can't go just yet. Let's get . . . hey, folks, let's all go to the living room. Steph? Where is she?"

Stephanie appeared from somewhere below. This house was still a mystery to me. People popped up, down, and disappeared around corners. We all gravitated back to the living room and Chet, standing in the middle of the room, raised his arms calling us to attention.

"I have a presentation to make. That is, Stephanie and I have a presentation to make." Chet looked at Stephanie, and then held out a hand to Erin. "Come here, baby doll. You, too, Patrick." His right hand rummaged around in his jacket, and he wobbled a bit before pulling out a key on a brass ring. He paused for several seconds as if he had forgotten what he was about to say. "You two have been looking for a place to live, haven't you? Somewhere convenient to both of your places of work. And you've put down a deposit on an apartment on Stanford Street."

Patrick and Erin eyed the key.

I couldn't believe what I knew I was about to hear.

"Well!" Chet went on. "Do you remember the condo you both looked at a couple of months ago? The three-bedroom place a couple of blocks down? The one you said you liked but couldn't afford?" He held out the brass ring, jangling the key. "It's yours now. I bought it for you."

I confess that my first reaction was chagrin. I gave them silver and he gave them a *house*. Patrick and Erin smothered both Chet and Stephanie with kisses. Babs stood with her hands clasped and a perfectly smooth smile on her face. When I looked at Juergen, I caught him looking at me. He smiled and nodded. Was that sympathy I saw in his smile? I sincerely hoped not.

Patrick grabbed his coat and left to pick up Lettie. Juergen offered brandy or coffee to the rest of us. While we were listening to Chet's presentation, Gisele had set a coffee pot and cups near the brandy decanter on a side table.

"Thank you," I said, "but I think I'll go for a little walk."

"Be careful, Dotsy. You don't know these hills yet so don't go too far," Juergen said, pouring a cup of coffee.

I promised I would be careful, then climbed the stairs to my room. I grabbed my new jacket off the bed and spotted the price tag and the little envelope with an extra button and matching thread still dangling from the sleeve. I'd been wearing it like that all afternoon. Snapping the plastic thread, I pulled on the jacket and put the envelope on top of the dresser. In the mirror, I studied my own face and deliberately brightened my expression, reminding myself how much easier Patrick and Erin's new life would be with no rent or mortgage payment. It shouldn't matter to me who gave them the condo or how it compared to my now-paltry-looking gift. Nothing but foolish pride on my part. I ran a brush through my hair and freshened my lipstick. *Now. How do I get out of this house? Must I go through the living room or is there an outside door on this floor?*

On the far side of the dining room I discovered that the door

Gisele used while serving our dinner led to a descending staircase on the right and straight ahead to an exterior door. Clanging pots and clinking glassware told me the kitchen was at the bottom of those stairs. I tried the door and it opened with a loud pop.

I felt a tap on my shoulder. Juergen held out a flashlight to me. "You don't know these hills yet, Dotsy. Take this and watch your step."

"Thank you, Juergen." I was touched by the concern I saw in his face. "I'll be careful."

"Keep it in your room. We have plenty of flashlights."

The cold night air felt good when it hit my face. I trudged up the slope and around the back of the house, keeping the beam of my light on the ground a few feet ahead of me. As I passed the dining room windows, I peered in. The fire had died down and now cast a faint red glow against the walls. Across the meadow, maybe a hundred yards beyond the house, lay the bunker, masquerading as a sheer rock cliff. Tomorrow, I decided, I'd ask Juergen or Gisele to take me into it. Would I find anything left from World War II? I imagined ammo belts and saucer-shaped helmets. Machine guns mounted on tripods. I recalled my visit to Winston Churchill's war rooms with their bomb-proof concrete walls under the streets of London.

I stepped around and over rocks along the west side of the house where, looking up, I saw lights aglow in my room and in Babs's but both rooms appeared vacant. My beam found a comfortable-looking boulder and I sat, just out of view from the living room, the light from its picture windows slanting yellow rectangles onto the meadow south of the house. The air smelled of green cedar. A few stars were out—not many—telling me it might be clouding over. The hulk of the Matterhorn loomed darkly in the east, beyond the lights of a little village. So peaceful. Such a contrast to the tension inside that house. Could I be imagining it? I didn't think so. Several times during dinner I had felt the room was about to explode.

Continuing my circuit of the house, I passed the living room with its long porch outside the picture windows. Juergen stood on the porch, gazing up at the heavens, his hands braced against the porch railing. On a lower level, jutting out from under the living room at an angle, a large indoor swimming pool glowed blue from recessed lights beneath its glass-smooth surface.

Climbing the steep slope on the east side, I glimpsed a dark form ahead. A man, his head bent forward, loped eastward and slipped around the hill. It was Chet. I could tell by his walk. *Where was he going, all alone?* It was after ten o'clock.

I passed the kitchen door and paused.

Angry voices punched through the screen of an open window. Women's voices, I thought, although I couldn't make out whose. A croak, as if from pain. A keening whine. No sound at all for a minute.

Then, quite loud, Stephanie's voice boomed. "If you don't tell him, I will! I swear I will!"

I joined Juergen in the living room and poured myself a cup of coffee, now lukewarm in the pot. He sat in the big leather chair with his laptop computer on his knees and his feet on an ottoman. As I walked behind him, I saw he was studying an online star chart. He looked up and smiled at me. From his casual demeanor I concluded that the angry words from the kitchen hadn't reached his ears.

"Is astronomy your hobby?" I asked.

"My passion," he said. "That's the main reason I keep this house here. It's inconvenient as hell to get here from my home in Zurich, but with the altitude—the stars! Tonight is not so good with the clouds rolling in. But if we get a nice clear night while you're here, I'll show you things you've never seen before!"

I smiled innocently, not wishing him to think I had a dirty mind. He seemed to blush a little.

"What are your plans for tomorrow?" he asked, pausing his fingers above the keyboard.

"I don't have any, really, but I think Lettie Osgood and I will probably do a bit of sightseeing. I want to see the church where the kids will be getting married, and I'm sure there will be other things to see in LaMotte."

"I'll show you a faster way to get there. Let me know when you want to go."

"Does it involve the elevator Patrick told me about today?"

"Damn him. I like to keep it a surprise."

Babs descended the stairs from the landing. "I'm trying to adjust the hem on Erin's wedding gown," she said, folding herself into one end of a sofa. "It's a bit long, and I don't want to run the risk of her stepping on the hem when she's walking down the aisle."

Juergen excused himself, closed his computer, and left Babs and me alone.

I asked her what she knew about Juergen. Beyond the facts that his primary home was in Zurich and he was CEO of the Merz family enterprises, whatever they were, I knew nothing.

Babs folded her hands and crossed her gracefully slanted legs at the ankles. "Juergen is an adventurer. In fact, until recently when he had to take over control of the family businesses, he was a real daredevil." She glanced toward the stairs as if assuring herself Juergen wasn't still within earshot. "He has climbed every face and ridge on the Matterhorn. Ten times, Patrick told me. He's climbed Everest and Kilimanjaro. He's done the motorcycle race on the Isle of Man. He's ballooned across Asia and I don't know what all. He's done a research trip to Antarctica."

"Is he married?"

Babs paused, her folded hands tensing slightly. "No. I don't believe he's ever been married."

Something told me Babs had designs on Juergen. He would make a great catch, wouldn't he? As far as I knew, Babs had stayed single since her marriage to Erin's father ended. I changed the subject. "I know Erin intends to continue at the zoo after the wedding. Do you know how far it is from their new condo to where she works?"

"Wonderful of Chet, buying them their first home! I was completely surprised, weren't you?" Babs's tone of voice was the only indicator of her excitement since her expression was incapable of showing anything. I waited for her to answer my question. "Oh, you asked how far it is. I don't know. But Erin is determined not to give up her career. That's how it is now, I guess."

"Patrick says Erin is great with animals."

"A girl used to be considered an old maid if she wasn't married by thirty, but I think that number is higher now, don't you, Dotsy?" She droned on, oblivious of my comment. "Of course, you and I have jobs. But then we have to, don't we? It's an economic necessity when you don't have a man to see to that side of things for you."

Babs made my neck itch. I tried to recall what I'd been told about Erin's father. Had he died or had they divorced? The family was Roman Catholic, I knew, so it may have been one of those annulment things the church sometimes allows in certain circumstances. Whatever had happened, I was sure Mr. Toomey was in a better place now.

I heard the crackle of a door opening somewhere below, and then the sweet, familiar voice of my lifelong best friend, Lettie. "Where *is* everybody?"

I jumped up and, arms out, waited for her to appear. There she was! Red, spiky hair, red nails, bright purple luggage. Five feet one and appropriately round for her age. We hugged and she made her normal little squealing noises. Juergen had reappeared so I introduced him and Babs to Lettie.

"I didn't think I was ever going to get here. Those roads! Are they as scary in the daytime as they are at night? We were flying along in this little toy cab sort of thing and the road was going like . . ." Lettie demonstrated hairpin turns with her stubby little hands.

"There are more ways to kill yourself in the Alps than just skiing. Believe me," Juergen, standing in the doorway, tilted his head to one side and grinned.

"Don't I know it!" Lettie's eyes widened. "Everywhere you look they have Red Cross stations. On every corner. All over the country. I've never seen so many Red Cross stations. Everybody here must need a rescue every day!"

"Red Cross?" Juergen asked, his brows lowered.

"Are you sure they were red crosses, Lettie? Or were they white crosses on a red background?" I asked, already anticipating the answer.

"Well, I . . . now that you mention it, they *were* white. With red backgrounds."

"That's the Swiss flag, Lettie."

"Oops," she said, covering her mouth with her hand.

Erin joined us. She and Patrick took the sofa, Juergen reclaimed the big leather chair, but Lettie declared she'd rather stand since she had been sitting all day. She patted her backside to emphasize the point. Babs watched from her nest in one of the chintz-covered chairs.

"Well! Let me tell you how I almost got arrested in Geneva!" Lettie said, stepping forward to take center stage.

Oh, golly! I loved hearing about Lettie's harebrained predicaments—*afterward*. I hated being there at the time, and Lettie seemed to have particular problems with airports. I recalled the strip-search a few years ago at the airport in Milan when the water pistol in her carry-on showed up on X-ray.

Juergen interrupted her. "Before you begin . . ." He paused and pulled a cell phone from his pants pocket, looked at its screen, then held up a finger. "Excuse me. Just a minute." He answered the incoming call. "Yes. The Italian wine." He pressed the phone to his sweater and looked at me. "Dotsy? Do me a big favor, will you? Go to the kitchen and ask Gisele to start a pot of decaffeinated coffee for us. Do you know how to find the kitchen?"

"Yes."

"If she isn't there, would you mind starting the coffee yourself? The decaf should be in the cabinet above the coffee maker."

He went back to his phone conversation, mouthing, "Stephanie," to the rest of the room. "No, no. The *Lacryma Christi*. With black labels."

The kitchen was large, with a bright red Aga cooker dominating one end. I had never seen a real Aga, but since they were often mentioned in detective stories set in England, I had looked it up on the Internet and found they cost more than some cars. I could see why they were found only in the large manor houses. This one had several ovens, and six burners.

While the coffee brewed, I snooped. The refrigerator seemed too small to hold provisions for a house party the size of ours. I speculated that they might also keep supplies in the bunker. That made sense. It would be like a cave inside. Caves, I knew from Luray Caverns near my home in Virginia, maintained a steady ambient temperature year round. An ideal place to store food and wine. That must be where Stephanie was now. Juergen had been talking to her about wine a few minutes ago and he apparently knew I wouldn't find her in the kitchen. Gisele maybe, but not Stephanie.

I waited until the coffee maker finished gurgling and heard laughter as I carried the pot upstairs. Patrick was convulsed, holding his sides. Juergen, red in the face from laughing, arched back in his leather chair until his eyes found me. "You missed it, Dotsy. You must hear about Lettie's airport adventure!"

"I'll tell it to her later," Lettie said. "Now, if you'll excuse me, I'd like to turn in. It's been a long day."

Lettie and I stayed awake talking for another hour until my watch said one A.M. We crawled into our twin beds, pulled up the covers, and squashed pillows so we could see each other as we talked. Lettie thought she had picked up on some uncertainty in Patrick and she was concerned. He hadn't told her anything specific, but there was something in his manner. Patrick was Lettie's godson, and they had always had a special bond.

"He seems distracted, Dotsy. Have you noticed?"

Lettie, although a complete scatterbrain in matters of logic, is one of the most emotionally perceptive people I know. Her heart is big enough to enfold the world. Over the years, I've come to respect her "vibes" and learned to heed them. She's not to be trusted around heavy machinery, but if she says someone is worried, *someone is worried.*

I told her about the strange reactions to Stephanie's phone call at dinner, about Marco's gift, about Chet's gift, about my hour alone with Babs, and what Patrick had said about Babs. "And Chet looks really bad, Lettie. He's drinking too much and he's lost weight."

"Serves him right, after what he did to you."

"I'm over that. Truly I am. Stephanie can have him with my blessings." I turned over and jammed my pillow against the headboard. Someone tapped softly on our door. "Come in," I said.

Juergen opened the door a crack and stuck his head in. "Have you seen Gisele?"

"No." *Strange question,* I thought. Until then, I hadn't wondered where Gisele lived. Did she live here? I asked him.

"She has a room downstairs. She actually lives in town with her parents, but she stays here when we're entertaining guests."

Lettie reminded him that she had not met Gisele yet.

I thought back. "I can't recall actually seeing her since dinner, Juergen, but I think I heard her. Cleaning up, you know."

"She wasn't in the kitchen when you went down to make coffee?"

"No, but the kitchen was clean. The dishes were done."

"Thank you," he said and closed the door. I heard his knock on Babs and Erin's door a second later, and his same question asked again.

"As I was saying, I don't even want Chet anymore." I reshaped my pillow and turned back to Lettie. "I spent the last couple of days with Marco, in Capri. Did I already tell you that?"

"Now that's more like it! You should marry Marco, Dotsy."

"I don't want to marry anybody. Besides that, which side of the Atlantic would we live on? We both like our jobs."

Heavy feet clattered down the stairs, sounding almost as if they were tumbling or falling down to the lower level where I had seen the indoor pool. I heard nothing for a few minutes. Then heavy feet, now climbing to our level, crossed the landing, faded as they entered the dining room, and—I could barely hear them now—continued climbing, a few stairs creaking. I heard steps overhead, back and forth, back and forth, then down again, down some more, back to the pool room.

"Why do you suppose he's so anxious to find Gisele?" Lettie asked.

"I haven't the foggiest, and I'm too tired to worry about it."

We said goodnight and I switched off the bedside lamp.

Much later I jerked awake. Someone was coming up the stairs. I heard a thunk, as if the climber had hit the wall, and a loud belch. After a minute the steps retreated, descending, then faded away.

"Now what?" I heard Lettie mumble.

"That's Chet, I'll wager. Lettie, I'm so glad you're here now, because I feel like something is about to explode."

FOUR

I slept until nearly nine the next morning, got up, and followed the smell of coffee to the kitchen. Babs and Erin were already there, Babs at the counter smearing a toasted bagel with cream cheese. Erin was spooning a chunky cereal with raisins and nuts into her mouth.

"Help yourself," Erin said through a milky mouthful of cereal. "We're the only ones awake so far, I think. Coffee's ready and there's bread, butter, jelly—and eggs, if you can figure out how to work the stove."

I opted for toast and orange juice.

"Look outside," Babs said, pointing toward a window with her knife.

I looked. It had snowed. The craggy world outside had been covered overnight with a thick blanket of glistening snow. The view from the window was so bright it hurt my eyes. "I guess I shouldn't be surprised," I said. "Snow in April. After all, this is Switzerland. But isn't it lovely?"

Chet, still wearing the same blue shirt and corduroy pants he wore last night, stumbled in. "Coffee," he croaked.

"It snowed last night, did you know?" I said, handing him a cup.

"Uh—no." Chet opened the refrigerator door and then spotted the cream on the butcher-block table that dominated the center of the room.

"Stephanie not up yet?" I asked.

"Couldn't tell you." He pulled out a stool and sat at the table, one foot searching for a stool rung to hook onto, missing, and hitting the floor. "I slept on the sofa last night."

We three women just looked at him.

Chet sipped his coffee, grimaced, and scanned our faces with his bloodshot eyes. "What?" he said, defensively. "I came in late, and I didn't want to wake her up. It's not what you're thinking."

"I wasn't thinking anything," I said.

Patrick bustled in, rubbing his hands with glee. "Snow! Did you see? Snow! We're going to have some fun today! How about it, my love?" He kissed Erin on the forehead.

For the next few minutes, we discussed plans for skiing and sledding and where the necessary equipment for each could be found. I debated within my own head the wisdom of sledding or skiing with my sixty-something bones and a wedding on Thursday. I tentatively decided I'd probably risk it. A leg cast might look trendy with my green dress.

"Guten morgen, meine Freunde!" Juergen breezed in. He glanced around. "Where's Gisele?"

"We haven't seen her."

"I never did find her last night. If she went home and didn't tell anyone—" He looked at his watch. "It's after nine. She normally has breakfast ready by nine."

Patrick directed him to look out the window.

"Ah. Snow." Juergen turned to Chet and surveyed my ex-husband's scruffy appearance, scanning him from head to toe. "Where's Stephanie?"

"Still in bed, probably." Chet answered. He looked as if he couldn't bear explaining again.

"I'll bet Gisele has gone to the bunker. We keep our extra food stored there." Juergen turned to Erin, who had finished her cereal and was rinsing the bowl at the sink. "Would you go out and see, love? You know the combination, don't you?" He turned to me, and said, "We have a combination lock on the bunker door, because in an emergency we might not be able to find the key."

Erin went to her room for her boots and Patrick followed her. A minute later, they walked back through the kitchen and out the side door. "Snow! Glorious snow!" I heard Patrick exclaim as they shut the door behind them.

Two minutes passed before we heard Erin's scream. A horrible, trembling cry, it grew louder and louder as she approached the kitchen door. "Oh, my God! Oh, my God! Come out! Juergen, come out!"

Patrick came down right behind her. "I'm afraid it's Gisele. Juergen, you need to come out. Mom, I'd rather you didn't."

"I'd rather I did." I dashed out behind Juergen, my bedroom slippers sinking in the new snow. I might as well have been barefoot.

Patrick headed across the fresh white blanket, not toward the rock wall where I thought the bunker was, but to the left, into the middle of the meadow west of the house and straight toward a splotch of crimson, incongruously marring the pure white all around. Patrick threw his arms out, holding me back as Juergen closed in on the spot and knelt.

I recognized Gisele's jeans-clad leg and running shoes. An inch or two of snow lay over her and the red stain, near where her chest would be, spread out in a rough circle fading to pink at the edges. Patrick had already pushed back the snow from her face. Milky pale, almost like the snow, her face wore a startled look, the blank blue eyes fixed beneath crystallized, frozen lashes.

Juergen reached out and gathered her up in his arms, rocking silently. A full minute must have passed before he made any sound at all, then it came out as a high-pitched whine. My previous experience with dead bodies and the police urged me forward to pull him back. You weren't supposed to touch the body. The whole scene took me back, with a sharp pang, to Scotland and the body of a dear young friend—stabbed and wrapped in a blue tarp behind the castle where Lettie and I had been staying.

I couldn't tell Juergen to leave her alone. It wouldn't have been right.

"She's been shot, I think," Erin said.

"What do we do, now?"

"Call the police."

"Should we call a doctor first?"

"No need."

Patrick headed for the house, passing Chet on the way.

"I checked our bedroom," Chet called up the hill as he approached us. "Stephanie isn't there."

Erin and I looked at each other. Her eyes bugged out and I knew what she was thinking.

"Have you checked the bunker yet?" I asked her.

"No. Patrick and I saw Gisele, and we ran straight back to the kitchen."

I looked around. The only prints in the snow ran between Gisele's lifeless body and the house. My feet, now frozen numb, stumbled across the field after Erin. She stopped when she reached the rock face. Now that I knew what lay behind, it was easy to see the outline of the door, painted the same grey as the rock, and an industrial-type touch pad for entry.

Erin punched in four numbers.

I said I've dealt with dead bodies before, but never with anything close to what lay beyond that door. I will never forget it. I fear I will never quite get over it.

I saw the feet first, then the blood. Erin fainted dead away and left me with an unobstructed view of the horror. Blood everywhere. Splattered, splashed, streaked across the concrete floor from the door to the walls. Stephanie Lamb lay face up, part of her head blown away, so that nothing but a plum-colored mass of tissue and stringy hair remained on her right side. She lay in an awkward twist, with her right leg folded up under her hips and her torso bent to the left. Her head, what was left of it, lay against her left shoulder.

Within seconds, Chet was on his knees beside me, sobbing. I pulled myself together, took a deep breath of putrid air, and told myself it was up to me. Something, I wasn't sure what, was up to me. Erin lay crumpled in the doorway, now beginning to stir. Chet knelt beside me, to the right of Stephanie's body and about two feet from it. His shoulders trembled. I heard Juergen behind me. *"Oh, nein! Ach, nein, nein, nein!"*

"Don't touch anything." My voice sounded surprisingly strong to my own ears. "Juergen, help Erin. Get her outside. Now."

I knelt down to Chet, and put an arm across his shoulders. "I'm so very sorry. So sorry." His hands seemed glued to his face. "Can you stand up, Chet? You can't stay here. I'll help you."

He pushed himself up with one hand, the other still covering his face. "I can walk. Don't help me." He stumbled out the door. I couldn't help feeling as if his main concern was to get out of there. As if he had no desire to cradle the body of his wife. Chet had always had a weak stomach.

I stood for a moment before leaving and tried to take in the whole scene. I could see no sign of a struggle. Shelves arrayed with food, a large floor-to-ceiling wine storage rack along one wall. Ski poles, snowshoes, and skis leaned against the opposite wall. A cell phone, it looked like one of the pricey kind that do all sorts of things, lay off to one side. A black handgun lay on the floor, inches from Stephanie's right hand. I backed out and closed the door.

The helicopter arrived first.

Patrick had called the police and the police called the rescue helicopter. He told them Gisele was dead, but their procedures called for a swift helicopter pickup and transfer to the nearest hospital where, if she was indeed dead, she could be pronounced so. The pilot circled, searching for a suitable spot to put down, then settled the chopper, kicking up a cloud of snow and exposing green meadow and early spring flowers beneath.

They weren't prepared to pick up *two* bodies.

Minutes later, the LaMotte police came careening over the hill in an all-terrain vehicle with tires the size of inflated kiddie pools. In the interim, I had gone back to the house, dressed, and borrowed a pair of boots I found in a closet. Chet and Juergen had both disappeared. Only Patrick stayed outside with me, but several pairs of eyes stared out from windows on the upper floors of the chateau. The police surveyed the situation, pulled out notebooks, scratched down our names, and asked how to open the bunker door. Patrick told them the combination. One of the two policemen stepped inside, glanced around, put a hand over his mouth, and stepped back out, waving his partner back. He stood outside the door staring off toward the distant peaks for what seemed a long time while I waited silently.

At last, he spoke to me, in accented English. "I must be honest with you, Mrs. Lamb. Neither of us has investigated a homicide before. LaMotte is a peaceful town and the worst thing we ever deal with is a bar fight. And not many of *them*."

The second officer nodded.

"We are out of our—that is—we are not equipped to investigate something like this. I'm calling the Cantonal Police.

They will take it from here." He closed the bunker door and sent his partner to the big-wheeled ATV to make the call.

FIVE

Detective Kurt Kronenberg arrived by helicopter and ordered his men to work photographing, measuring, and staking out the perimeter with crime scene tape. I slipped into the house, leaving Patrick and Juergen, who had reappeared and was helping Kronenberg with the minutiae of names, times, relationships, etc.

Lettie and I watched from a bathroom window on the top level of the chateau. At some point, I noticed the bathroom had two doors, the one we had used to enter from a little narrow hallway, and another on a wall perpendicular to the hall. It stood slightly open. I peeked through.

I saw Chet sitting on the edge of a double bed, his back to me. He was bent forward so that I could see nothing of his head above his shirt collar. I eased the door shut, leaving him to mourn in private.

Footprints in the snow multiplied until a continuous path of slush connected Gisele's body and the door to the bunker. At noon, one of the helicopters airlifted both bodies away, swerving around a jagged peak and disappearing in the west.

Detective Kronenberg talked to us, one at a time. He and I sat at the dining room table with a silent note-taking policeman seated in the corner. In response to his first question, I explained that I was Chester Lamb's first wife and Patrick's mother. Kronenberg's eyebrows went up, but he said nothing.

"It was you who found the body of Mrs. Lamb, was it not?"

"Erin—Miss Toomey—and I. We went in together, but she passed out for a minute, so I guess you could say I was the first to really look at the . . . at Mrs. Lamb's body."

"When was the last time you saw Mrs. Lamb?"

I had to think. I had heard her in the kitchen when I went out for a walk last night, but I hadn't actually seen her. "When we were all in the living room after dinner. Mr. Lamb and Mrs. Lamb presented their wedding gift to Mr. Lamb and . . . look. This is going to confuse me. Can we refer to everyone by their first names? We have two Mr. Lambs and two Mrs. Lambs and two Toomeys."

"If that will help you, certainly." He turned to the note-taking policeman for confirmation that he understood the change.

"The last time I saw Stephanie was in the living room after dinner and that would have been about nine-thirty or ten o'clock."

"When was the last time you saw Miss Schlump?" That was the first time I could recall hearing Gisele's last name.

"I didn't actually see her, but she brought us coffee in the living room at about that same time. That is, when Chet was making his presentation. She's the only one who could have left the coffee tray on the sideboard because it wasn't there when Chet started talking, and when he finished, it was."

"What time did you go to bed?"

"About midnight, but Lettie Osgood and I stayed up and talked for a while in our bedroom."

"Did you, at any time, hear gunshots?"

"No.'"

"Did you hear anything unusual? A scream? Any strange noise at all?"

"No."

"On which side of the house is your bedroom?"

"On the southwest side. I remember seeing the glow of the setting sun out my bedroom window shortly before dinner."

"You were on the side that faces the meadow where Gisele's body was found."

"It does seem as though I would have heard a gunshot. Unless the gun had a silencer."

"It had no silencer, Mrs. Lamb." He studied his fingernails. "And you're certain you did not see either Stephanie or Gisele between nine-thirty or ten and midnight, when you went to bed?"

"I didn't *see* them, but I think I *heard* them."

"Explain."

"I took a walk outside sometime after ten. I only walked around the house and sat on a rock for a little while. But when I walked past the kitchen door, I stopped because I heard voices. I couldn't hear most of what was said, but I'm certain they were women's voices."

"Go on." The detective leaned forward, his eyes intense.

"I'm pretty sure one of them was Stephanie, and it was she who said, rather loudly, 'If you don't tell him, I will! I swear to God I will!' "

"And the answer?"

"I didn't hear an answer."

Kronenberg shot me a withering glare.

"I didn't. Truly I didn't. But I did hear something else. Earlier in the day." I told him about the argument Patrick and I had overheard when, according to Patrick, Stephanie had yelled something like *I know what you're up to.* That remark was in German and the response was in a woman's voice.

I flew straight to my bedroom after the interview and found Lettie there, cutting her hair with nail clippers. With the door open, I could see Detective Kronenberg's back as he sat at the dining table, and I could hear most of what was being said. The most important thing I learned was that they were treating this horror, at least for now, as a murder-suicide. It looked as if Stephanie Lamb, for whatever reason, had shot Gisele Schlump and then turned the gun on herself. I gathered nothing from Kronenberg's interview with Juergen because they spoke in German, but bits and pieces of the interviews with Patrick, Babs, and Erin told me the general direction in which the investigation was heading.

Kronenberg asked Patrick, who had arrived at the chateau several days earlier than I had, if he knew of any problems between Gisele and Stephanie. Patrick denied knowing any, but he did describe the comment we'd heard Stephanie make to Gisele, repeating it verbatim in German.

"What do you think she meant by that?"

"I don't know. I'm just repeating what I heard, as well as I can remember."

"It sounds rather . . . threatening, doesn't it?" Kronenberg paused, as if he wasn't sure "threatening" was the right word.

From where I stood, I could see Patrick's face beyond Kronenberg's back. I glanced at Lettie, now sitting on her bed with her hands clasped under her chin, her eyes narrowed in concentration. Lettie is blessed with an amazing memory. She remembers license numbers from her childhood, the color of her children's third-grade lunch boxes, and how many pairs of black socks her husband currently owns. When there's confusion, it's good to have Lettie around.

Patrick paused before answering Kronenberg's question. "Stephanie, my stepmother, was a direct sort of person. She could be very confrontational, and there are those who thought she was too controlling."

"You did not like her."

"Oh, no, no, no! I liked her." When Kronenberg said nothing

in response, Patrick added, "If I didn't like her, would Erin and I have decided to have our wedding here?"

Kronenberg tossed a casual arm over the back of his chair. "When did you leave the house to pick up Mrs. Lettie Osgood?"

"It must have been around ten."

"And when did you return?"

"Maybe, eleven? I was gone about an hour, because I had to wait at least a half-hour for Mrs. Osgood's cab. I drove Juergen's little cart down to the road so it would be easier to bring her and her luggage back here."

"Did you see anything out of the ordinary? Either on your way down or on your way back?"

"No. Nothing."

Lettie whispered to me, "Of course, we wouldn't have seen anything unusual that early. Juergen talked to Stephanie on the phone after I got here and everything must have been normal then, because they were very calmly discussing Italian wine."

"That's right. So Stephanie was definitely alive after eleven. But what about Gisele?"

"Juergen thought she might be in the kitchen, remember? He asked you to go down and tell Gisele to make a pot of decaf."

"*If* she was there, but she wasn't."

Lettie put the back of her hand against the side of her mouth and whispered, "I seriously doubt that Stephanie would shoot Gisele and then call her brother to discuss Italian wine!"

I sneaked across the landing and down the stairs to the living room, then tried to figure out how to get to the kitchen without letting Detective Kronenberg hear or see me. I liked the idea of eavesdropping from my own bedroom, and I didn't want to call attention to its proximity to the dining room. By winding down, around, and through the swimming pool room, I found a way. The pool room was warm. A wispy layer of steam drifted on the surface of the water.

In the kitchen, I slapped mustard and a bit of ham on some pumpernickel bread, added a couple of pickle wedges to two plates, and balanced a glass of water on each. I had no appetite, but it was lunchtime and Lettie said she was starving. She claimed to have eaten nothing since breakfast on the plane yesterday.

Under the telephone on the kitchen wall, a notepad caught my eye. I recognized Stephanie's handwriting and the sort of morphing figure-eight doodle I had seen her trace absentmindedly. With a jolt, I flashed on a memory of the same doodles she drew all over the margins of a letter in the lawyer's office while Chet and I banged out the terms of our divorce.

I tore off the top sheet and tucked it in my pocket. Since these notes turned out to be important, I reproduce them now:

Back in our room, I handed Lettie one of the plates and checked on the scene in the dining room. Erin had replaced Patrick in the hot seat. Lettie waved me to a corner of the room out of the line of sight from the door.

"He asked Erin if she knew anything about those things you heard Stephanie say. You, know, 'I know what you're up to,' and 'If you don't tell him, I will.' Remember?" Lettie took a bite of her sandwich and swiped a bit of mustard from the corner of her mouth with the back of her wrist.

"And?"

"And she said she didn't know anything about either of those comments, but Dotsy, she sounded funny when she said it. I think she was lying."

Six

Kronenberg and his assistant climbed the stairs to interview Chet in his own bedroom. I supposed Chet didn't feel up to coming downstairs. Meanwhile, Lettie and I descended to the living room where Juergen soon joined us. He'd been on the phone for the past hour. I'd seen him pacing the porch outside the living room, a cell phone to his ear. Awkward. If I'd known him better, I would have hugged him. Words were hopelessly inadequate to comfort a man who had just lost his sister and his—his what? His employee? Why did I feel as if she was more than an employee? Had they been lovers? Babs told me he was single, but as far as I could recall, Juergen himself hadn't said anything about his marital status. Gisele kept a bedroom here. Juergen's reaction to finding Gisele in the snowy meadow had been painful to watch. And then when he came into the bunker and saw his sister—the sister he'd grown up with and known all his life—lying there, her head a mass of blood.

A gust of cold air swept in with Juergen as he slid the glass door closed. He nodded to Lettie and me, jammed his fists in his pockets, and cleared his throat. "I need to go to Zurich."

The announcement startled me. "Now? Have you told Detective Kronenberg?"

"He's with Chet at the moment. I don't want to interrupt them." His eyes darted toward Lettie, then me, then back to Lettie. "I suppose I should ask him first."

"Yes, I think you should," I said.

"I'm not in the habit of asking permission to drive to my own home." He said this, not angrily but as if he was struggling to sort out a new order. Things had changed. New priorities. New demands.

"These are not normal times," I said, with as much kindness in my voice as I could muster.

"My father—our father—Stephanie's and mine. He's ninety-five and in poor health. Very poor. In fact, he could die at any time. He's bed-ridden and he has a nurse with him around the clock."

"I didn't know your father was still alive."

"He hasn't much more time. But this will be on the television news by evening. I can't keep it off the air for long. Our family is well known. This will be big news in Zurich."

"Don't they have to wait until the next of kin is notified?"

"Stephanie's next of kin *has* been notified. Chet." He nodded at the stairway. "He's upstairs. Gisele's parents have been notified as well." Juergen shifted his meaty frame to the sideboard and poured himself a couple of fingers of scotch. He held up his glass to us, offering.

I shook my head. "No, thanks."

"My father's nurse will turn on the evening news in his bedroom. She always does, but whether he pays attention to it or not, I don't know. I could call her and tell her to leave the TV off, but that won't work for long, will it?"

"Juergen, are you sure he should be told at all?"

His head jerked toward me.

"He's ninety-five and in poor health," I said. "The death of a child is absolutely the worst pain a parent can endure. *Could* he endure it? Might it kill him?"

Juergen walked back to the windows, turning his back on Lettie and me. For a long time, he said nothing, and then, "You are right. I'll call his nurse and alert her. He must *never* be told."

I had forgotten all about Brian. He was due to arrive that morning, and if I had thought about him at all, I would have wondered why we hadn't heard from him. He found his own way up the mountain. Lettie and I, still sitting in the living room, heard his voice.

"Dad! Stephanie! Where is everybody? What the hell's going on?"

I dashed toward the sound of his voice and found him in the kitchen. I hugged and kissed him, then held him at arm's length. "Awful news. Horrible. Let's go to the living room. You need to hear this sitting down." With one arm around his sturdy waist, I steered him to a chair. He had seen the helicopter and the crime tape so I started with the worst. As I told the story, Brian's face reflected a tumult of emotions.

"Where's Dad? I have to see him."

"He's talking to Detective Kronenberg in his room—upstairs, on the top floor."

Lettie interjected, "Maybe he shouldn't just barge in."

"He's Chet's son. He can barge in." I stood and gave Brian one more hug before he headed up the stairs to locate his father. Brian, my stalwart son. Just having him here buoyed me up. In the last few years, I knew, Chet had shoveled more and more responsibility for the John Deere dealership onto Brian's shoulders. Stephanie, as their accountant, maneuvered relentlessly to take over the policy-making end of the business, and Chet couldn't or wouldn't stand up to her. Brian told me about this during the Sunday dinners we always shared. He told me that Stephanie's ideas for business models in general weren't so bad, but the problem was she didn't know a thing about farming or farm machinery. He'd had to be rather blunt with her a couple of times. I pointed Brian toward the correct stairway and moped back to the living room.

I heard Kronenberg and Brian in the dining room above us. It sounded as though Brian had taken the same chair at the table the rest of us had occupied—the hot seat. It was hard to hear from this distance. I caught only bits and pieces of Brian's answers and nothing at all of Kronenberg's questions.

"Actually, I spent last night in Geneva—United flight—from Washington. It was late, you know, and I didn't want to barge in after they were all asleep . . . I'm devastated, of course . . . Of course not."

I motioned to Lettie, pointing up the stairs. As quietly as possible we climbed the stairs to the landing and slipped into our bedroom, casually, so that if either Brian or Kronenberg saw us, we wouldn't seem to have been sneaking. I left the door open halfway, then moved around the room until I found the spot that afforded the clearest reception of voices from the dining room. I heard:

"I have never met Gisele Schlump; in fact, I've never been to Switzerland before."

"Do you know who she was?"

"I've heard Patrick mention her. She lived here, didn't she? She was their cook. I may have heard Stephanie, my stepmother, mention her a time or two as well."

"Did Stephanie and Gisele get along?"

"I don't know! Really, I'm not even sure I ever heard Stephanie mention her."

"Can you think of any motive she might have had for wanting to kill Gisele?"

"Absolutely none."

"Can you think of any reason Stephanie might have had for wanting to kill herself?"

"Absolutely not! Stephanie is the *last person in the world* I'd expect to kill herself."

"Why do you say that?"

"Because Stephanie was confident. Sure of herself. Those sorts of people don't kill themselves!"

I turned to Lettie and whispered, "Those sorts of people *do* kill themselves, I'm afraid."

By late afternoon, I was going stir-crazy. I had to escape. From the living room windows, I spied Brian and Patrick heading eastward and over the crest of a hill. Lettie, nestled in the sofa with her feet tucked into the crack between the seat cushion and the back, fiddled absently with her cell phone.

"Let's go for a walk," I suggested. I tramped up the stairs to our room to get my jacket and ran into Juergen, coming down.

"Put on a warm coat if you're going out, Dotsy. The temperature is falling again. It's going to be a cold night."

"That's the warmest I have," I said, pointing to the new jacket I'd draped over the post at the foot of my bed.

"Come with me." Juergen led me to a coat closet on a lower level and pulled out a zip-up parka and a pair of yellow galoshes. "Keep these. You'll need them whenever you go out." He scrambled through the closet floor and located a smaller pair of galoshes for Lettie.

Lettie and I headed out and eastward, away from the off-limits crime scene. Breaking new snow as we went, our progress was slow, but it didn't matter because we had nowhere to go. I only wanted to get away from the house. "Your thoughts, Lettie. What happened here?"

"My head is spinning! Nothing makes sense."

"You're right. What could possibly have possessed Stephanie to grab a gun, shoot the cook, and then shoot herself?"

"All I can think of is that Gisele knew something that

threatened Stephanie. Scared her. Something she couldn't let get out."

"If so, it must have been a whopping big threat. Stephanie was not the sort to scare easily. She thrived on conflict. Trust me—I *know*. Stephanie's reaction to a threat would be, 'Bring it on! You want a fight? You got one!' "

"And to kill herself! It makes no sense."

"And what I heard her say, 'If you don't tell him, I will,' sounds more like *she* was the threat."

We reached a spot that looked like the place where Patrick and I had turned left. The trail we had followed yesterday lay covered by the blanket of new snow. I nudged Lettie toward the left. "I have an awful feeling," I told her, "the police will decide this isn't a murder-suicide but just plain murder. A double murder. And if so, who is the most logical suspect?"

Lettie stopped and looked into my face but said nothing.

"Me, Lettie. Me! The woman scorned—staying in the same house as her ex-husband and the woman who stole him from her!"

Lettie blinked and her head jerked. "What about Gisele? Why would you kill her?"

"She saw what I did."

"Oh, dear. I have to admit it has a certain logic to it." Lettie resumed her path. "Do you have an alibi?" She said this in the same tone she'd have used to ask, "Do you have a tissue?"

"I was in the living room with the others for most of the time between ten-thirty and midnight and after that I was with you. Erin, Babs, Juergen, can all vouch for me. Plus you and Patrick came in later."

"That's all right, then."

"But there was the time when I went to the kitchen and brewed the coffee. That's the only time I can't be vouched for, and it would hardly have been time enough to kill two people."

Lettie held up one finger and moved it around as if she was scanning an invisible timeline. "Time enough to grab a gun, run to the bunker where you already knew Stephanie was because of the phone call, shoot her, run back out, see Gisele getting ready to scream her head off, shoot her, toss the gun inside the bunker, slam the door, run back to the house."

"That would take," I muttered, "maybe two or three minutes."

"*If* you knew where to get a gun."

"Right. Who would ever think I'd find a gun in a World War II bunker? In a country where gun ownership is *mandatory?*"

"Don't talk like that. You're scaring me."

We had come to the boulder where Patrick and I sat yesterday. The Matterhorn dominated our eastern horizon and the cedars, their branches covered with snow like white lace, skirted the slope below us. Sweeping the snow off the top of the boulder, we sat and bandied other possibilities about. Who, other than myself, had a motive? Chet might have felt dominated and emasculated by Stephanie. Juergen might have a financial motive, depending on how much money their father had and what was in his will. Gisele had probably been smarting from Stephanie's verbal attacks.

"Gisele is out, Lettie. She'd have had to shoot herself *after* she shot Stephanie, but the gun was in the bunker beside Stephanie."

"You're right. I can't believe we're calmly talking like this."

"There you are."

We both turned and spotted Babs picking her way toward us, Erin in tow. Babs wore a mint green knit cap with a matching scarf and a navy pea coat. Erin's coat was brown and black checked. Her little face peeked out between a cable-knit cap and several wraps of an incredibly long, rainbow-striped muffler.

"What a day. What an awful day," Babs said, in a flat tone.

"Poor Chet must be devastated. Erin and I are just back from LaMotte. We had to talk to Father Etienne. He'd already heard about poor Stephanie and poor Gisele. I don't know how he'd heard about it, but news travels fast in a small village and the Merz family is well known around here. I assured Father Etienne that this tragedy wouldn't change our plans for Thursday's wedding, and I'm very glad we stopped in when we did! He thought the wedding was postponed!" The pitch of her voice rose but her eyebrows, thanks probably to Botox, did not. "Anyway, we assured him it wasn't. I mean, after all, Stephanie wasn't the mother of the groom. You are. She had no official role. And Gisele—she was invited to attend, but she wasn't part of the actual wedding party. I explained that the whole family was here for only a short time and we all have to fly home soon." She shook her head. "Of course, we can't postpone the wedding!"

I'm sure my mouth was hanging open as widely as Lettie's was. While her mother was talking, Erin stood with her back to us, swirling arcs in the snow with one boot. I suppose I must have thought about Thursday's wedding a couple of times that morning and assumed it would be postponed. How could they think of going on with it as if nothing had happened? I was appalled. The wedding hadn't been mentioned all day except to explain to Detective Kronenberg why we were all here.

"Babs, have you and Erin talked this over with Patrick?"

Erin turned and peaked at her mother through her wraps.

"We haven't been able to talk to him about anything! He and Juergen have been busy with that little detective all day."

Little detective. Those two words told me more than anything else she had said. Kronenberg was about six feet-two and two hundred pounds. *Little* was Babs's assessment of Kronenberg's importance, not his physical size.

"Babs, we've had two deaths today. Two people who were at

dinner last night won't be there tonight. Or ever again. Even though Stephanie and I weren't best of friends, and even though I hardly knew Gisele, I'm saddened by their deaths. I can't imagine celebrating a marriage right now. Can you, Lettie?"

Lettie raised her chin, looked down her nose at Babs. "No. And before you go any further with your plans, you should talk things over with Patrick."

"But by Thursday, surely, this will be behind us."

"Thursday's only three days away."

"Busy, busy! You realize, don't you, that everything Gisele and Stephanie were planning to take care of—the bar, the wine, the coffee—all of that will have to be done by the caterers now. Unless you and Lettie could take over."

I didn't answer her. I couldn't. I elbowed Lettie and mumbled, "Get me away from here before I hit her."

Back at the house, I found Brian and Patrick in the pool room. Patrick, fully clothed, sat on the side of the pool, pant legs rolled up and his feet on the top step in ankle-deep water. Brian was swimming laps. I wondered where he had found the swim trunks. In my heavy wool sweater I was uncomfortably warm in the room's balmy atmosphere. Condensation dripped down the windows in rivulets, and the whole room smelled of chlorine.

I told Patrick he needed to talk to Erin as soon as possible. "Babs is assuming the wedding will come off as planned on Thursday. Do you really think that's wise?"

"The wedding? Thursday?" His head jerked around. "No! Not with all this!" He stood up and stepped out of the water. "I've hardly had time to . . . what I mean is, I don't think it's a good idea now. This Matterhorn thing was cool before, but now it's not. I'm thinking a wedding back home, maybe later in the summer, would make more sense."

"I agree. More of our family and Erin's would be able to attend. And your father needs time to mend."

Patrick, his pant legs still rolled up, grabbed his shoes and padded across the tile floor to the stairs. Brian, meanwhile, had climbed out and grabbed a towel. He scrubbed his hair, draped the towel around his shoulders, and pulled up a deck chair to face the one I had taken.

"Where's Detective Kronenberg?" I asked.

"Gone. Helicopter took off a half-hour ago."

"How's your father doing?"

"It's hard to tell, isn't it? He's gone all broody, but that's getting to be his norm."

"So you've told me."

"This makes no sense, Mom. Stephanie's the last person I'd expect to kill herself. There must have been something going on that we don't know about." Brian blew a drop of water off the tip of his nose and wiped his face with the towel.

"What about the business? What shape is the John Deere franchise in?"

"Aha! Damn you, Mom. You're always a step ahead of me! That's exactly what I'm worried about."

"Tell me."

"There's money missing. I've been chalking up the sad state of our balance sheet to the economy. Sales are off. Farmers are hurting. They can't afford to float any more loans so they can't buy new equipment. That's part of it, but not all of it. We haven't actually been selling that much less than we were five years ago, but—" Brian folded one hand inside the other and cracked his knuckles, then gazed out a fogged-up window.

"Go on."

"I had another accountant, a friend of mine, take a look at our books. As a favor to me. I don't understand all the little conventions and devices those guys use, but he told me there's money missing."

"How much?"

"Maybe a couple million."

"Ouch!" That sounded like big money to me, but in the heavy machinery business one tractor can cost a couple hundred thousand, and most of the money on the books is in a sort of revolving credit account they call a floor plan.

"Our business is basically bankrupt. We're robbing Peter to pay Paul."

"I assume you've discussed this with your father." I searched Brian's face, his eyes, the tightness of his jaw line. My sweet baby's forehead was developing deep lines.

"Sure. But he doesn't want to talk about it. You know how he is." Brian glanced at me, then looked away.

"What are you not telling me, Brian? There's something else, isn't there?" I knew my son. I could read his face like a billboard. "You told Detective Kronenberg you spent last night in Geneva because you didn't want to walk in here too late, but your flight was supposed to get to Geneva at ten in the morning. What happened?"

"How do you know what I told Kronenberg?"

"I overheard."

He stood up, snapped his wet towel against a supporting column. "I didn't spend last night in Geneva. I was in LaMotte. I stayed at a hotel there."

I waited.

"I had an appointment with a guy who's been looking into the Merz family financial position. Particularly Stephanie's share of the family holdings."

"I didn't know she had any."

"Oh, she has—had—a lot. Importing, exporting, and banking. Old man Merz is super-rich, although it's practically impossible to find out *how* rich. Juergen and Stephanie both have minority shares in the family enterprises." He exhaled loudly and sat back down. "Anyway, that's what I was doing last night. I was in LaMotte talking to this guy who's been checking into things for me. I had to lie to Kronenberg because I don't want Dad or Juergen to know about this."

"You may have made a bad decision, kid." I had never before had to criticize Brian's common sense. It didn't feel good. "What's going to happen when Kronenberg finds out you lied to him?"

"Why would he find out? He isn't interested in me. I had nothing to tell him about why Steph would have done what she did. End of story."

"I have a horrid feeling it isn't the end of the story." I watched his face for a minute. "What did this guy—spy—whatever—come up with? What did he tell you?"

"It's hard to find out anything for sure, Swiss banking regulations being what they are, but it seems their import-export enterprise is worse off than our John Deere business. In fact, they've already declared bankruptcy, gone through a reorganization thing, and reopened."

"Under new management?"

"Not really. Seems like old man Merz is still, nominally, the chairman of the board but with Juergen actually making the decisions. He and Stephanie are both theoretically equal in terms of their voting shares."

"I thought you said old man Merz was super-rich. Now you're telling me he's bankrupt."

"I said their import-export business went bankrupt. Old man Merz still lives in a castle, he still has banking interests—artwork probably worth millions."

"What happens when old man Merz dies? He's ninety-five years old."

"Depends on what's in his will, doesn't it?"

I looked around at the blue tiled room, the pristine pool, and imagined the breathtaking view beyond the fogged-up windows. If the business was bankrupt, did that mean this house would have to be sold? Juergen's home in Zurich? Were the personal finances of Juergen and Stephanie in jeopardy, or were they separate from the business? I asked Brian.

"The business is incorporated. The only thing Juergen and Steph lose is the value of their shares in the business. What I'm worried about is finding out what happened to the two million, more or less, that seems to have gone missing from Lamb's Farm Equipment, Inc. I suspect Steph funneled it into Merz Import and Export."

"And your father doesn't know about this?"

"He knows we're bleeding red ink." Brian stood up again and stretched. "But I'm not going to tell him about this until I know for sure what's going on."

SEVEN

In spite of the day's horrors, night fell on schedule.

Lettie slipped into the living room where several of us were watching the snowy peaks beyond the windows darken and said what we'd all have said if we'd been in normal frames of mind. She said, "I'm hungry."

I sat up straighter, tuned in to my inner self, and felt the telltale edginess that signals the onset of hypoglycemia. I'm diabetic; I have to eat regularly. "Is there anything like orange juice in the kitchen, Juergen? I need sugar."

"I don't know." Juergen also didn't know about my diabetes and probably thought my question was prompted by a simple hunger. "I've ordered dinner for all of us. One of us needs to go and pick it up." He looked at his watch with the dancing dials.

I stood up, intending to go the kitchen, then stopped, my head spinning. I sat back down. "I'm sorry. Would somebody get me something with sugar in it? I don't care what."

"Oh! I forgot your diabetes," Erin said, jumping up and heading toward the stairs. "I'll get you something."

"I beat you to it," Lettie said. She dashed in holding a napkin under a glass of orange juice, the sweet solution to my problem sloshing over the rim.

Within a minute or two, I rallied. Dinner. What had Juergen said? *I've ordered dinner? We need to pick it up?* How? We were a thirty-minute cab ride from LaMotte. Then I recalled the lift. "Did you say someone needs to pick up dinner? How?"

"It's in the tunnel," Juergen, now wearing muffler, hat, and gloves, stood in the doorway. "You haven't seen the tunnel yet, have you, Dotsy? Would you like to? Do you feel up to it? Come along, then. Lettie, would you like to come, too?"

Lettie declined the offer. I climbed the stairs to our room and donned the parka and galoshes Juergen had lent me earlier. He led me out a side door into snow now bathed in moonlight. *We're going to the tunnel to pick up dinner.* I couldn't recall ever saying that before.

I followed in Juergen's footsteps, grabbing the back of his jacket now and again when I felt myself slipping. In the dark, it was impossible to know where to step next, but it seemed as if we followed the path Lettie and I had taken earlier, then veered off to the right and downhill across virgin snow. We traipsed through the cedar trees and came to the quaint little house I'd glimpsed the day before. Sided with cedar shakes and topped with slate shingles, it looked like the witch's house in *Hansel and Gretel*, but smaller.

Juergen opened the door, flipped a light switch, and waved me in.

I don't know what I was expecting, but a shiny, modern elevator wasn't it. I suppose I thought it would be sort of like Willy Wonka's "Wonkavator."

"Oh, you crazy Swiss," I said. "This is incredible."

"Just because we're in the twenty-first century doesn't mean we should forget our past. We're keeping up appearances, as you Americans say."

"This is too much!" I pulled off one glove and touched the gleaming door. It was ice-cold. The distance from the exterior door to the elevator door was, at most, two feet.

"It goes down through the mountain to a spot on the road at the edge of town. The residents of a couple of other houses and I"—he pointed vaguely in directions where I hadn't noticed any houses—"own it jointly. Down below there's a buzzer you have to push if you don't have a key. The signal comes to our houses. So no one can use it without our permission. Shall we go?"

Juergen pushed a button, and the elevator door slid open. The panel within displayed three more buttons: up, down, and stop. Based on the feel in my stomach, it seemed as if we descended rapidly and a long way. My ears popped about halfway down. When the door opened, I stepped out into a tunnel hacked out of solid rock. A couple of overhead bulbs lit the passage to a door at the far end. Left rough and unpainted, the tube made no attempt to look like anything other than what it was—a hole through a mountain. On the floor beside the elevator door sat a large green canvas tote bag. Juergen unzipped the top. Inside the bag sat several insulated boxes and a cash register receipt. "I ordered bratwurst, potatoes, and some other stuff. I've forgotten what else I ordered." He looked at the receipt more closely. "*Ja*. Apple strudel." Juergen slung the straps of the canvas tote over his shoulder and stepped back inside the elevator.

On the ascent, I asked, "So when you want to order food, you call a restaurant and they bring it to the tunnel?"

"*Ja*. All the local restaurants know us. They bring the food to the elevator entrance, buzz us, and we let them in to deposit the food. The door outside the tunnel is well disguised, so you'd never notice it unless you knew what you were looking for."

"Another reason not to invade Switzerland. You have a thousand ways to escape." Trekking homeward again, we both fell silent and the only sounds were the crunch of snow beneath our feet and the crack of branches heavy with ice. Juergen stopped me when we came to the clearing and pointed upward. "Orion," he said. "It gives me great comfort to see the stars. They never change."

★ ★ ★ ★ ★

Erin slipped into my bedroom after dinner when everyone else was downstairs. I put aside the page of Stephanie's notes I'd torn from the pad near the kitchen phone, and patted the bed beside me. Instead, she chose to sit on the side of Lettie's bed, facing me.

Erin's round, gamin face was paler than I'd ever seen it, her eyelids pink and puffy. As she sat, her feet left the floor and her black flats slipped, one hitting the floor and the other dangling from her toes.

"Don't you think you could wear a couple sizes smaller, Erin?" I said, smiling. I intended this as a good-natured tease, not a criticism. When Erin came to know me better, she'd learn how to take my oblique sense of humor.

"These are Mama's shoes. I only brought wedding shoes and hiking boots. Mama said my boots didn't go with slacks." She let the other shoe fall and folded her legs, yoga-style, on the bed.

"I see."

"Have you talked to Patrick today? About the wedding?"

"We discussed it."

Erin's eyes seemed focused on a spot to the left of my head. "You want us to postpone the wedding, don't you, Mrs. Lamb? Please! Patrick listens to you. Please tell him it's okay to go ahead with it!" She laced her fingers so tightly together, they turned white and red. "We've planned this for so long, and Mama has spent everything she can afford on this wedding. I know it's going to be odd, so soon after Stephanie's and Gisele's deaths, but don't you think they'd want us to go on with it? This was something Stephanie looked forward to and helped me plan for. Surely she wouldn't want to know she'd caused it not to happen!"

"Think, Erin. When will the funerals be held? And where?

Gisele's will be here in LaMotte, I'm sure. Probably on Wednesday or Thursday. Stephanie's also. I overheard Chet and Juergen discussing it this afternoon. Juergen doesn't want his father to discover Stephanie is dead because his health is so fragile. Chet couldn't possibly attend his wife's funeral and his son's wedding in the same town and, very likely, on the same day. That's unreasonable. For Patrick it would be *bury your stepmother and go get married*. Boom, boom. Hopefully, with time enough to change clothes between services."

"But everything is planned! All our old friends are coming!" she whined. Erin and Patrick had met at a summer retreat near LaMotte and had stayed in touch with the young people they'd met there, most of whom were from this part of Europe. The majority of the attendees were to be those friends, our family being few in number.

"If money is the problem, I'm sure Chet and I can both help her out. Wouldn't it be nice if you two could get married, perhaps later in the summer, at home where our friends and family could also be there?"

Tears ran down Erin's cheeks. She swiped at them with the palm of her hand. "You don't understand! I knew you wouldn't."

I yanked a tissue from the box on my bedside table and handed it to her. "I do understand, Erin. You and Patrick have your hearts set on your Matterhorn wedding, and now this. It's heart-breaking, but try to imagine how Patrick's father feels. Think how Juergen feels."

Erin gathered up her too-big shoes and left the room. I replayed the whole conversation in my mind and came to a startling conclusion. Erin's haste to marry Patrick was about something else. Something she couldn't talk about. Erin wasn't a whiner and she wasn't excessively sentimental. There must be another problem. A threat of some sort that had nothing to do with the Matterhorn.

I found Patrick in the bedroom he shared with Brian. Stopping in the doorway, I chuckled to myself. As when they were kids, they'd already divided the room into Brian's side and Patrick's side. Brian's side was a mess of clothes, paperbacks, shoes, and boarding passes. A blue Oxford cloth shirt lay crumpled and wet on the floor beneath the boots he'd worn in the snow. On Patrick's side, three pairs of shoes were lined up, toes against the wall, exactly three inches between pairs. Bed made, luggage stowed, loose change in a little bowl on the bedside table.

"Dad and Brian went out somewhere together," Patrick said.

I recounted what Erin and I had talked about a few minutes earlier.

Patrick scooted his chair back from the desk where he had been writing in his journal. "I told her I wanted to postpone the wedding until August. I can get a week off then and she can, too. We could have it at Sacred Heart and most of our friends could attend, but Erin doesn't want to talk about it."

"Why do you think she's so adamant?"

Patrick stood up, laced his hands behind his head, and walked to the window. After a full minute, he said, "I don't know. I really don't. Erin isn't normally like this." He turned toward me, pulled his glasses off, and rubbed the lenses with the tail of his sweater. "She's always so easy to get along with. Sometimes I have to ask her, 'What do *you* want?' She always goes along with whatever I want."

"Aren't there any alarms going off in your head, Patrick?"

He didn't answer me.

"Might she be pregnant?"

Patrick's shoulders jerked. I think my question caught him off-guard. "No. She isn't pregnant." He coughed and stared at the floor. "I'm sure she isn't."

Patrick's discomfort was palpable. I gave him a break and changed the subject. "I've been trying to make sense of this note I found. It's Stephanie's writing and it may have been the last thing she ever wrote." I pulled the note from my pocket, unfolded it, and handed it to my son. "I found it on the pad by the kitchen phone."

"Why did you take it?" He put his glasses back on.

"I'm not sure. I suppose it's the lack of a suicide note that's bothering me." I paused, wondering if that was really it, or if it was something else. Something about the scene in the bunker this morning? Something I'd heard? "Something's not right. Don't you feel it, too?"

"Brian said Stephanie was the last person he'd expect to kill herself. I think he's right, Mom. Yes. I agree with you. There's something we don't know, but what?"

"Look at the note." I pointed to the Au and the Ag.

Patrick squinted at the page and muttered, "Ag, agriculture, agnostic, agent . . . Au, auto, Auburn University, awesome . . . no, that's Aw."

"How about chemical symbols? Stephanie studied chemistry in college, didn't she? And all the A's are capitalized, the way chemical symbols are supposed to be written."

"Brilliant. Sure. Au is gold, isn't it? What's Ag?"

"Silver. I looked it up."

"Silver and gold." Patrick resumed his seat in the straight-back chair, crossed his skinny legs, and bent over the note in a Sherlockian manner. "You may be right, Mom, but that doesn't tell us *why*. Or who she was talking to at the time, or what they were talking about. I assume she was on the phone when she wrote this."

"I thought maybe jewelry?"

"Possible. I suggest we ask Dad and Juergen." With his little finger, he pointed to some numbers Stephanie had written off to one side of the sheet. "Looks like a phone number."

"Too many numbers."

"Not if it includes a country code. It starts with 001. That's the U.S."

"I think we should call it."

"Okay, but let's talk to Dad and Juergen first. No hurry." He turned the paper sideways. "What's this? It looks like Jo bury or Jo berg."

"Looks like her pen was skipping. I'd say Jo bury."

I found Juergen in a small office-like room tucked between the living room and the stairwell. A couple of filing cabinets, a desk strewn with papers, a laptop computer, a swivel chair on a clear vinyl mat. Juergen sat with his back to the open door.

"Knock, knock," I said.

He was on the phone.

"Excuse me," I whispered. "I'll talk to you later."

Brian and Chet had retreated, inexplicably, to the kitchen with a bottle of Macallan's Scotch. Brian sat on the counter, his feet crossed at the ankles. Chet sat on a stool at the butcher-block table, hunched over his glass of single malt, neat. It shocked me to see how much larger than Chet Brian was now. Brian was talking about money. Chet may or may not have been listening. I didn't interrupt them.

Lettie emerged from the bathroom adjacent to our room, dressed for bed, her face smeared with the green wrinkle-reducing goo she'd been using for years. She carried a bottle of lotion to her bed and began slathering her legs.

I was making a copy of Stephanie's note because I had decided to give the original to Detective Kronenberg. I assumed they'd be back soon because they'd left crime scene tape up.

"Will the police come back in the morning, do you think?"

"I wouldn't be surprised. What do you think now, Dotsy? I've been mulling it over in my head all evening. I haven't heard a word anyone else has said to me."

"Me, too," I said, placing Stephanie's note on top of the dresser and slipping my own copy into a drawer. "I don't believe Stephanie committed suicide. It makes no sense. She wasn't depressed. She was picking out wine a few minutes before . . . well, actually I don't know that. I don't know how long it was after that phone call to Juergen. It couldn't have been long though, could it? Unless she came back from the bunker and then went back again later."

"Were there any footprints in the snow leading to the bunker?" Lettie cocked her head and looked up from her slathering.

I thought carefully. "No. Erin and I were the first to walk over that direction and there were no footprints. Ours were the first. The snow was pristine, I'm sure."

"So no one entered or left the bunker after it snowed. Wonder what time that was?"

"You know what, Lettie? I think it was someone from outside. Someone from the town, maybe. At first I thought the only way to get here was the long route by the road, but then Juergen showed me the elevator. We talked about the elevator at dinner, remember? How easy would it be for someone to have come up in the elevator, and slipped back down into town without anyone here seeing them?"

"What about Gisele?"

"What about her?"

"Did she have a key to the tunnel? Did she use the elevator?"

"I don't know, but I'll bet she did. Her parents live in La-Motte."

"Who else? Don't they have a handyman or something?"

"Don't know." I kicked off my shoes and flopped down on my bed. "This is rather useless speculation, isn't it? We haven't the vaguest idea of a motive—motives. Whoever killed Gisele probably had a different motive for killing Stephanie, assuming the same person did both."

"One was killed for some unknown reason. The other one saw the murder and had to be killed as well."

"Either Gisele or Stephanie might have been either one." I stopped and, reluctantly, brought the grisly bunker scene to the front of my mind. "Why was the gun lying there, beside Stephanie? Why did the killer leave it?"

"So it would look like murder-suicide, which it does."

I got up again and knelt beside my suitcase, scrambled through it for my moisturizer. "Basically, it could have been anyone in the whole world. And until one of us comes up with a convincing reason someone would have to kill either Stephanie or Gisele, we have nothing to go on."

EIGHT

Lights burned later than usual in the forensic lab and in Kurt Kronenberg's office. The Cantonal Police, like the LaMotte city cops, were unaccustomed to murder, and murder of a domestic nature was even more rare. Most of their work involved traffic. Most premature deaths involved snow—skiing or avalanches. The few murders they did have usually involved illegal immigrants and smuggling. Their last domestic killing had been five years ago when a man shot his wife and didn't even bother to cover his tracks. Police arrested the husband within hours and had nothing to investigate because he promptly confessed.

The technician in the lab didn't understand the significance of what she saw. Bullet A, removed in the autopsy from Victim A, was a Winchester 9 mm Luger jacketed hollow point. Bullet B, extracted from the chest of Victim B, was a Remington 9 mm Luger metal case. Kronenberg had brought her only one shell casing, a Remington 9 mm.

She dropped by Kronenberg's office expecting to find it closed and dark, but he was still there, squinting at his computer screen as if his eyes hurt. "Here's what I've found on the bullets."

Kronenberg studied the form she handed him, blinked and rubbed his eyes, and studied it some more. She turned to leave. "Wait a minute!" He threw up one hand and waved her back. "This can't be right!"

"I assure you it is," she shot back. "This wasn't rocket science."

"The shell casing I gave you came from inside the bunker. Near the body of Victim A."

"Okay," she said, not seeing the problem.

"It matches up with the bullet we took from Victim B."

"Right."

Kronenberg placed the ballistics report on his desk and covered his face with both hands. "There was no other shell casing in the bunker. I'm certain. We searched that concrete floor on our hands and knees."

"So Victim A shot Victim B."

"We already assumed that. But what happened to the shell casing from Bullet A?"

"Pardon?"

"If Victim A shot herself, what happened to *that* shell casing? Did she pick it up and throw it out the door? The blast blew most of her head off!" Kronenberg folded his arms on his desk and laid his forehead on them. A second later his head shot back up. "And if Victim A was standing inside the bunker when she shot Victim B, who was standing outside a full twenty meters away, and then shot herself, *who closed the door!*"

NINE

I heard the helicopter as I stood at the big windows in the living room, cradling my morning coffee in my hands. The unmistakable *whump-whump* of the rotors sounded, as a dragonfly-shaped shadow swept across the meadow outside. I looked at my watch. Eight-fifteen. Why so early? I expected the police to return, but at eight-fifteen in the morning? What time did these guys go to work?

I heard their knock at a door somewhere above and behind me. I still didn't get the overall plan of this house, and noises were always coming at me from unexpected directions. Wooden stairs creaked and popped beneath a multitude of feet in the stairwell. Juergen entered first, followed by Erin, Babs, Detective Kronenberg, and his sidekick.

"We have to get everyone together," Juergen announced in his high-pitched voice. It sounded as if he was carefully controlling his tone. "Where are the others?"

I ran upstairs for Lettie while Juergen went to look for Chet. Erin was sent to fetch Patrick and Brian, who were supposedly in their room and probably still asleep. Eventually we all settled in the living room. Kurt Kronenberg spoke to us from a standing position, his back to the windows. I had trouble seeing him clearly, with the glare of the morning sun behind him. He looked like one of those light-at-the-end-of-the-tunnel-after-death movie scenes. When I thought back on this later, I decided Kronenberg had seized the spot deliberately so he could see our expressions clearly when he broke the shocking news. We couldn't see his face that well, but he might catch a look of guilt or panic as it flitted across one of ours.

"Yesterday we were called to a scene that looked like a murder and a suicide." He paused, dramatically. "Today, we have a double murder on our hands." He paused again.

I felt the color rise in my face. A little squeak from Erin, several gasps around the room, and Lettie, sitting beside me on the sofa, grabbed my elbow and squeezed it. Without being too obvious, I tried to see the faces of the others. Chet and Juergen were standing behind the sofa, so I couldn't see them at all, but Brian's head swiveled toward his father, his eyes so wide they showed white all around the irises. Patrick and Erin exchanged looks of shock. Babs looked frozen, as usual.

Kronenberg explained what he'd discovered about the bullets and the shell casing and why it meant, unequivocally, that Stephanie couldn't possibly have died by her own hand or by that of Gisele Schlump. He had to explain it three times before Lettie, still frowning, nodded.

"We'll be working here for several days, and I have to set up an incident room. We can move our small van in, but it would be difficult to drive it over the ridge. If you have a room here that we could use, it would make things simpler."

Juergen's words passed over my head. "Bring in your van. I'm sure you can understand the stress all of us are under. We need to talk to each other privately, to comfort one another! I've lost my sister and my good friend." His voice rose an extra octave, trembling. "Chet has lost his wife! These boys have lost their stepmother! We're all at the breaking point!"

Kronenberg waited several beats before he answered. "*Ja.*"

Brian spoke up. "In the meantime, what do we do? Can we leave? Go into town? Go to Geneva?"

"*Ach, nein!*" Kronenberg's face darkened. "You cannot leave.

I will need to talk to you all again. I will . . ." He turned his back to us and jammed his fists into his pockets. When he turned around again he spoke slowly, as if consciously choosing each word. "I do not know how long this will take. Of course, I cannot hold all of you hostage. You will need to buy food, you will need to walk, to exercise. I must ask you to give me your passports. You cannot leave the country and if you are leaving the house, you must tell me where you are going."

"But this could take weeks! I have to be back at work next week!" Babs cried.

"I'm sorry about that, but finding out who murdered these two women is more important."

"Sounds like you think one of us did it," Chet said.

"Given the isolation of this chateau and the time frame, Mr. Lamb, I'm afraid that's the most likely answer."

The room went silent while we took in Kronenberg's statement. I glanced around again and caught Babs looking at me. Was she thinking, *Dotsy, the woman spurned? The one most likely to have wished Stephanie dead?*

"I assume you have tested both victims' hands for gunshot residue," Juergen said. Good old Swiss practicality.

"We found gunshot residue on Stephanie Lamb's right hand. None on Gisele Schlump. The absence of residue on Miss Schlump's hands and clothing tells us she was shot from a distance of more than five feet and did not fire a gun herself."

"Have you narrowed down the time any better since yesterday?" Chet asked.

"I won't to go into the issue of time right now. I'll be talking to each of you individually."

It seemed significant to me that Kronenberg easily answered the gunshot residue question but balked at the one about time. Why? I said, "We know it happened before it snowed. It must have, because there were no footprints there until"—I nodded toward Erin, sitting meekly beside her mother—"until Erin and I went in the next morning."

"I would like to start with Mrs. Lamb." Kronenberg scowled at me. "Let's talk upstairs in the dining room. The rest of you can go about your business, but when I call you in, please bring your passport with you."

I handed Kronenberg my passport and the phone pad note in Stephanie's handwriting. It gave me pause, handing over my only means of leaving the country to a man who looked as if he could hardly wait to sink his teeth into me. Today he wore a coat and tie rather than his uniform, and his blond hair was slicked back without a part. His tweed jacket smelled of dry cleaning fluid. His eyebrows slanted up as they stretched from his pale blue eyes to his temples. He flipped my passport open to the photo page, glanced at it and then at me. We both sat in the same positions at the dining table as we had the day before.

"What's this?" He frowned at the phone pad note I'd handed him.

"I thought I'd better give this to you. I was planning to give it to you even before you told us about—what you just told us about." My voice didn't sound like it belonged to me. "I found this by the phone in the kitchen. It's Stephanie's handwriting. It might be the last thing she ever wrote. I assume she must have been talking on the phone and . . ."

"How do you know it's her handwriting?"

"I recognize the doodles."

He studied the note but said nothing.

"I thought the Ag and the Au might refer to silver and gold. Chemical symbols, you know."

"Do you work, Mrs. Lamb? What do you do?"

"I teach history at a junior college in Virginia."

"Not chemistry?"

"No." Did the man think you had to be a chemistry teacher to know a chemical symbol when you saw one?

He put down Stephanie's note and flipped through a few pages on his own small pad. He nodded to his note-taking assistant in the corner. "Yesterday you said the last time you saw either Stephanie or Gisele, was about nine-thirty or ten o'clock, but you *heard* them later, through the kitchen window, when you took a walk."

"I heard Stephanie. I don't think I heard Gisele."

He flipped back a few pages. "You heard Stephanie say something like, 'If you don't tell him, I will. I swear I will.' Is that right?"

"Yes."

"Was anyone with you on this moonlight walk, Mrs. Lamb?"

"No."

"You just decided to go out by yourself and have a little walk around the house?"

I felt heat in my neck. "I needed to clear my mind. I needed some fresh air."

"Why?" His right eyebrow shot upward.

Oh hell! How did I get myself into this? "We had a roaring fire in the fireplace, and I was a bit overheated. Plus, I'd been riding on trains all day. I was tired of sitting."

"You weren't upset? Angry?"

"No." Okay, I *was* upset because Chet and Stephanie's wedding present had made mine look paltry, but I didn't need to tell him that.

"When did you go to bed?"

I had to think. Hadn't he asked me this yesterday? What was my answer? If I gave him a different answer today, Kronenberg would ask me which answer was a lie. If I gave the same answer, it would sound rehearsed. "It must have been about midnight, I think."

"Can anyone else verify that?"

This was awful. "Lettie. Lettie Osgood."

"Did you go out again after that?"

"After I got dressed for bed? No!"

"Calm down, Mrs. Lamb."

There must be a course in detective school called, *How to make absolutely anyone lose their cool.* I took a deep breath and clamped my hands together under the table.

"How did you feel about Stephanie Lamb? What was your relationship with her?"

"We didn't have a relationship."

"She was married to the man you were married to until she came along."

"I know that." I'd regained my composure. He couldn't shake me now. "That's all water under the bridge. Stephanie was my children's stepmother. I neither hated her nor particularly liked her."

"And yet you were willing to sleep here, in the same house with her and your ex-husband upstairs."

"It was important to my son for all of us to be together."

Kronenberg summoned Juergen to the hot seat after he finished with me. Unable to understand what they were saying in German, I left my bedroom with my cell phone and my copy of Stephanie's note. Lettie and Erin sat curled up in armchairs in the living room, whispering, their heads inclined toward each other. I left them alone and descended one more level to the kitchen.

Before I left home, I'd called my cell phone company, and they'd assured me my device would work in Switzerland. I could call the States with no problem. I checked my signal strength and dialed the number on the note.

"You have reached the Cook County Bureau of Vital Records.

Our office hours are Monday through Friday, eight-thirty to four-thirty. If you wish to leave a message . . ."

I hung up. *Bureau of Vital Records?* Cook County—Chicago? But there were probably dozens of other Cook counties across the U.S. Why would Stephanie have been calling the Bureau of Vital Records? They kept records of births, marriages, divorces, and deaths. "Hatch-match-dispatch," Lettie called it. If I called them back during office hours, would they tell me if Stephanie had requested information? Probably not. How could I find out what she wanted? I could ask Chet. If I did nothing, Kronenberg might do the sleuth work for me. He had the number because it was on the note I gave him, but he wouldn't tell me, would he? His prime suspect? Not unless it gave him more ammunition to fire at me.

I heard voices. From the kitchen window I spotted three women and a man plodding down the slope outside, the women wearing scarves tied around their hair and each carrying a lunch box or bag. I answered their knock and struggled to understand what they were trying to tell me, all talking at once, in German, Italian, or broken English. They had come to clean.

Knowing Juergen was in the hot seat, I hesitated, then realized he had to know they were here. I thought that Kronenberg might put the skids on cleaning lest their cloths erase latent clues, and that's exactly what Kronenberg did. A few minutes later, the crew left by the same door they'd entered.

Passing through the living room again, I interrupted Lettie and Erin's *tête-à-tête*. "Lettie, what's three-twelve the area code for?"

"Chicago," she told me with hardly a break in her other conversation.

Lettie—my own little data bank.

I recalled that both Erin and Patrick lived in Chicago when they were in college.

TEN

After our cold lunch of sandwiches and chips, Patrick grabbed me by the arm. "Let's go for a walk, Mom."

I snagged the coat Juergen had lent me and followed my son outside.

By this time the police had managed to drive, push, and muscle a little van into a spot not far from the bunker. Everyone breathed a sigh of relief when Kronenberg picked up his papers and left the house. Of course, he'd still be calling us in to talk to him, but at least we could talk normally inside the house. I felt conflicted—glad to see the back side of Kronenberg, but sorry I'd lost the eavesdropping potential of our bedroom so close to the dining room. The big detective had never discovered I was listening.

Patrick and I skirted the crime scene tape and headed off toward the west, in the general direction of the spot along the road where the cab driver had deposited me and my luggage. Before we actually reached the road, Patrick pointed north and we walked that way, following a lightly trodden path.

"I know more about the time now, Mom."

"How?"

"I overheard part of Dad's interview with Kronenberg."

"Good boy."

"I wasn't eavesdropping. I happened to be going up the stairs and I couldn't help overhearing."

I decided not to tell him I'd been shamelessly doing that for the past two days. It was beside the point. I stepped around a half-frozen cow patty in my path. Much of the snow on this side of the hill had already melted, or perhaps it hadn't received as much snow to begin with. "Kronenberg thinks I did it, you know."

Patrick stopped and looked at me. "Uh-uh. He thinks Dad did it. He was giving Dad the third degree. I wanted to run in and tell him to leave my father alone."

"Why? My motive is obvious, but why does he suspect your father?"

"Probably because the spouse is always the number-one suspect."

Had Kronenberg learned of their money troubles? Brian told me in confidence about the missing money from the John Deere accounts, so I didn't want to mention it to Patrick now. Ridiculous! Chet wouldn't kill anybody. I glimpsed another potential problem. What if Chet and I became suspects one and two? Would I defend myself at his expense? Would he, if he knew something that would throw a bad light on me, do so in order to save himself? I pushed those thoughts back.

"They found Stephanie's BlackBerry in the bunker."

"I remember seeing it there, lying on the floor." Reluctantly, I recalled the gory scene. The blood, the matted hair, the gun. The BlackBerry phone lay a couple of feet away from the body.

"They checked it and found her call to Juergen was made at eleven thirty-one P.M. It was the last call made from that phone. Kronenberg figures the snow started falling about four A.M. so that narrows it down a bit. Yesterday, all they knew was that it happened between nine P.M. and six A.M."

"That makes sense. It was about eleven-thirty when I heard Juergen talking to her. We were in the living room. They were discussing wine, and I sort of figured she was in the bunker."

"Could she get a cell phone signal in the bunker? It's inside a mountain."

I thought about it. Patrick had a good point. "She could have stepped outside to make the call."

"Maybe she did." Patrick stopped and looked back over his shoulder. Back toward the bunker and the Chateau Merz.

"Do you suppose that was when it happened?" I grabbed his arm. "Do you suppose she stepped outside to make the call and saw someone shoot Gisele? Ran back into the bunker?"

"It had to be *after* she talked to Juergen."

"Of course. Maybe she finished the call, hung up, and then saw the murder."

"Ran back inside."

"But not fast enough. No time to close the door behind her."

I wondered if Kurt Kronenberg had it figured the same way. I thought some more as I walked, following Patrick along the narrow trail. We had left the road behind. The road switched back and down the mountain while our trail swerved the opposite direction into a broadening meadow dotted with flowers and patches of snow. After a couple of minutes, I said, "It won't work. If it happened like that, the shell casing for the bullet that killed Gisele wouldn't have been inside the bunker. And the shell casing for the one that killed Stephanie probably *would* have been."

Patrick turned, raised one finger and said, "Plus, they found gunshot residue on Stephanie's hand." He resumed his path. "I have to think about it, Mom. Oh, what a tangled web!"

The path sloped upward to the north, toward a ridge beyond which I couldn't see. I slowed my pace and Patrick matched his to mine. By this time, I estimated, we had walked more than a mile, maybe two. "This is lovely," I said, "but where are we going?"

"I don't know. I've never been here, either."

At the top of the ridge, I saw that the other side was another broad meadow, but to our left the ridge rose higher and flattened out to a plateau. In front of us, the meadow was strewn with brightly colored fabric and a half-dozen people.

"Paragliders," Patrick said. "This must be their jumping-off spot."

Looking more closely, I spotted a multitude of strings attached to each silk-like swath. The people milled around, straightening, spreading, fluffing, and checking. A young-looking man and woman, apparently lashed together, took off toward the north followed by a billowing cloud of orange and red. The cloud rose, fluttered briefly, and then filled with air as the couple disappeared over the edge of the meadow. My heart skipped a beat.

"Do you want to try it, Mom?"

"No, thanks."

Another man took off a minute later, followed by a solid red canopy. Then I noticed the chair lift. A pair of taut wires emerged from below, from the chasm into which the paragliders had vanished, extended over the crossbeam of a supporting pole and across the meadow to another pole, then up to yet another pole at the top of the plateau. Several empty chairs dangled from the wires, still and silent on their continuous loop. *This must be how the paragliders got up here. They probably have a button or something to start and stop the chair lift.*

I looked to the summit of the plateau, into the glare of the afternoon sun. Something white and thin jutted out over the edge. Sunlight glinted off its tip. "What's that?"

Patrick squinted up, following my gaze, and shaded his eyes with one hand. "I don't know. I told you, I've never been here before."

"Let's find out." I started climbing.

"Mom!" Patrick whined. When I didn't stop, he started

climbing, too, but with enough sighs and groans to let me know he wasn't real happy with me. I slipped on a patch of ice and had to grab a sapling to keep from sliding into Patrick and returning both of us to our starting point.

Patrick blew out an impatient breath and grabbed the sleeve of my coat. "I don't believe you sometimes! Why are we doing this?" He widened his stance and helped me to my feet.

It was worth the climb. At the break in the slope, I hefted myself up and looked out onto a paved landing strip. A short one, yes, but an actual landing strip. "Wait till you see this!"

The thin white thing that had prompted me to climb the slope to begin with loomed directly over my head now. I scrambled onto the tarmac and walked around the most emaciated plane I'd ever seen. It had a tiny bubble-like cockpit with two narrow seats, one behind the other. Elevated tail and long, thin wings tipped up on the outer ends. The wingspan must have been sixty feet or more, but I saw no propeller, no jet engines. "What do you call this thing?"

Patrick, who by this time had scrambled up and onto the flat asphalt, touched the wing that rested on the tarmac, then let his gaze flit up the elevated wing. "It's a glider."

"How do you fly it?"

"You have to launch it with another plane or something. Cool. They call it soaring. It's popular here. I'd like to try it myself."

From long experience, I knew that Patrick's mouth was braver than the rest of him. I imagined someone appearing out of nowhere and asking him if he'd like to go for a soar around the Alps. Patrick would stammer and stall until he thought of an adequate reason for staying on the ground. I looked across to the other side of the shortest runway I'd ever seen and spotted a small, metal-sided hangar. A little airplane, the kind that has wings across the top, sat inside the open bay, its propeller sticking out as if it were curious about the two intruders. I didn't see anyone around and wondered if they'd leave the glider out and the bay open when no one was here. "Do you see anyone?"

"No," Patrick said, already picking his way down.

Back in the meadow, we hung around and watched the para-gliders. Patrick struck up a conversation with one of the men. I walked close enough to the jumping-off spot to look down on the bright silky rectangles swinging gently, riding the currents into the valley below, zig-zagging across a ribbon-like stream on the valley floor. A beautiful sight, but I dared not stand too close to the edge. *Could I ever get up the nerve to paraglide?* With my acrophobia? Not without a double shot of Demerol.

I jumped at the loud thunk that suddenly came from the lift pole beside me. What was happening? The wires began moving and the dangling chair nearest me jiggled toward the plateau. I expected to see an occupied chair rising up from below but all I saw, ascending or descending, were empty. I turned to Patrick.

He joined me in looking for some reason the lift had suddenly jerked to life. "Ready to go, Mom?" He waved goodbye to the man he'd been talking to and we headed back toward our trail.

Something made me look up as I passed beneath the lift support near the base of the plateau. Directly over my head an occupied lift chair on the down-moving side bobbled as its rollers slid over a crossbar. All I could see was a man's pant legs and his shoes. Cordovan Italian-made shoes with randomly placed patches.

I don't know why I bother snooping. I learn more just walking around and minding my own business. Climbing the stairs to my bedroom following my walk with Patrick, I slipped past the open door of Juergen's little office behind the living room and overheard his end of a phone conversation.

"No, no. Not Jo burg airport! Some little airport near Pretoria."

Of course. The "Jo burg" on Stephanie's note was Johannesburg, South Africa. Why hadn't I thought of that? Friends of mine who went there on safari last year came back talking about Jo burg this, Jo burg that. Like a name you really shouldn't use unless you'd been there and were on intimate terms with the place. I paused again on a higher step and listened a bit more.

"They were supposed to have sent twelve." *Twelve what?* "How should I know?" *Know what?* "What else can I do? I have enough to worry about, already." *You can say that again. Don't we all?*

Back in my room, I kicked off my hiking shoes and prepared to take a shower. I could see the police van and the southernmost stretch of the crime scene tape from my window. A light still burned inside the van.

I thought about the phone conversation I'd overheard and about the fact that Juergen was speaking English. That indicated, I thought, that he wasn't talking to a fellow German-speaker, but it didn't mean he was talking to someone whose native language was English, either. The accepted language for international dealings, I knew, was English. Aren't we lucky? When, say, a Dutchman is talking to a Japanese businessman, he'll probably do it in English. That made me recall the argument in German I'd overheard between Stephanie and Gisele. Stephanie, after all, was born in Zurich and German was her first language, but she spoke English with no accent.

Wait a minute. The other conversation, the later one when I'd heard Stephanie yell, *If you don't tell him, I will,* was in English. *So she wasn't yelling at Gisele,* or she'd have been yelling in German. That meant she was yelling at one of us, and I knew it wasn't me.

ELEVEN

We went to a restaurant in LaMotte for dinner that evening. The eight of us bundled up and tramped to the little elevator hut, across the snow that by now had acquired an ice glaze on top like the sugar crust on a crème brûlée. Surprisingly, everyone but Lettie already knew about the elevator. Perhaps Juergen had treated each guest to a guided tour as he'd done for me. Lettie, awe-struck, compared the hut to Alice's rabbit hole, falling down into another world.

The restaurant was expecting us, but we weren't expecting our entry to be as uncomfortable as it was. Maybe Juergen was, but I wasn't. All heads turned when we walked in. The wait staff seemed to freeze in place. The maître d' conferred discreetly with Juergen as he led us toward a table for eight near the center of the rustic dining room. Juergen said something to him and, like so many baby ducks, we turned and followed them to a more secluded part of the restaurant, to a large round table behind a quaint wooden screen. It hadn't occurred to me until now that we were the subjects of keen local gossip, but we obviously were. LaMotte, after all, was a small town if you disregarded tourists, and we had come in the slack season between skiing and summer hiking. The year-round residents probably wouldn't number more than five thousand. The Merz family, wealthy financiers from Zurich with a vacation house above the town, had brought this tragedy down upon them. Stephanie, daughter of the patriarch, had shot herself. But far worse, she had killed one of their own. Gisele—daughter of Herr *und* Frau Schlump, a well-respected local couple. The fact that police now knew it was a double murder wouldn't be generally known yet. The town was in mourning, and, undoubtedly, outraged.

And here we were.

When we first entered, the chatter and laughter of patrons had drowned out the music, but now I heard only the piped-in strains of a string quartet and the scraping of our own chairs on the floor.

I intended to sit as far away from Chet as possible, but it didn't work out that way. Juergen took the chair nearest the wall and motioned Erin to sit on his right, Lettie on his left. He gently nudged Babs, who already had her hands on the chair next to him, away and pulled Lettie toward him. Brian, maintaining the boy-girl-boy-girl alternation, stepped in beside Erin and pulled out the chair on his right for me. Chet followed and sat on my right. Babs and Patrick took the last two chairs.

So suave, the way Juergen stage-managed the seating without appearing to do so. Everything about him said "class." The way his flannel trousers fit just so. The way his hair fit his head without appearing to have been styled. And that watch—that multi-tasking watch with its built-in compass and twirling gears. I wondered how much it cost.

While Juergen selected the wine and discussed menu selections with the waiter, I studied the faces around the table, trying to see each one as Detective Kronenberg might have seen them yesterday—as if I had never seen them before. Erin, so thin and mousey with her big brown eyes, looked vulnerable. I couldn't imagine dark passion or rage hiding behind that little round face. Erin seemed oblivious of her own appearance. She wore no makeup and her hair, pulled straight back into a low ponytail, did nothing to amend the basic roundness of her head.

Juergen sent the waiter off to fetch our wine. I tried to imagine our host in the business suit he'd probably wear on a normal weekday. Tonight, he wore a leather jacket over an edelweiss sweater. He couldn't leave business behind completely, even in these horrid circumstances, because he had spent a large part of the day in his little office behind the stairs. Each time I walked by, he'd been on the phone, talking business. I wondered how his plan not to tell his aged father about Stephanie's death was holding up and opened my mouth to ask, then realized now was not the time. The strain of the last two days showed in a tightness around his mouth. In the restaurant's lamplight, he blinked and squinted as if his eyes hurt.

Our waiter brought three large carafes of wine and placed them strategically around the table. Sidling up behind Juergen, he waited while Juergen asked us, "How do you feel about a cheese fondue? This place has the best in all of Switzerland."

"Oh! It's been ages since I had fondue." Lettie clapped her hands and wiggled in her seat. Patrick whispered something to her and she put her hand over his—gave it a small squeeze. Lettie had learned a lot about Babs Toomey since she'd arrived, and she had relayed it all to me while we were getting dressed to come here. When Lettie, with her near-photographic memory, relays information she does a thorough but lengthy job of it. I've learned not to ask her anything unless I really want to know *everything*. Lettie had talked with both Erin and Patrick that day, but separately.

She told me about Babs Toomey and Mr. Toomey, Erin's father. It seems they weren't married long. When Erin was a baby, Mr. Toomey left and took the entire contents of the couple's bank account with him. His occupation had always been rather hazy, but he claimed to be a pharmaceutical representative. He kept a copious supply of prescription drugs, according to what an aunt had told Erin. Erin, at this late date, had only vague memories of her father. Since Mr. Toomey had managed to obtain an annulment, by long distance and over Babs's protests, Babs had been engaged three more times, but in each instance the deal fell through.

A young man, passing along the hall behind our table, spotted Patrick and did a quick about-face. He dashed over and took Patrick's hand, bringing my son to his feet. "Patrick, my man! I've been trying to call you, but I get nothing but your voice mail."

"Ethan, I . . ." Patrick's face turned red and he choked on his words.

"The wedding, man! It's this Thursday, isn't it?" The young man called Ethan looked across the table and beamed at Erin. "Hey, babes! The bride! Looking good!" He turned back to Patrick, his head jerking backward as soon as he saw the look on Patrick's face. "It *is* this Thursday, isn't it? The hostel is already full. All the old gang is here. We even brought clean clothes. What is it? The wedding's still on, isn't it?"

Patrick took Ethan by the arm and led him away, muttering something the rest of us weren't meant to hear.

"Did I say something wrong?" Ethan said, as he disappeared into the hall, Patrick close behind him.

"Who was that, Erin?" Babs tossed this question across the table, her casual tone and immobile face hiding her private panic, I thought.

"Ethan. He's one of the guys we met at the retreat."

Poor Patrick. If he told Ethan the wedding was still on, he'd have shocked and outraged Lettie, Brian, and me. We had all told him it would be wrong to have it now. I suspected Chet and Juergen felt the same way, although I hadn't talked to either of them about it. On the other hand, if he announced the wedding was postponed, Babs would've passed out and hit the floor, unless he had already talked to her and received her blessing—

and I knew he hadn't.

In a family with five children, I suppose one is bound to be left out or at least to *feel* left out, and it's often a middle child. Chet and I treated each child as an individual, as we would have done if he or she were the only one. But you can't always correct for that birth-order thing, and children are born different. Patrick seemed to have been born a shadow child, vague, fragile, elusive. A steady C student. His only sport in high school was track. The high point of his athletic career was when he came in sixth in the high hurdles at a district meet. Our phone at home rang continuously for more than a decade while the brood progressed through middle school and high school, but few of the calls were for Patrick. He had two dates in high school, and I arranged both of them.

My other four all had something unique going for them. Brian never met a stranger. Most Likely to Succeed, class president, team leader. Charlie, the brain, was valedictorian of his graduating class, now a high school principal and father of three. Jeffrey—biracial, adopted, a natural-born performer, handsome—he had a way of getting down around your heart and warming it. Anne, the baby, the only girl, predictably pampered by her father. I endeavored to counteract Chet's overindulgence with firmness and thereby earned Anne's undying resentment, but I still had hopes of bridging the gap between us. I shook myself out of my reverie. Chet, sitting on my right, was already pouring himself a second glass of wine and the rest of us had barely touched our first.

Patrick slipped back in and took his seat.

"What did you tell him?" Brian asked.

Patrick muttered something about meeting up with him later. I assumed he meant Ethan.

"You'd better man up!" Brian shot this across the table like a slap to Patrick's face.

With my left hand, I grabbed Brian's knee under the tablecloth and squeezed hard. Under my breath, I hissed, "Knock it off!"

The cheese fondue arrived in two large pots set over ceramic warmers and accompanied by baskets of crusty bread. I couldn't remember the last time I'd had fondue. A Swiss invention, it had a brief run as a fad in the U.S. in the seventies, then sort of died out. Lettie said, "I know there's an etiquette for eating fondue, but I'm damned if I can remember what it is." She grinned. "Juergen, before I make a fool of myself, would you refresh my memory?"

I'd have bet more than one of us was glad Lettie had asked.

Juergen slid a cube of bread onto his long fork. "It's not complicated. You aren't supposed to double-dip. Don't bite off part of your bread and stick the rest back in." He demonstrated. "Don't lick your fork and don't spit in the pot." We all laughed, and it felt good. "Try not to drop your bread in the pot, but if you do, don't go hunting for it. Just leave it."

Lesson over, we all dived in. Brian was the first to drop his bread in the pot.

"Tradition says," Juergen announced, raising one eyebrow and his wine glass, "if you do drop your bread, you have to buy the next round of drinks."

Brian affected indignation, but looked around at our three carafes. The one nearest Chet was nearly empty. Brian signaled the waiter for a refill. I was the next one to lose my bread to the cheese.

"*Jawohl!* Another tradition!" Juergen said, and all eyes turned to me. "If a woman drops her bread, she has to kiss the man next to her."

Oh, golly! Was this supposed to be funny? Fortunately I had two choices, with men on both sides of me. I turned to Brian, to give him a motherly peck on the cheek, but he was bent sideways, searching for something on the floor. I yanked on his sweater, then felt Chet's hand on my neck as he pulled me toward him and with his other hand turned my face. He kissed me on the mouth and his lips were not entirely closed, either.

That irked me to no end. After all, two of my children who had finally made the adjustment to our divorce and Chet's remarriage had to sit there and watch their newly widowed, and currently inebriated father, kiss their mother as if this were a stupid game of spin-the-bottle.

TWELVE

I was the first to spot the moving light inside the pool room.

The eight of us tramped from the elevator hut back to Chateau Merz in pairs, Juergen and me out in front. Through the night air, crisp and clear, hundreds of tiny yellow lights from houses in the valley and up the slope on the other side, thousands of stars in shades of white, sparkled as if the very air were alive. Juergen pointed out places of interest along the valley floor while I pretended to see what he was pointing to, his outstretched arm barely visible to me as a dark gap in the distant, twinkling lights.

We had left a couple of lamps burning inside the house, and a floodlight attached to the eave at the highest level cast a cone of light down the corner of the house and onto the snow beneath it. I froze in place when my peripheral vision detected movement in the bluish light coming from the lowest level of the house. Looking straight at it, I couldn't be sure. Maybe it hadn't moved. Maybe a swaying tree limb or a passing bird had produced the illusion of motion.

Patrick, a few feet behind me, bumped into my immobile form and said, "Oops. Sorry."

The light did move. No doubt about it.

The pool room, in what might be considered the basement of a normal, vertically stacked house, was surrounded by large, plate glass windows and was sometimes illuminated after dark by underwater lights, but those lights weren't on now. Instead, a single beam moved to the left, then swerved across the pool water, casting wavy reflections along the far wall, bouncing eerie phantoms off the glass.

"What's that?" I pointed, and, one by one, my seven companions zeroed in on the light.

"Don't panic," Juergen said. "It may be Zoltan."

Zoltan? Did I hear that right? Wasn't that the name of an extra-terrestrial or something? Were we about to get beamed up? I remembered the landing strip Patrick and I had discovered that morning and wondered if the next thing we'd hear would be those five notes from *Close Encounters of the Third Kind.*

The light swerved again. As if attached to a metronome, it swung across the ceiling, down one wall, and back again.

Juergen strode across the last stretch of snow and downhill to the level of the pool. Brian, my fearless firstborn, dashed ahead and caught up with him. The rest of us kept our distance. Cupping his hands around his eyes, Juergen peered in, rapped on the glass. He shouted something in German.

"What did he say?" I turned to Patrick.

"He said something like, 'You're scaring the shit out of my friends.' "

Juergen and Brian disappeared around the corner and I assumed they were entering through the door on the far side. A minute later, the overhead lights inside the pool room popped on and Juergen waved us all in.

Zoltan turned out to be not an alien but Juergen's local handyman. He lived somewhere to the west and he regularly dropped by, Juergen told us, to do routine maintenance on the house. Under a ragged knit cap, his rheumy eyes surveyed our group with little interest. He carried a coil of rope slung over one shoulder and anchored by a gloved hand. The back of his leather glove glistened with the slug tracks left from wiping his nose.

Juergen told us Zoltan was only looking for a sweater he had lost. They talked in German for a minute before the handyman left through the door we had just entered, and my heart returned to something like its normal rhythm.

"You see, Lettie? Kronenberg's *completely* ignoring the most likely scenario." I pointed my toothbrush at her like a teacher chastising a student.

Lettie slapped a glob of age-reversing goo across one cheek and looked up at me from the side of her bed, an attentive expression on her green face.

"I've known all along it was most probably an outsider," I said. "This house is not as isolated as you think. There's the elevator. Anyone from down below who has a key—and who's to say Gisele didn't have copies made?—could zip right up from town. You saw how Zoltan can drop in whenever he feels like it. Has Kronenberg even considered who else, other than us, might have a motive for killing either Gisele or Stephanie?"

"If anyone did come up from the elevator or from the other direction, the snow would've wiped out any trace, like footprints or whatever."

"Right. Chet came back here sometime late that night and there's no evidence of that."

"Maybe they'll find something when the snow melts."

"After all their tramping around on top of the snow—helicopters and all—I doubt it."

Lettie thumbed the lid of her jar of age-reversing goo. "You know what's bothering me? The way we're all acting normal. Laughing, dropping bread in the cheese, kissing the man next to you. It's not right! Two people are dead."

"Time out," I said, making a T with my hands. "I didn't kiss Chet. He kissed me. I could have slapped him."

"That's not what I meant. I know you didn't start it. What I meant was, it doesn't seem right that we're all going along our merry way, all cheerful, and acting like we don't even care that Stephanie and Gisele are dead."

I plumped down on the side of my bed, opposite Lettie, our knees nearly touching. "Because we aren't phonies, Lettie. That's why we're acting normal." My mind flew back to a night ten years ago and a lily-draped casket. "I remember being embarrassed at my father's viewing when I realized I was laughing too loud. I'd been crying for two days, dealing with morticians and organists—and my mother. I was cried out. At the funeral home that night, I saw friends I hadn't seen for twenty years, and we started talking about stupid stuff we did when we were in school. It was still funny, so I laughed. What if I'd refused to laugh? What would that make me?"

Lettie put the back of one hand beside her mouth. "A phony."

"Don't you feel sorry for those poor folks they put on TV a couple of days after a tragedy and stick a bunch of microphones in their faces? If they don't cry, everyone says, 'They aren't sad so they must be guilty.' So they get this kind of forced quiver in their voice. But it's phony."

"And people who really aren't sad do that, too." Lettie placed her jar of goo on the nightstand. "Did you notice how nervous Chet was tonight?"

I pictured the dinner table, the fondue, the tension between Patrick and Brian. I didn't recall noticing anything about Chet other than the amount he was drinking. Was he drinking to calm his nerves?

"He got up three times and sneaked a peek around that partition between us and the rest of the room. Twice, he went to the bathroom, but he took the long route, through the restaurant instead of just down the hall. And he kept turning and peeking through the slats of the partition."

I thought about it. "Maybe he was looking for an alibi."

"An alibi?"

"Chet was in LaMotte at the time of the murders. Drinking, I'm sure, so he was probably at a bar. Until he finds someone who remembers him, he has no alibi."

I took my toothbrush and face cleanser across the hall to the bathroom, leaving Lettie alone to think about my last statement. When I came back, her thoughts had moved on to another aspect of the murders. "Who was the real target, Dotsy? Stephanie or Gisele?"

"Assuming one was the original target, and the other was killed because she saw what happened?"

"Is there any other possibility?"

I ticked off a few on my fingers. "Suppose Stephanie killed Gisele, someone saw, and killed Stephanie in revenge. Maybe someone saw her, tried to wrestle the gun away from her, and it went off. Maybe vice versa—Gisele killed Stephanie. No, that won't work. Gisele's hands had no gunpowder residue. Maybe a third person killed both of them and left the gun beside Stephanie's hand to implicate her." Unconsciously I had stood up and begun pacing the floor.

"Then what happened to the shell casing from the bullet that killed Stephanie?"

"The killer took it because . . ."

Lettie looked at me and grinned. "Yeah. Won't work, will it?"

For the next half hour, Lettie and I reenacted various scenarios, using my Revlon "Natural" as the shell casing for the bullet that killed Gisele and Lettie's Clinique "Raspberry Rush" for the one that killed Stephanie. We dragged a couple of chairs around to make a gap representing the open bunker door. We made too much noise, because Babs Toomey, looking like a duck in a yellow T-shirt and with orange toe-spacers on both feet, burst in brandishing a rolled-up *Bride* magazine.

But our work was not in vain. We reached the conclusion

that, barring a couple of improbabilities, the police were right. A third person killed both Gisele and Stephanie, and unless someone discovered evidence currently unknown to us, these murders would never be solved.

THIRTEEN

The next morning, Chet got the third degree from Kronenberg. His summons to the police van came as we all milled about in the kitchen fending for ourselves—toasting, brewing, and getting in each other's way. He didn't return to the house for nearly three hours. When he did, he merely paused on the stairwell landing and looked into the living room where several of us sat, reading or doing things on laptops, but said nothing.

Patrick said, "You're back. Good."

Chet didn't react or respond. He turned and continued up the stairs.

The day was warming up to the point that I opted to wear the jacket I'd bought in town the other day rather than the heavy parka Juergen had lent me. I left by the kitchen door, climbed around the north side of the house and across the slushy meadow to the police van.

I rapped on the door and heard, *"Geben Sie."*

Kronenberg snapped his feet off the desk and sat up straight. He seemed shocked that one of us would come here unbidden.

"I simply can't stay quiet any longer," I said. "While you're harassing all of us, the murderer is getting away scot-free! You need to be looking for someone who came from outside! Gisele was a local girl. How many people in LaMotte knew her? Was she seeing anyone? Stephanie grew up in Switzerland. How many possibilities does that suggest?"

The pencil in Kronenberg's hand bent with the pressure of

his thumb and pinkie. "I am not ignoring those possibilities, Mrs. Lamb, and may I point out that you know nothing about what I am doing. But I assure you I am considering many possibilities that I have not discussed with you!"

"Not in the last three hours, you haven't."

"Oh! You're angry with me for accusing your husband—ex-husband—is that it?" He stood up, looming over me. "For investigating his possible role in the death of his new wife?"

The implication was clear, but it wasn't as if I hadn't expected it. I shot a glance toward the junior officer, working quietly in one corner of the crowded space. He looked as if he wanted to melt and flow through a crack in the wheel well.

"I'm not accusing you of anything. I'm simply pointing out that we have seven Americans in that house, two of whom never even met one of the victims. But we're surrounded by hundreds of people who *live* here, who knew Gisele or Stephanie or both of them, and who aren't even being considered."

"I promise you, I am considering everything." Kronenberg's pitch lowered, but his mouth remained tight. "Bear in mind, Mrs. Lamb, that LaMotte hasn't had a homicide in more than twenty years. How many towns in America can make such a claim?"

"You've been watching too many American movies," I said. The voice in my head warned me I'd said just about enough. I opened the van's metal door and stepped backwards onto the muddy wooden steps they'd placed at the threshold. As a parting shot I added, "We're not all gangsters."

On my return, I approached the house from the west, where a flight of stairs led up to a deck outside the living room's sliding glass doors. I didn't see Chet until my line of sight cleared the plank flooring. He stood facing the valley, both arms stiff, the balls of his hands pressed against the wooden railing. I wondered if he'd seen me coming and deliberately put himself in my path. Leaning into the railing, his gaunt shoulders jutted upward like two wings between which his head nestled. I felt as if I might start crying in spite of myself. This, after all, was the man with whom I'd watched all 180 episodes of *Seinfeld*. The man who automatically sat on the left end of the sofa so I could plop my feet on his lap for my nightly foot rub.

"Dotsy," he said as I headed for the glass doors. "Come here a minute."

When I stepped up beside him I saw the glass of scotch in his left hand. "Bit early for that," I said, eyeing my watch.

"It's five o'clock somewhere." He squinted out toward the distant mountains. Noon already, the sun hovered over the southern peaks and shone straight into our eyes. I waited a full minute for Chet to say something. After all, he had called me over, hadn't he? At last he said, "Why did you go up there? To the police van?"

"I told Detective Kronenberg he might be well advised to look beyond this house for his killer." I expected at least a grin for that statement, but I got nothing.

"He thinks I did it."

I counted to three. "Where were you that night?"

"In town. At the Black Sheep Bar." He looked at his glass. "Drinking. I came back here about three o'clock and went to sleep on the sofa. I heard nothing. I saw nothing. I did not go up to my bedroom because I assumed Stephanie was there, and I didn't feel like dealing with her mouth."

"Did you talk to anyone at the bar?"

"Yes, but I'm damned if I can remember anything about him except that he was wearing a red ski jacket and he was from Ukraine—that's Russia, isn't it?"

"It used to be part of the Soviet Union."

"He spoke English. I do remember that."

"Didn't he tell you his name? Where he was staying? Any-thing?"

Chet shook his head and took another mouthful of scotch. He swallowed and then crunched the ice in his mouth. His ice-crunching had always irritated me. It still did. "He might have, but I can't remember."

"How did you get back up here?"

"I took the elevator."

"Who let you into the tunnel?"

"I had the key."

"How many keys are there? Juergen told me you had to call up here and someone had to buzz you in."

"Two keys. Only two. Juergen keeps one on his key ring and the other one is kept on a hook in the kitchen. He's careful that no one makes copies."

"But didn't he say a couple of other houses up here also use the elevator?"

"They have the same rules, he told me. They've all agreed that each house will have only two keys—one for the owner and one for the house."

I thought about this. How nice it was that neighbors trusted each other so much. But still, trust can be broken. Someone could have made copies of the key to the tunnel.

"I need help, Dotsy."

His words cut into my chest like a rusty saw. I couldn't look at him because I was afraid I'd see tears and I couldn't handle that. "What can I do, Chet?" *Please don't tell me you need a hug!*

"I don't know, sweetheart. But you're a smart woman. Think."

Now, that I can do! I patted him on the arm and slipped through one of the sliding glass doors, walking determinedly past the decanter of brandy on the sideboard. I craved a stiff drink more than I ever had in my whole life, but it was a bit early for that.

From my bedroom window, I watched Juergen plod across the slushy meadow toward the police van. He carried something shaped like a book in one hand. He stopped, scanning the expanse from the bunker to the southern lip of the meadow where it plunged down and out of sight, as if he could still see Gisele's body lying near the spot where he now stood. He crouched, planting one knee on the ground, and touched a green tuft peaking through the snow. He picked something small—a flower—and tucked it into his inside jacket pocket.

Of all of us, only Juergen had known both Gisele and Stephanie intimately. But how intimately had he known Gisele? I suspected they may have been lovers, but I had no evidence. I recalled the way they had flirtatiously teased each other and the anxiety in his voice that night at bedtime when he couldn't find her.

A phone rang.

I let it ring a couple of times, then realized it was the house phone. I'd grown accustomed to a variety of ring tones from our several cell phones, but I hadn't heard the house phone until now. I doubted I could reach the kitchen before it stopped ringing so I stepped out into the hall, waiting for someone else to answer it, but no one did. After many rings, I found a phone on a wall in the stairwell. *"Guten tag,"* I said, surprised at myself for answering in German.

The caller, logically assuming I spoke the language, launched into a long description in German of something that sounded like a serious problem and ended with, *"Sie nicht?"*

"Por favor. Ich sprechen nicht Deutsch. Bitte," I spluttered.

"English?"

"Ja. Yes." There are few exercises in humility more effective

than playing language roulette with a European.

It turned out to be a florist in LaMotte, frantic to know what Mrs. Toomey wanted him to do with the truckload of flowers. His efforts to dump them in the church had been thwarted by Father Etienne, who told him the next service scheduled was a funeral and that the Toomey/Lamb wedding was canceled. I listened in horror.

"I'm awfully sorry about this," I told him. I took his number and promised to call him back with an answer. To the house in general, I yelled, "Is anybody here?" Apparently not. From the balcony over the living room I looked out to the deck beyond the glass. Even Chet had disappeared. His empty glass sat abandoned on the corner post.

I slipped into galoshes and went looking for somebody—anybody. Rather than hang around the house waiting for the poor florist's next call, I set off along the trail leading east. If I ran into Babs, Erin, or Patrick I'd tell them to get this wedding straight and do it now. *Decide.* Call Father Etienne. Call the florist and whomever else they'd left hanging in limbo.

I thought about Erin's visit to my room the other night and the desperation in her voice. Why so desperate? Erin and Patrick loved each other; what was the big deal about waiting a few months? I felt, strongly, it had something to do with Babs, but what? The wedding dress could be packed up and sent home. Friends who had already arrived in town—I understood most of them were staying at a youth hostel—could wish them well and go home. Postponed weddings happened, and this one certainly should be. No one would fault them for postponing a wedding because of a double murder.

Might Babs have a fatal illness? Only a short time to live? Why wouldn't she say so? Might she be determined to keep it a secret and not put a damper on the nuptial celebration? I could

117

imagine Babs saying to little Erin, at age seven, eight, nine, "On your wedding day . . . If I live long enough to see you married . . . When you walk down that aisle . . ." *ad nauseum.* Little Erin might have grown up knowing that marriage was her mother's idea of a young girl's destiny.

I thought about Stephanie's phone pad note with the Chicago phone number. What did that have to do with anything? Cook County Bureau of Records? Births, marriages, and deaths? Somehow, I knew there was a connection. Patrick and Erin had both lived in Chicago, but had they lived there at the same time? I didn't know.

I had to find Patrick.

When I reached the boulder where Patrick and I had sat that first day, I ran into Babs and Erin. Somehow, telling them about the reason for my errand in the absence of Patrick seemed the wrong thing to do. Erin sat on the boulder, her knees pulled up and her arms folded tightly against her waist. Babs stopped talking as soon as she saw me coming.

"Patrick?" Babs responded to my question. "He and Brian went that way." She pointed ahead, where the trail stretched over a hill and disappeared.

I thanked them and took off, bracing myself for a steep climb. I found my sons in a pretty little glen overlooking another valley. Telling Patrick about the florist, I gave him my most disapproving scowl and ordered him to come back to the house with me. I led both of them back by a more westerly route in order to avoid another meeting with Babs and Erin. Before we did anything else, I wanted to call that Records Bureau again.

I returned to my room and located my copy of Stephanie's note, slipped down the stairs to Patrick and Brian's room, and handed Patrick the note. "They open at eight forty-five, Central time." Checking my watch I said, "We'll have to wait a bit."

"What's this about, Mom?"

"I don't know. But as it stands right now, there's a priest in town who's planning on a funeral tomorrow and a florist who's planning on a wedding, same time, same place. The flowers are on the truck. You've put it off too long, Patrick, and I have a feeling the shove you need is at this number!"

"Why?"

"I don't know. But it's the Cook County Bureau of Records—Chicago. I already called it, but they were closed. For whatever reason, Stephanie either called or was trying to call this number on the day she was killed."

"So?" Patrick almost sneered. His face reddened. In his whole life, Patrick had never used that tone with me. I felt my own face flush.

Brian, who had been lying there on his bed all along without my noticing, said, "Bureau of Records, Patrick. Why does anyone call the Bureau of Records in a place they don't live in?"

"You tell me," Patrick shot back. "I'm serious! You tell me."

"Make the call, Patrick."

I ticked off time zones on my fingers. "You'll have to wait an hour."

"That won't be necessary," said a little voice from the hall behind me.

I turned and saw Erin.

"Patrick and I need to be alone," she whispered.

Fourteen

Brian and I took a walk together, leaving Patrick and Erin alone. We decided to mosey westward along the trail Patrick and I had taken yesterday—the trail that ended near the high altitude landing strip. Patrick's attitude was still on my mind. Did he actually know what Stephanie's call was all about? Why was he acting so defensively? Brian kept his arm around my shoulder as we walked, throwing me off-balance every time he slipped on a patch of ice or slippery rock. Chet, he told me, had gone to his room and closed his door.

"I'm going to have to tell Kronenberg I lied," Brian announced in a casual tone, his head lowered.

I waited, knowing he would explain.

"I told him I was in Geneva the night I flew in, but I was actually in LaMotte."

"Didn't I tell you you should have told the truth to begin with?"

"Kronenberg is sure Dad killed Stephanie and tried to make it look like suicide. Probably wrapped her hand around the gun and fired it again to leave gunpowder residue on her hand, then left and ran into Gisele. Gisele saw what happened so he had to kill her, too."

"Then how did the casing for the bullet that killed Gisele end up inside the bunker?"

"I don't know. I'm just telling you what Dad told me."

We cleared the crest of the hill and our trail wound around

toward the north, paralleling the road down below for a short distance. By tacit agreement, we stuck to the trail.

Brian said, "So Dad has no alibi for the time of the murders because he was in LaMotte, drinking at a bar, but he was sloshed so he doesn't remember anything about the guy he talked to there, except that he wore a red ski jacket and came from Ukraine. The bartender doesn't remember Dad, and the police can't find the guy. Not surprising, with no more information than that to go on."

"So you were in LaMotte at the time. How does that help?"

"Because I saw Dad! I saw him and the guy in the red jacket because I was there, too."

"But you didn't speak to them because . . . ?"

"Because I didn't want Dad to see me. I was talking to the guy who was helping me find out about the Merz business, which, by the way, he called MWU. Stands for Merz-something-something in German."

"Where is this guy now?"

"I assume he left town after he talked to me."

"So. You're in this bar eight thousand miles from home talking to this guy who's been spying for you. You see your father sitting there talking to another man, but you *don't speak to him?*"

"Dad doesn't know I was looking into the Merz business dealings, and he'd have been pissed if he found out. He's sensitive about Stephanie and me getting along. This would be like admitting I didn't trust her. I kept my back to them while I paid the tab and walked out."

"You need to tell Kronenberg before he goes any further with this nonsense."

Five white sheep grazed around a rocky outcrop a few feet away from us. They paid us no attention. Brian took his arm from around my shoulders and loped ahead, cracking his knuckles, one hand folded inside the other. "What do I say when Kronenberg asks me what we talked about?"

"What *did* you talk about?" I paused, then added, "I know what you talked *about,* but what did you *learn?*"

"MWU went bankrupt last year. Very odd because it seemed to be in sound shape, and then all of a sudden—" Brian made a raspberry sound and a "thumbs down" motion. "The John Deere franchise seems to have lost money *just prior* to MWU's declaration of bankruptcy, as if money was being funneled in to prevent the bankruptcy from happening. Looks like Stephanie did it to help out MWU."

"How much stock did she have in MWU?"

"Thirty-three percent. Juergen had thirty-three percent and their father had thirty-four. Juergen has been making the decisions for the company, since old man Merz got too old to do it himself. It's hard to say how much input Steph had." Brian jammed both hands in his jacket pockets. "This guy I talked to says it looks like a case of raiding. He had a Russian word for it, but I can't remember the word. It seems the Russian mafia are in cahoots with various public officials, and they can get an honest company raided and then take it over. Boom! Their records are confiscated, their employees' retirement plans vanish, their assets evaporate."

"This happens in Russia?"

"Right. But MWU does business in lots of countries, including Russia. It's hard to pin things down these days. Large businesses operate all over the globe, you know, especially an import-export business. What this guy thinks is that MWU got slammed and tried to fix things with money from wherever they could find it—like our John Deere franchise."

"Did it work?"

"Obviously not. They did go bankrupt. But somehow they've reorganized and Juergen is still chairman of the board."

"You and your father need to talk to Juergen about this."

"I'd like to, but I don't know where to start. I don't really know anything for sure and Dad . . . well, you know. What could I say? 'Hey Juergen, just wondering. Did you and Stephanie take a bunch of our money?' "

I grabbed him by the elbow. "How about, 'Hey Juergen, how's business? How's your import-export company doing these days?' "

"I suppose I could . . ." Brian's voice trailed off as if he was trying to remember why he really couldn't. I put myself in his shoes and understood. This was a horrible time to worry Juergen with business, and Chet was stressed to the breaking point.

"But first, you have to talk to Kronenberg and tell him *exactly when* you saw your father."

A shadow shaped like an X zipped across the rocky slope from north to south. I looked up. A glider, thin and swift and eerily silent, soared overhead, turned left, and passed directly over the meadow to the east and Chateau Merz. I tried to read the numbers under its wing but it was gone in an instant. But I was pretty sure I knew where it came from.

When I thought back on it later, I knew Patrick and Erin had been watching us from a window because when Brian and I stepped through the sliding glass doors into the living room, the whole group converged as if by magic. Chet walked in from the kitchen stairwell carrying a mug of something I hoped was coffee. Lettie and Babs were already sitting there, Lettie laying aside her magazine and Babs sitting on one end of the sofa, her hands clamped tightly in her lap. Patrick followed Erin in from the stairs leading down from the balcony near my room. Only Juergen was missing.

"Mom, Brian, have a seat. Erin and I have something to tell you."

Erin took a seat beside her mother on the sofa and Patrick

perched on the front edge of the leather chair. Brian waved me into the upholstered armchair not already occupied by Lettie and pulled up an ottoman for himself. Erin's eyes, so puffy they were nearly swollen shut, leaked tears down her splotchy cheeks. She held a tissue-wrapped forefinger under her red nose.

"Go ahead," Patrick told her.

Erin made a noise, a sort of squeak, then covered her mouth with both hands. "I can't!"

"All right, I'll start," Patrick said, clearing his throat. "Erin has been married before. I've just talked to the Cook County Bureau of Records and asked them to check for anything they had on Erin. Seems she married a guy in August of 2006. In Chicago."

A long, anguished moan slipped from Erin's throat.

"Oh, God!" Babs growled between clinched teeth.

"Go ahead, Erin. Your turn," Patrick said.

"It was nothing, really! We never actually lived together! Not like a marriage at all."

"It was legal. That's what matters."

"And you never told Patrick?" Chet, still standing near the door, craned his neck forward, his eyes dancing with anger.

"Slipped her mind," Patrick muttered. "Erin, buck up! Tell the whole story."

Babs stood and dashed from the room but I listened for her footsteps on the stairs, heard none, and realized she was still listening from around the corner.

"I met Rafael when I was in school in Chicago. We went out for a while and he asked me to marry him so I did." Erin took a deep breath but when she went on, her voice was even shakier than before. "What Rafael actually wanted was a green card so he could stay in the U.S. He was from the Philippines and his visa was expiring. Or maybe it already *had* expired, I don't know. We never lived together and, as soon as he got his green card, he disappeared altogether. I haven't seen him since. No one seems to know where he is."

"So how did you get a divorce? *In absentia?*" Brian asked. "Divorce by decree or something like that?"

Erin nodded her head.

Patrick's elbow pressed into the arm of the big leather chair, his forehead resting in his hand. Hearing no answer from Erin, he looked up. "Well . . . that's yet to be determined. So far, we haven't been able to actually find a record of divorce."

"Erin?" I said. "If you're divorced, you must have a divorce decree. Do you?"

"I don't know. I have—something at home. A paper or something."

I had heard more convincing lies from three-year-olds.

"So, Houston, we have a problem!" Patrick's voice suddenly sounded stronger. As if he'd poured a can of spinach down his throat. "Divorce or no divorce, we have no annulment from the church. Without that, no priest can marry us, and I wouldn't want to anyway!"

A loud wail from Erin.

Lettie sat, her head swaying from side to side. She looked as if she wanted to jump up and run to Patrick, to shield him from this pain. I glanced at Chet. He was smiling! Not a big grin of the sort that anyone would notice but just a small upturn on one corner of his mouth, of the sort that an ex-wife could see.

"That's right, Dotsy! Go ahead! Gloat!" Babs Toomey rounded the corner from the back hall and smacked her cardigan against the newel post of the stairs. Shattered buttons rattled as they hit the floor. "It's what you've been wanting all along, isn't it? Can't stand to see people happily married!"

My face must have registered shock. I felt her assault as surely as if it had been physical. "Babs, please!"

"Hey! Watch it!" Brian leaped to his feet.

I grabbed his wrist. "It's okay, Brian. Sit down."

That made her even madder. "The mere fact that you . . . you kept that note! You've been digging for anything you can find to use against my poor Erin, haven't you? You've been hammering away all week to get the wedding canceled!"

In the steadiest voice I could muster, I said, "What are you afraid of, Babs? Surely you don't want your daughter to become a bigamist. She could go to jail." That word didn't sound right. Bigamy, I knew, means having more than one wife. *What's the word for having more than one husband? Bi-andry?*

Chet stepped toward Babs and gently cupped his hands around her shaking shoulders. At first glance it seemed like a sympathetic gesture, but it wasn't. Chet was positioning himself to hold her back, should she lunge in my direction.

"Have you called Father Etienne?" I asked Patrick.

He nodded.

I opened my mouth to ask if he'd called the poor florist but decided that would sound impertinent. Like rubbing salt in Erin's wounds. Instead, I turned to my former future daughter-in-law and said, "I overheard an argument, Erin. On my first night here. Stephanie and someone else were in the kitchen, and I heard Stephanie yell, 'If you don't tell him, I will!' Was it you she was yelling at?"

Erin nodded and blew her nose.

Babs crumpled against Chet's shoulder.

Patrick's left leg jittered. His heated face had fogged the bottom of his glasses in two crescents that lay against his cheeks.

Babs, a few feet behind the sofa, stepped forward and clamped a hand on her daughter's shoulder. "Come along, Erin. Let's pack our things."

"I'm afraid you can't," Chet said. "We still have the small matter of a double murder, and Kronenberg has our passports. None of us can leave."

FIFTEEN

Following the confessional in the living room, tension weighed so heavily on the house I felt I might suffocate, so Lettie and I took the tunnel key from the hook in the kitchen, hurried through the wood to the elevator hut, and descended through the core of the mountain. I tried the key after we stepped through the exterior door of the tunnel to make sure it worked and that we could return home the same way we'd come. Frankly, I didn't much care if we could or not, because the idea of having to take a hotel room for the night sounded good to me.

A short walk down a narrow road, across a little stream, past a few residential houses, and we were back at the train station. "This is where I came in," I told Lettie. We wandered along, dodging the sneaky little silent cars, until we found a restaurant that looked cozy and inviting. We went in.

Lettie peered over the top of her menu. "Are you deciding what to order or studying people's feet?"

I laughed, not realizing until she mentioned it that I hadn't been reading the menu at all. "I'm looking for a certain pair of shoes. Red leather, Italian-made, with odd sort-of patches in odd places."

"Of course. I should've known," Lettie answered with a straight face.

I explained about the man whose shoes I'd seen both outside

and inside the store where I bought my jacket and how I knew they were Italian and expensive. Relating the story of the glider at the high-altitude landing strip and seeing those same shoes on feet dangling from the chair lift, the next thing I heard was our waiter's impatient tapping of pen on order pad.

Lettie ordered leg of lamb and I, having not actually looked at the menu yet, ordered the same. I asked for a glass of orange juice as soon as possible because I was starting to feel a bit hypoglycemic.

"It's fantastic, Dotsy! A landing strip that close to our place? I wonder if Juergen ever uses it. Seems like it would be an easy way for him to shuttle between here and his home in Zurich, doesn't it? If he has access to a plane, and I'll bet he does, don't you? He's rich."

"I know, but the strange thing is the glider. Several times, I've seen a glider or the shadow of a glider pass over our house. You can rarely tell they're coming in time to look up and see them because they're perfectly silent. They have no motors. But I suspect someone is watching us, and I want to know who it is."

"The man in the red shoes?" Lettie wiggled in her seat like she does when she's excited.

"Maybe so, maybe no. But if you see a glider, Lettie, try to remember the numbers under the wing. That would tell me if it's the same one Patrick and I saw on the landing strip."

"Roger, wilco."

The waiter brought my orange juice and Lettie's wine. Lettie took a sip and said, "So the outburst you heard from Stephanie that evening was for Erin, not Gisele. Have I got that right?"

"I had assumed it was Gisele because of the argument I heard earlier that day. Obviously Gisele and Stephanie were having some sort of row. But yesterday it occurred to me that if Stephanie was yelling at Gisele, she'd have been yelling in German. As long as we were assuming Stephanie had shot Gisele and then herself, this made sense, but when Kronenberg told us it was definitely a double murder, I started to rethink what I'd heard."

"Stephanie was having a bad day, wasn't she?"

"She was a domineering woman. I can say that to you, Lettie, because I know you won't think it's sour grapes."

"Right. If you said that to Kronenberg, he'd say, 'Aha! You hated her! Did you hate her enough to kill her?' "

"Exactly." We stopped talking while the waiter deposited our entrées in front of us and asked if we needed anything else. When I was certain he'd gone, I asked, "What do you think, Lettie? If Stephanie *had* found out Erin was already married and confronted her with the fact, would Erin have killed her?"

Lettie hesitated, slowly turning the salt shaker. "She certainly had a good motive, but would she have the guts? I don't think so. I can't see mousey little Erin committing murder. And would she have known how to get a gun? Where *did* the gun come from, by the way?"

"I suspect it was already in the bunker. These bunkers were built for defense so they'd keep weapons in them. Plus, that morning when we discovered the bodies, Erin and I were the first to go in. She already knew the entry code, so she must have been there before. If she'd been there before, she might have seen whatever guns they keep inside."

"What about Babs? Did Babs know about Erin's marriage problem?"

"Oh, I'm sure she did."

"Remember when she yelled, 'Oh, God'? That sounded like she knew what was coming."

"Exactly. And I can *see* Babs wielding a gun."

After our meal, I suggested a bit of barhopping. We ambled down the cobbled main street lined on both sides with ski gear emporia. While passing several bars, I confessed to Lettie that I was looking for one called the Black Sheep. We found it at the far end of town between a Catholic church and a large hotel. In fact, the street ended in a horseshoe-shaped driveway that curved past the front entrance of the hotel.

I grabbed Lettie's arm and pointed toward the church. "That's where the wedding was supposed to be. Tomorrow." I felt tears rising, my nose burning. "Let's go, Lettie. I'll buy the first round."

I chose a small table in the back, close enough to the bar to chat with the bartender but with a clear view of most of the other tables. Several patrons sat at the bar, but no one was waiting on tables. You had to place your order at the bar. I walked to the far end of the bar, several feet away from the nearest customer, so the bartender would have to walk down and out of the thick of things to take my order.

"What a pretty little town you have here," I said as he slid two wine glasses from the slotted rack over his head.

"Just got here?"

"Yes. I'm taking a sort of grand tour—with my friend." I nodded in Lettie's direction. "We started in France and we're making our way through Switzerland, Austria, the Czech Republic, and Ukraine."

"By yourselves?" He filled both glasses with the house white wine.

"Yes. We decided to brave it alone because organized tours are so confining, aren't they?"

He shrugged, wiped a section of his workspace with a towel. "Be careful. Two ladies alone. There are people who will take advantage."

"We know that." Taking one of the glasses and a couple of napkins, I paused, swiping the bottom of the glass before reaching for the second. "Something I've been worrying about, though. Ukraine. I haven't managed to find out much about Ukraine. Bank machines, for instance. Do they have ATMs? You have them all over Switzerland, of course—and France, too. But Ukraine, I gather, is not so modern."

"I think they have bank machines everywhere, now." He shrugged. "But I've never been to Ukraine myself."

"That's just the problem. No one has! I can't find anyone who's ever been there. I mean, when was the last time you met someone from Ukraine?"

"It's been a long time."

I dawdled as long as I could, returning my wallet to my purse, closing my purse, settling it on my shoulder, lifting the two wine glasses, putting them down again, and grabbing a couple more napkins. Giving him plenty of time to recall a customer from Ukraine in a red ski jacket. Getting no further response from him, I carried the glasses to our table.

Lettie took a sip of her wine, looked up, and nodded at someone behind me. I turned.

It was the bartender and he held out a credit card toward me. "You dropped this."

I thanked him and took it.

"Lamb," he said. "I noticed the name. Odd thing. The Cantonal Police were in here earlier asking about an American named Lamb."

I tried to maintain a look of simple curiosity, as if he wasn't talking about my ex-husband but someone else with the same last name.

"They showed me his passport photo and asked me if he'd been in here. I told them I didn't recall ever seeing the guy before."

"Oh dear. I hope it isn't anything serious."

"Would they bother to walk all over town showing his passport if it *wasn't* serious?"

I felt strongly that he knew exactly what it was about. Everyone in LaMotte knew about the shootings at Chateau

Merz. Would he realize the two Lambs were probably related? When he left, I tried to recall what Chet's passport photo looked like. If it was the same one he had before we split, it would be more than five years old by now. Chet had lost weight and his face had grown more haggard in the last five years. Passport photos being what they are, I doubted if the bartender would recognize Chet from that photo even if he *had* been here.

Lettie put the back of her hand up to her mouth and leaned over the table. "Do you think it was Chet's passport, Dotsy? Or Brian's or Patrick's?"

"I'm sure it was Chet's."

Lettie balled up her fists and slammed them against her thighs. "What can we do? This is terrible! I mean, what if they arrest Chet or something? Do you think they have any evidence against him?"

"They don't believe Chet's alibi. He says he was here but, as you just heard, the bartender doesn't remember him. If they check into the John Deere franchise's books, they'll find it's nearly broke. They may even find out that Brian suspects it was Stephanie who was taking their money and putting it into a Merz family business."

Now that I started it, I had to tell Lettie the whole thing. But Lettie would never tell anyone else. I could trust her. The story lasted longer than my wine, so I ordered another for both of us. Lettie sat, fidgeting, until I finished.

"Do you think he did it, Dotsy? You know what? I heard him come in that night. I heard him stumbling up the stairs after we were in bed."

"I heard him, too. And no, he didn't do it! Chet may be a jerk and a spineless egotist, but he isn't a killer."

Lettie stepped to the bar and returned with our fresh drinks.

"I don't know what to do, Lettie. I can't just sit around and let Chet get blamed for murders he didn't commit. There's something else going on here, but I haven't the vaguest idea how to find out what it is. There's the man in the red shoes. There's my son's fiancée, who happens to be already married. There's her plastic mother. Gliders flying over our heads. Tunnels through mountains. Weird notes on phone pads. Johannesburg. World War II bunkers with guns and wine bottles and . . ." I let my voice trail off, realizing how far afield my brain had wandered.

"You know what you should do?" Lettie slapped a pudgy, red-nailed hand on the table.

"What?"

"Call Marco!"

Brilliant! Why hadn't I thought of that?

Lettie and I picked our way from the elevator hut through the trees, then westward toward the Chateau Merz. A crystal clear night with no moon; stars were out by the thousands. To the north, a large mound warped the horizon, dividing starry black above from solid black below and at the top of this mound, a black silhouette. A telescope angled upward on a tripod. A figure, kneeling, with head close to the telescope's lower end.

"Juergen?"

"Dotsy. I thought I heard someone. I'm glad it's you."

"I have Lettie with me."

"Come on up. I want to show you. But be careful. I almost broke my leg climbing up here."

Feeling the slope with my hands, I began climbing.

Lettie said, "I'm going back to the house. Give me the tunnel key so I can put it back on the hook."

I picked my way up the hill, touching rocky outcrops, feeling around and testing each foot placement before putting my full weight on it. When Juergen's outstretched hand touched my arm, I smelled the leather of his jacket. He helped me up. "Close your eyes for a minute so they can become dark-adapted."

I did as he said.

When he told me to open them, I saw he had a green laser aimed at the heavens. "Do you know Orion?" He swerved the green beam around the constellation I had always thought looked more like an hourglass than a hunter.

"Where I live in Virginia, we have a fairly dark sky. I can often see the Milky Way."

"As well as this?" He moved his beam along the broad sweep of the Milky Way.

"It's never this clear or this bright at home." For the next half-hour Juergen showed me star clusters, nebulae, and constellations with an eagerness in his voice I hadn't heard before. He told me about seeing the Southern Cross directly overhead when he was in Antarctica. He fiddled with his telescope and, guiding me to the chair he'd brought out with him, let me sit, twist my neck into a painfully torqued position, and see Saturn—rings and all. His wristwatch had a dark blue face now, and a back-lit crystal that rotated when he moved his arm.

"I had to escape the house, so I came up here," he said.

"Did they tell you about the dust-up this afternoon?"

"Oh, yes. I could hardly miss it. I came back to the house after you and Lettie had left for dinner and found rooms being switched. Like—what do you call it?—musical chairs. Babs and Erin are moving their things to a room down below, near the pool. Patrick and Brian were discussing moving up to the room the women vacated, but I don't know whether they did or not."

"It's awkward. Not that I have any sympathy for them. It's Patrick I feel sorry for, but it's too bad they can't leave."

"Kronenberg might let them go to a hotel in town. After all, they can't leave the country as long as he's got their passports."

"That's what I'd do, if I were in their place. I'd go to a hotel."

"You understand, though, that I can't suggest it, because it would look as if I was throwing them out." Juergen turned a red light onto a star chart at the foot of his telescope.

"I can't suggest it either. Babs and I don't get along. She already thinks I'm out to get her."

His flicked the red light off. "I wish she would stop flirting with me."

I nearly choked on a laugh. That came totally out of the blue. "She's flirting with you?"

"Watch her. You'll see what I mean."

"Did you stick with your decision not to tell your father about Stephanie?"

Juergen walked over to a boulder and sat. "Yes. His nurses are censoring the news and warning his visitors to stay off the subject. It's hard, though. He wants his evening news on the television but the nurses are only allowed to let him watch the weather channel."

"I'm sure you'd like to go see him yourself."

"Until today, I couldn't. If I'd seen him, I'd have broken down. Maybe tomorrow I'll talk to Kronenberg about making a quick trip to see him."

Careful not to upset the telescope, I stood up. My dark-adapted eyes saw Juergen dimly, hunched over with his elbows on his knees. I waited for him to go on.

"I spent most of today with Gisele's parents in LaMotte," he said. He sucked in a lungful of air. "I'm afraid they blame me, partially. If she hadn't been here that night, she'd still be alive."

"But didn't she stay here often? Didn't she keep a room here?"

"Right. But she didn't always stay. Just when . . ." his voice trailed off and I wondered what the end of that sentence would have been. I waited a minute in silence, heard a soft keening moan. He was crying. "She was—she was a good friend." This came out as a high-pitched whine.

I wanted to ask, "Did you love her?" Instead, I said, "Such a beautiful woman. I wish I could have known her better."

"Beautiful. Yes." He blew his nose, waited, inhaled deeply. "She was so good—so clean—like the air here." He paused and cleared his throat. When he went on, his voice quavered and rose to a squeak. "Now that she is gone, I feel as if I should sell this house. I don't want to come here anymore."

I was glad I couldn't see his face clearly. I wondered if Gisele knew how he'd felt about her. I wondered if she had felt the same. I wondered if Gisele's parents knew about them.

From down below came the voice of Babs Toomey. "Juergen? There you are! Everyone's been asking where you were!" Juergen stood up, stepped over toward me, and whispered, "Don't leave, Dotsy. Stick with me."

SIXTEEN

Sergeant Seifert's head bobbed, warning him he'd fallen asleep
again. Sitting the midnight to nine A.M. shift in the police van,
his two duties were: (1) keep an eye on the taped-off zone
around the bunker door, and (2) watch the videotapes from the
security cameras. Kronenberg had forbidden him to use the
fast-forward button for fear it might cause him to miss some
tiny little movement. A head peeking around a corner for a split
second. A shadow dashing across the bottom of the screen. This
was not what Seifert had in mind when he decided to become a
cop. Since midnight, he'd walked the perimeter of the yellow
tape a dozen times just to give his eyes a break; an owl swoop-
ing down on a rodent provided the major excitement of the
night.

When Juergen Merz brought these tapes to them yesterday,
Kronenberg nearly had a coronary. They had noted the position
of the security cameras soon after their investigation began, but
the devices had apparently been turned off for months. An
antiquated system, rarely used. Herr Merz had apologized for
its age, as if the police had a right to expect state-of-the-art
surveillance in remote mountain homes. He had come to them
that day with the tapes and told them he had, in fact, turned
the security cameras on that evening because he was concerned
about Gisele. He'd asked her to spend the night so she could
start breakfast early for the houseful of guests. Each of the three
cameras had recorded over any previous images, running out of

tape when Herr Merz forgot to turn them off.

One camera hung from the northeast corner of the house, one from west end of the upstairs hall, and one from the corner of the deck railing outside the main living room. The first kept watch over the east side of the house, down the slope past the kitchen door and the pool room. The second looked down a hall with several doors, one of which—the door to Merz's bedroom—had been left open all night. The third pointed in such a way as to see the exterior stairs leading up to the deck as well as most of the living room and the balcony above it. It could see only a sliver of the passage outside the doors of the Toomey women and that of Frau Lamb and Frau Osgood. The bathroom across the hall from their rooms couldn't be seen at all, but Kronenberg had pointed out a glow cast on the opposite wall when someone turned on the bathroom light or opened its door. All three recorded their vistas dimly, in shades of blue, because, except for the beginnings and ends of the tapes, the only light sources were the halogen floodlights under the eaves.

Seifert heard the scraping of shoes on the wooden steps outside the door, the turn of the knob, and he felt the van dip toward the south as Kronenberg's bulk crossed the threshold. The smell of coffee came in with him.

"Wake up. Breakfast." Kronenberg plopped two paper bags on his desk. One held a croissant, the other, two cups of coffee. Herr Merz had borrowed one of the precious keys to the tunnel, lent for the duration of the police investigation, from another upslope resident. The coffee, from a restaurant down below, was still warm. Handing over the croissant and one of the coffees, Kronenberg said, "What do we know that we didn't know yesterday?"

"Camera one, two-eighteen A.M. Chet Lamb walks around the house from the north, past the kitchen door, past the pool room, and disappears."

"Two-eighteen," Kronenberg echoed. He dragged a chair around and sat beside his junior officer in front of the monitor. "What else?"

"That's it."

"Damn!" He took a sip of his coffee. "That doesn't necessarily contradict the story he told us, but it doesn't back it up, either. If he was in town, as he said he was, and came up from the tunnel, he would have walked down that way, but it seems as if he'd have gone in one of the two doors on that side of the house. It was cold. Started snowing about four. But instead, he walks *around* the house. Did he go through the door to the pool room? He could have gone up the steps to the deck. But why?" Kronenberg jiggled his foot. "He could have walked across the meadow and up to the bunker. Could have gone completely around the house, looking in windows. Could have seen the bunker door open and a light inside."

"I've been wondering, sir. Isn't it rather a coincidence that Herr Merz turned on the cameras on this particular night? Of all nights?"

"What are you suggesting, Seifert?" Kronenberg barked. "That Herr Merz knew there was about to be a murder and turned on the cameras to catch the action?"

"No, sir. I didn't mean that."

"Herr Merz has already explained that he turned the cameras on because he was concerned about Gisele."

"How would turning on the cameras help?"

Kronenberg's foot jiggled faster. A bit of coffee sloshed onto his pant leg. "I wonder if he called down to the village. Called her parents and asked if she was with them. Did I already ask him that question?"

"I don't believe so, sir."

"What about camera two? The one on the porch? I watched most of that one yesterday before I left. Did you finish it?"

"No one went up or down those outside stairs all night. The light in the living room went out at twelve thirty-two as you already noticed, and after that, you can't see anything inside the house except a small flash at the top of the screen whenever someone turned on the bathroom light. I've written down those times, sir."

"They don't mean anything. Just women going to the bathroom."

"What about camera three?"

"In the upstairs hall, the door to Herr Merz's room was open and it stayed open all night. Others stayed closed. Herr Merz's bed was right in line with the camera and you can actually see him in the bed. He first entered the room at twelve thirty-four, came out, in pajamas, at twelve forty, looked out the hall window for a minute, and went across the hall to the bathroom. Went to bed. Went to the bathroom again at two fifty. Do you want me to tell you how many times he rolled over? I wrote down the times."

Kronenberg craned his neck toward Seifert's notepad as if he didn't believe he'd actually done that. "What about Patrick Lamb?"

"No sight of him in any of the tapes, sir."

Kronenberg sat back and exhaled loudly. "It's too damned bad none of those cameras was pointed toward the bunker."

Seifert picked up his pad and glanced at his notes. "The snow started falling on the east side of the house at four oh-two, sir. On the south porch, not until four oh-three."

"That's very helpful, Sergeant."

"And I think an owl caught a mouse about three this morning." Seifert was making a point: I'm conscientious, I'm smart enough to see the humor in this, and I need more to do.

"Chet Lamb is our man. We know he was out there even if we don't know exactly where he came from or went to, outside camera range. Herr Merz is completely accounted for, and we have no reason to think that Frau Osgood, Frau Lamb, Patrick Lamb, Fraulein Toomey, or Frau Toomey were anywhere other than in bed, where they told us they were."

"And Brian Lamb hadn't arrived yet." Seifert bit into his croissant, swigged his coffee, wiped his mouth on his wrist. "What about that phone pad note Frau Lamb gave you? Anything to that, you think?"

"That woman needs something to keep her busy. Knitting or something."

"And the wedding is off because Erin Toomey may already have a husband." Seifert lowered his head, careful to make his next statement in a way that didn't sound insubordinate. "If Stephanie did know about this, then Erin had plenty of motive to kill her. And the Chicago phone number was on the note. In Stephanie's writing."

"I realize that," Kronenberg shot back. "But I can't see Erin Toomey wrestling Stephanie Lamb into a head lock long enough to shoot her. Can you?"

"How about the mother? Babs Toomey was keener to get that wedding over than Erin was."

"Babs Toomey wouldn't have had to use a gun. She could have frozen her with one look." Kronenberg looked at Seifert as if he realized he should stop belittling the sergeant's ideas. "But you're right. Both of the Toomeys may have had motive, and, if so, they'd have had to act quickly before Stephanie told what she knew."

"At least Patrick Lamb and Lettie Osgood are in the clear, aren't they? No possible motive there."

"Ah, ah, ah! Not so fast. None that we *know* of."

"Have you wondered if Herr Merz and Gisele were more than they let on? If they were lovers? It might account for Herr Merz getting so upset when he couldn't find her at bedtime."

"Let's don't go there. Stephanie Lamb was the intended victim, and Gisele was collateral damage. She was killed because she saw too much."

"Sir?" Seifert raised his eyebrows, then quickly diverted his gaze to the wall and said nothing.

"Chester and Stephanie Lamb were having problems." Kronenberg stood up, began pacing the only five feet of unobstructed floor in the van. "Their farm equipment business in Virginia was in trouble and Lamb thinks his wife was skimming the profits. Brian Lamb has hinted as much—and, by the way, that man knows more than he's told me so far. Stephanie led Chet around as if he had a ring through his nose. He says he was in the Black Sheep from ten-thirty until whenever, but no one remembers him and he can't tell us anything about the man he allegedly talked to for hours. Chet Lamb is definitely our man."

As if he had heard Kronenberg call his name, Brian knocked on the van's door a few minutes later. At Dotsy's insistence, he hiked across the meadow as soon as he finished his morning coffee. Entering, he took a deep breath. "Is this a good time? I need to tell you a few things I omitted earlier."

Kronenberg pulled out a folding chair for Brian, then seated himself in the power position behind the van's only free-standing desk. Seifert grabbed his notepad and scooted his chair to the corner behind his boss.

Brian's tongue darted over his lips. "I need to fill in a few blanks in what I've already told you—no, that's not quite right." He cleared his throat. "I haven't told you the truth about where I was on the night of the murders."

"I trust that's what you plan to do now."

"Exactly." Brian leaned forward, pressed his elbows into his knees. "I wasn't in Geneva that night. I was in LaMotte. I spent the night in the big hotel there and took a taxi up here the next morning."

"Why didn't you tell me that to begin with?"

"Because I didn't want my father to know I was in LaMotte, and I felt like I had to tell you the same story I told him. I didn't think it would make any difference—at the time."

"Now it does."

"Right." Brian told the story of his meeting at the Black Sheep with the man who had been checking into the Merz family businesses. Words flew from his mouth faster and faster as he talked about Stephanie's role in Lamb's Farm Equipment, her stake in MWU, the Merz family's import-export business, and Chet's ostrich-like refusal to see the problem.

Kronenberg stopped him with an upraised hand a couple of times, letting Sergeant Seifert catch up in his notes. "And this meeting took place in the Black Sheep Bar. Now you're going to tell me you just happened to run into your father there."

Brian's face reddened. "Well, yes. I did. But I couldn't let Dad see me, so I got out of there as fast as I could."

"What a coincidence. You were actually there, and saw your father where he said he was, on the evening for which he needs a witness to his whereabouts." Kronenberg slapped his open palm on the desktop. "I don't believe in coincidences!"

"I'm telling you the truth."

"You understand, Mr. Lamb, that I'll need confirmation of your story. What was the name of this gentleman you met in the Black Sheep?"

"I don't feel comfortable telling you his name, because—"

Kronenberg withered him with a stare.

"But, of course, you need the name. I understand. Of course." Brian threw up two hefty hands, protectively. "He's going to be furious when you call him. I promised the guy nothing he told me would go any further and I wouldn't involve his name in anything that came up later. He was probably thinking about a possible lawsuit. But not murder!"

"His name, please."

Brian cleared his throat and croaked, "François Bolduc. Lives in Zurich," then pulled out his cell phone and dictated the number.

"Can anyone verify that you really went to the hotel after you left the bar?"

"Talk to the concierge. A man was on duty that night. I asked him about getting a taxi in the morning."

"You've talked this over with your father?"

"No. He knows nothing about this."

"What about Juergen Merz?"

"I haven't talked to him, either. I'm not looking forward to him finding out I've had a spy looking into his business affairs."

"Have you any reason to think the murders of Stephanie and Gisele were related to these business problems?"

"I have no idea why either of them was killed."

Kronenberg glared at him.

"No idea at all."

SEVENTEEN

I felt as if I should tiptoe around the house and peek into each room before entering, the eerie calm a paper-thin blanket over the tumult beneath the surface. Lettie and I had talked until two A.M. after I came in from star-gazing with Juergen. It had taken Juergen and me quite a while to get rid of Babs Toomey, determined as she was to outlast me and have Juergen to herself. Under the Alpine stars. How romantic. Every time I tried to leave, he'd grab me by the collar and insist I wait until he located one more nebula, one more star cluster, in his telescope. I could tell he hadn't finished all he wanted to tell me about Gisele, but he finally gave up, packed up his equipment, and handed Babs something heavy to carry back.

Patrick moved his things upstairs to the room beside Lettie and me, the one Babs and Erin had vacated. Lettie told me Patrick and Erin had retreated to that room, closed the door, and talked for more than three hours, emerging occasionally to replenish the contents of their glasses. Coke, she thought.

I carried my morning coffee to the living room and found Juergen sitting in his favorite chair, the big leather one with the butt-sprung seat. His face now drawn and haggard, he looked years older than the energetic man who picked me up from the taxi four days ago. The laptop on his knees wobbled as he typed an email message to someone, hit "send," and picked up the cell phone chirping on the arm of his chair.

I slipped out the sliding glass door to the deck, respecting his privacy. To the south, I saw Chet sitting on a rock near the edge of the precipice that marked the limit of Chateau Merz's lawn, and from where I stood it looked as if one step forward would send him over the edge. I caught my breath. His silhouette sloped from his head to his elbows as if he had no shoulders left. Where was Brian? Still with Kronenberg in the van? Spilling his guts? I wished I were a fly on the wall inside that van.

Stepping back inside, I pulled the door shut behind me.

Juergen closed his laptop, set it on the ottoman in place of his feet, and scrubbed his face with both hands. "I have to go to Zurich. They've taken my father to the hospital."

"What's wrong?"

"They don't know yet." He stood, his gaze swerving to the windows. His eyes teared up. "What next? My God, what next?"

"How will you get there?"

"I left a car at a garage in LaMotte."

I wondered how many cars he had. I wondered if he had a plane and whether he ever flew into the landing strip I'd discovered.

"I must go and talk to Kronenberg," he said, and then he shocked me. "Would you like to come with me to Zurich?"

I'm sure I stammered a bit before I answered, "I'd like to, but I really need to hang around here. I haven't talked to Patrick since . . . since yesterday. And we do need to talk."

"Of course. I didn't think." Juergen turned his back to me and stepped closer to the windows. "I'll probably be back late tonight or early tomorrow. I'll call the house here and check on things periodically." He slid a door open and stepped through to the deck, then turned back to me. "Take care, Dotsy—keep your eyes and ears open."

From my bedroom window, I watched Brian slog across the meadow from the van to the house. A minute or so later, Juergen made the reverse trip. I watched for perhaps ten minutes, then saw him leave the van, taking the path north of the house that led eastward to the elevator hut. Meanwhile, Lettie came in and flopped onto her bed.

"Juergen's father has been taken to the hospital," I told her. "He's going to Zurich to see him."

"I assume he cleared it with Detective Kronenberg."

"Do you know what Juergen just asked me?" I turned from the window and looked at her. "He asked me to ride along with him to Zurich."

"Why? I mean, was it like a come-on or more like *so we can talk?*"

"I'm not sure. If it was a come-on, I'm flattered. He's probably ten years younger than I am."

"Have you called Marco yet?"

I had forgotten about calling Marco. When we were at the Black Sheep last night, Lettie and I had decided the smartest way to start making sense of my tangle of observations was to call Marco, the policeman. "I'll do it now."

I grabbed my cell phone and headed for the deck. Out there, I'd found, I could get a stronger signal. Passing through the living room, I noticed Juergen's laptop still sitting on the ottoman. I picked it up. Its cover was closed, but it was warm on the bottom.

"Juergen left this thing turned on and now he's gone to Zurich," I said to Lettie, who had followed me down the stairs. "The battery will go dead before he comes back."

"Do you know how to turn it off?"

I opened the cover and found the screen still lit, his email in-box displayed. "He forgot to log out of his mail, too."

We weren't really snooping, I reasoned. We were doing him a favor. Lettie shouldered up to me and we scanned his incoming messages. Most of the senders and subjects were in German, but a few were in English. A couple of the names sounded Russian. Lettie pointed to one with a subject line that read, "Done."

"Click on that one, Dotsy. Apparently it's in English. Let's see what it's about."

"No way. You see the little bullet on the left side? That means Juergen hasn't read it yet. If we click on it, the little bullet will go away and Juergen will know someone read it before he did."

"Whatever."

Lettie knows I hate that word. It's her way of saying, "Whatever." The last three incoming messages, all unread, came from a Kamilla Duerr. Two of those had arrived within the last ten minutes. I shut down the computer and took it to Juergen's little office on the stairwell landing behind the living room.

Marco answered on the third ring with, *"Pronto,"* an Italian greeting that always makes me feel I should hurry up. "What time is the wedding?" he asked. "Are you getting dressed now?"

"There *is* no wedding. It's been called off." I explained and could almost hear Marco slapping himself on the forehead when I told him Erin might already be married.

"Stai mentendo!" he said. "Tell me you are lying!" He asked how Patrick was taking it, and I had to confess my son and I hadn't really had a chance to talk yet. "So what are you waiting for? Come to Florence! We are having a festival and I miss you!"

"I can't. The Swiss police have my passport and I can't leave the country. I'm afraid Chet's wife and the house cook have been murdered. We're all suspects." This prompted a torrent of Italian from the other end. When Marco's verbal monsoon abated, I said, "I need your help."

"I cannot help you. I told you, I cannot leave Florence until the festival is over."

"I don't mean *come here*, I mean *listen*. Several things have happened that I can make no sense of, and I want to pick the brain of a man who knows all about international crime and Italian shoes and spies—and Johannesburg."

Marco loves flattery. He laughed in that hearty way he has, then listened while I poured out my crazy laundry list of unexplained observations. He said, "Johannesburg is in South Africa, of course, where they mine gold, silver, and diamonds. Crime in South Africa is something you do not want to get mixed up in. It is horrible. The conditions in the mines are inhuman. As for your spies in gliders, you can find out who is doing this by simply asking. Go to the place—the landing strip—and ask them who flew on a certain day. It is not privileged information."

"And Marco? Somehow, Russian names—the Ukraine—there may be . . . oh, I don't know what I mean."

"Russian, did you say?" He paused. "That rings a bell in my head. Something."

"What?"

"I do not know. Let me think about it. I will call you back." He paused. "What do you need to know about the red shoes?"

I laughed. "Nothing. If I get a chance I'll take a picture of them and you can find out who made them. Maybe they keep a list of fools who pay that kind of money for a pair of shoes." I paused, and then added, "I miss you, Marco."

"I miss you, too."

I wore a silly smile for an hour after that call. Patrick found me in the kitchen and consented to let me make him a sandwich. We ate at the butcher-block table in the middle of the room.

"Where have you been all morning?" I asked.

"I went down to LaMotte and talked to Father Etienne."

I felt a little jab. He'd confided in Father Etienne rather than me, his own mother. I tucked that hurt away and said, "Did it help?"

"Sort of. He's hard to understand. His English is not good, but mostly he just listened."

Patrick tamped wayward breadcrumbs with his middle finger. "He asked me how I could have been so stupid—he didn't say stupid, he said naïve or something—means the same thing. He also told me I owe you a big one. A big thank you. If you hadn't picked up on that phone number and followed through on your hunch, I might be getting married," he looked at his watch, "in about one hour from now." He put down his sandwich and reached across the table. Laid his hands on mine. "Thanks, Mom."

"I wouldn't say it was a hunch. More like a loose thread. Besides, you were going to call it off anyway, weren't you?"

He helped me load the dishwasher, pausing at one point to slip his arm around my waist and kiss the top of my head. I knew he had more to say, but our kitchen chores were done. "I need to go back to that landing strip, Patrick. Will you go with me?"

"What for?"

"I've seen that glider again. The one we saw up there. It's flying over this house oftener than you'd expect if it's only for fun. I want to know who's doing it, and Marco told me all I have to do is go and ask them."

"Another hunch? Hey, what's up? Are you and Kronenberg in a race to see who can solve these murders first?"

"Never mind. Humor me. A walk will do us both good."

Before we could leave the house I had to shake Chet off. He wanted to come with us, but I knew that would kill the conversation I wanted to have with Patrick. "Don't leave me here with Babs Toomey," Chet pleaded.

I laughed. Babs was really casting her net wide. I reminded him that Lettie was upstairs and he could, if need be, hide behind her skirts.

When we reached the spot where the path turned north, away from the hairpin turn in the road, Patrick started to talk. "Erin thinks we can get beyond this. We can go home, check things out, discover that she really isn't married and everything will be hunky-dory. No problem."

"But it's not that simple," I prompted.

"Whatever the case turns out to be, she can probably get an annulment from the church. Then we could get married—legally and with the church's blessing. But I don't want to. I'd be marrying a liar! Erin can't see that." He stopped walking, clamped both hands on his head and gave out with a cry that might have been heard at the top of the Matterhorn. "She thinks all she has to do is prove to me she's not married and that fixes everything, but it doesn't! It doesn't even *begin* to fix it. She lied to me, flat out. If you married someone a couple of years ago and didn't mention it to your new fiancé, it's the same thing as lying. We've talked to each other about everything, Mom. Everything! I can tell you who she went out with in high school, I can tell you the name of her first grade teacher, I can tell you every little thing she remembers about her father. She only left out one small detail. *'Oh! Did I mention I got married?'* That's lying."

"And you're afraid you can never trust her again."

"Right. I can forgive, but I can't forget. That's impossible. To forget, I'd need a lobotomy. Every time I had reason to doubt her, I'd think, *She might be lying.*"

"It's been my experience that people don't change, basically. They can change their eating habits, but they don't change something as basic as their honesty."

We had come to the ridge. A half-dozen people and two or three paraglide canopies dotted the meadow beyond. Beside me, Patrick was dancing with pent-up energy.

"I want to do that."

"What, jump off the mountain? You don't know how, Patrick. You need training to do what they're doing."

"I'm going to go talk to them."

Before I could stop him, he trotted off across the meadow toward one of the men. Realizing it would be useless to go with him, I decided to climb up the slope to the airstrip by myself. Patrick was a grown man, supposedly. If he wanted to kill himself, I couldn't stop him. But that didn't mean I had to watch him do it.

Turning to the flat-topped hill, I studied its slope. The left side, where I climbed up the other day, wasn't the only way to go. There was the chair lift, its cables stretching across the meadow from one support beam to the next, angling up the slope, and vanishing at the summit. The lift wasn't running at the moment. I also spied a concrete structure with a hand rail on the far end of the hill. Stairs? I hurried in that direction, about a hundred yards, and found that there was indeed an easier way up than the hands-and-knees route I'd taken before. A set of steps rose, turned ninety degrees, and continued to the top, ending a few yards from the long building that seemed to be a combination hangar and office.

The glider, one wing-tip touching the asphalt, sat just outside the hangar. A small propeller-type plane peeked out the open hangar doorway. Piles of dirty snow lined the edges of the runway. I walked up to the office door and peered through the window, shading my eyes against the sun. Lights inside. The door opened easily with a little tinkle from its attached bell.

I called out, waited a minute, and was rewarded by the appearance of a grease-smeared man in a dark blue jumpsuit. I told him I was interested in soaring, and wondered if the glider outside could be rented. I'd never done it before, I told him, but I knew they held two people and thought perhaps a pilot might take people up for a price.

"The glider and the plane belong to Herr Spektor," he told me, nodding toward the small plane as he wiped his hands on a greasy cloth. "He doesn't take people up." The man paused, as if searching for a diplomatic way to put it. "That is to say, he doesn't take up people . . . the general public. He sometimes takes a friend."

I nodded but said nothing, leaving it up to him to go on.

"Of course, someone has to fly the launch plane. Or sometimes he flies the plane and someone else goes soaring."

"Do you fly also?"

"Yes." He scuffed one boot against the concrete floor. "I sometimes fly the launch plane myself, when he comes here alone or with a friend who wants to go in the glider with him. But it's his plane."

"Mr. Spektor, you say? Does he live near here?"

The man reddened. He was obviously uncomfortable with my blatant effort to wangle an invitation. "I don't know," he mumbled.

Of course he knew. One plane in the hangar, one glider, one employee on-site. How could he not know where the owner lived? I spotted an open logbook on the counter so I simply walked over and looked. It wasn't privileged information, after all. Marco had told me so. Plus, it was right there, open for anyone to see. It appeared to be not a flight log but a telephone log or something. Date, time, name, message. One name appeared more often than any other: Spektor, and on one line it said Anton Spektor.

Having learned all I could from the man in the jumpsuit, I tramped back down to the meadow just in time to see Patrick, tethered in tandem to a complete stranger, take off running toward the edge of the cliff. The yellow sail behind them billowed, dipped, and fluttered as the stranger pulled on the strings and my son vanished over the side of the mountain.

EIGHTEEN

In mid-afternoon, the golf cart bounced over the hill and down to our chateau, driven by Zoltan the handyman and piled high with bags of groceries. He brought a passenger as well, a middle-aged woman with frizzy hair and a bratwurst-like torso. She introduced herself as Odile Grunder and explained that Herr Merz had employed her as cook. She was to stay with us for the duration and illustrated her intention to do so by swinging an ancient leather suitcase from the space behind her seat in the cart.

A quick mental scan of the house told me there were at least two, and probably more, currently unoccupied bedrooms. Odile seemed to be familiar enough with the house that she didn't need my help settling in, so I helped Zoltan carry in the groceries. My questions and comments to him during this process were met with silence or, at most, a grunt. Guessing he spoke no English I said, *"Sprechen Sie Englisch?"*

He answered with another ambiguous grunt.

Odile waddled into the kitchen as I was trying to put the groceries away and pushed me aside. "I take over now," she said, leaving no doubt as to whether she required my help. Her English was heavily accented and rudimentary. Having been banished from the kitchen, I stepped outside and spotted Patrick running down the slope.

"That was the greatest, best, most exciting, amazing thing I've ever done in my whole life! Mom, you have to go paragliding! It's great!"

"Not likely to happen, Patrick."

"I've signed up to take lessons so I can solo."

"And how long will that take?"

"Couple of weeks."

"You think we're going to be here that long?"

"I hope not," he said, as if he had only now realized he wasn't a permanent resident. "I mean—if they let us leave, I can take lessons at home."

I started to mention paragliding lessons might not be readily available in downtown Cleveland, but I knew Patrick was using this new interest as a necessary diversion. He would need time to work through his pain, because his plans for the rest of his life had been trashed. Erin's shocking revelation that she had married and might still be married was an open wound in Patrick's heart. Until he could deal with it, any diversion he could find was better than sitting in his room and staring at the wall.

"Where is everybody?"

"Brian and your dad have gone for a walk. Lettie's in the living room."

"I want to talk to Lettie."

That was good. Lettie had always been a good godmother to Patrick, and she understood him better than almost anyone other than me. Wondering what I could do now that I'd been shoved out of the kitchen and didn't care to infringe on the conversation in the living room, I headed downhill.

"Hello! Mrs. Lamb?" Odile, the new cook, called to me from the kitchen window. I retraced my path, stepped inside, and found she wanted help with planning dinner. How many of us would there be? When did we want to eat?

When the plans were complete I stayed, sitting on a stool at the butcher-block table. "Is this the first time you have worked here? As a cook?" I talked slowly, enunciating carefully and reminding myself that limited English did not mean hard of hearing.

"I vork here two times with Gisele . . ." Odile lowered her eyes, clamped her hands together. "Ven big . . . lots of people come *und* der house is full. I help."

"I see. So you knew Gisele."

Leaving the refrigerator door open, she pulled out a stool and sat on the other side of the table from me. "Oh, so bad. So bad! I luff Gisele. So pretty. Everybody luff Gisele." Her face screwed up in pain. I was close enough to the refrigerator door to nudge it closed with my foot and did so without saying anything.

Having started, Odile opened up and talked for almost an hour. Gisele had been her niece, she told me. Gisele's mother and she were sisters. She went into great detail about Gisele's childhood mishaps and mischiefs. The whole town of LaMotte was in mourning over the loss of their lovely girl. Who could have done such a thing? The pointed glance I got from her eyes told me: We Americans were their prime suspects.

"Gisele haf a lover, you know." Odile cocked her head to one side.

I wondered if I'd heard her right. Did she mean Juergen? Obviously not. If she meant Juergen, she wouldn't have referred to him as *a lover.* "No. I didn't know that."

"*Ja.* He vork in der post . . ."

"Post Office?"

"*Ja.*"

"Have you seen him since . . . ?"

"*Nein.*" Odile shook her head and snuffled. Her face reddened. She turned her gaze to the window and I saw that her eyes brimmed with tears.

"Odile, perhaps I shouldn't ask, but I've been wondering

about Gisele and Herr Merz. Did you ever talk to her about him?"

"*Ja.* She tink he very . . . rich. Very good catch for right voman."

"But not for her, right?"

"Ach! I do not tink so! Marry Herr Merz? I do not tink so."

I couldn't figure what she meant by that. I waited, hoping she would go on, but she simply stared out the window until she jerked to attention and said, "You are Mrs. Lamb? Stephanie Merz was Mrs. Lamb, also. What is your relationship?"

"She was married to Chet Lamb, who was my first husband."

"Ach! Sorry! I didn't mean to . . ."

"It's all right. I'm used to it." I explained why we were all here and staying in the same house. I felt as if she already knew, as if it the whole story had already made the local gossip circuit. I asked her how well she knew Stephanie.

"I haf not seen her since she was . . ." Odile held her hand out, about shoulder height, then raised it. I took this to mean Stephanie had been a teenager when she last saw her. "She move to America, she vork, she marry. But you know that." She sighed. "When they were young, Juergen and Stephanie, they did not get along." She grimaced and shook her head.

"They fought?"

"They come here with their parents sometimes, for skiing. Ve vould see them in town, but never together. People who vork here, at this house, tell us about terrible fights between Juergen and Stephanie."

"Brothers and sisters often fight," I said.

"Herr Merz—Juergen—always try so hard to please his father. To make his father proud. But Stephanie, she tear him down. Make him look like a *dummkopf*—like a foolish boy."

"I can see Stephanie doing that."

Odile cocked her head to one side and smiled. "*Ja.*"

"I'll understand if you can't answer this, Odile, but I'd like to know what the people in town are saying. Who do they think killed Stephanie and Gisele?"

"At first ve hear Stephanie shoot Gisele und then shoot herself," she answered, her words carefully measured. "Then ve hear—no. Someone else shoot both of them."

"We thought the same thing at first. But now? I don't know. I'm completely baffled."

"Some say it vass Stephanie's husband who did it," Odile lowered her head and glanced up at me through her eyebrows. "*Und* some say it vass *you.*"

Odile might have been trying to make a point: Americans go home. The dinner she served, wiener schnitzel, sauerkraut, potato dumplings, and a selection of cheeses—all Swiss—carried with it, I thought, a message. Babs kept her head down except when Chet said something, and I got the impression she'd have stayed in her room if Odile provided room service. Patrick and Erin took turns glancing at each other but avoiding eye contact. Brian, uncharacteristically, ate almost nothing.

I said, "Juergen called a few minutes ago. Did you know?"

Chet said, "Where is he?"

"He's still in Zurich. His father's been taken to the hospital and now he's slipped into a coma. Juergen sounded as if he doesn't expect him to come out of it."

Chet set his fork down slowly and reached for his wine glass. Brian glanced sideways at Chet. I wondered what they were both thinking. If old man Merz died, would it have any ramifications for Chet? Was Stephanie in her father's will? Did Stephanie have a will? Was Chet the beneficiary? But Stephanie had already predeceased her father. What would happen to her share of her father's fortune in this case? I figured it would depend on how the will was worded. Sometimes they had the phrase "or her heirs or survivors" and the money would be passed along to Stephanie's beneficiaries, but lacking that phrase it might be distributed to the father's other heirs.

And the most important question of all, *did Chet know?*

After a long, rather awkward silence, Erin piped up. "When is he coming back?" She looked at me. "Does Detective Kronenberg know where he is? I thought none of us could leave."

"Juergen asked permission before he left."

"Sounds like special treatment to me," Brian said. "Rich guy gets to leave. What if I went up to the van and told him *I* had to leave because *my* father was sick?"

Chet swallowed a gulp of wine and winced.

"I didn't word that right, did I?"

"Kronenberg has Juergen's passport," I said. "Juergen can't leave the country any more than the rest of us can."

After dinner Patrick was called to the police van. I watched from my bedroom window as he trudged across the meadow in the rosy twilight. The sun had slipped behind the western ridge, casting the remaining patches of snow in gold, the meadow grass in amber. Patrick's silhouette, hands jammed into pants pockets, shrank and disappeared into the van. I wondered what this was all about.

I stood at the window for a while longer, scanning the sky for that glider. I still wanted to get the numbers on the bottom of the wing, even though I hardly needed more confirmation that the glider at the airstrip and the one that had been buzzing our house were one and the same. A large bird soared in lazy circles over the meadow. All seemed peaceful.

A man came flying out of the van, shouting, running northward. Seconds later, another man—this one I recognized as Kronenberg—dashed out in the same direction. They soon disappeared behind the rise that blocked my view of the bunker, so I ratcheted my window open with the little handle on the sill. Male voices, excited, angry. Had the first man been Patrick? I had to know.

Skittering down the stairs and through the living room, I took the outside flight of stairs to ground level and from there, up the hill and across the meadow. I stood on the little rise and watched two men escort a third across the area still set off by crime scene tape and into the van. The man twisted, growled, and kicked, but Kronenberg and his assistant had him firmly by each arm. Thank God, it wasn't Patrick. It was Zoltan, the handyman.

I waited on the porch for over an hour, wondering when Patrick would come back. I was dying to know what was happening inside that van. I figured Patrick must have left before the scuffle with Zoltan and then possibly headed elsewhere for a walk to clear his head. But perhaps he'd seen it all. I hoped he had.

Full dark now, I didn't see Patrick until his head popped up from the stairs. He grabbed me by the elbow and pushed me to the other end of the porch. "You'll never believe what's happened!"

"They've got Zoltan, don't they?"

"How do you know that? Never mind. They caught Zoltan poking around inside the police tape and ran out and grabbed him. They brought him into the van—I was just sitting there— and they threw him down in a chair. He was swearing and spitting and they were holding him down. They started questioning him: What were you doing there? Did you find anything? Did you go inside the bunker? Stuff like that.

"I figured they'd tell me to leave, but they didn't. Finally, I figured out why. They don't know I speak German. They probably thought, 'forget him, he doesn't know what we're saying anyway.' So I stayed.

"When Zoltan did start talking, he told them he thought it was okay to go into the bunker now, because it's been days since the murders. They didn't believe him, but Mom, here's the good part. Zoltan told them he saw Juergen and Gisele somewhere over toward that little shed where they keep the golf cart. On the day of the murders. They were kissing, he said."

"Uh-oh."

"Right. And then he said he saw some guy named Milo—this was later the same day—come over the hill and go into the house. Into the kitchen. Milo came out with Gisele. They walked over toward the bunker, and he started yelling at her." By this time Patrick was so excited, he knocked his own glasses to the porch floor. He snatched them up but didn't put them back on. "He was yelling, calling her a whore, calling her a bitch. Gisele was crying, he said. Then this guy, Milo, he drew back and swung but Gisele ducked in time so he didn't actually hit her, but he would have if she hadn't ducked."

"Who is this Milo?"

"All I got was that he works at the post office in town. Kronenberg seemed to already know who he was."

"Gisele's boyfriend," I said.

"Anyway, after he took a swing at her, she ran back to the house and Zoltan claims he didn't see anything else. After that, they looked at me and I was just sitting there, playing with my cell phone like I didn't know or care what this was all about, and Kronenberg told me I could leave."

Lettie and I had a lot to tell each other that night. She told me about her talk with Erin, and I filled her in on Zoltan's exploits, Patrick's paragliding adventure, and my discoveries at the airstrip. Now I knew who owned the glider and, in all likelihood, who had been soaring over the house at odd hours. His name was Anton Spektor. What I didn't know was why.

Lettie, bless her little photographic heart, said, "*Déjà vu!* Anton Spektor was one of the names on Juergen's email list."

Nineteen

"Did you see this?" Seifert, Kronenberg's junior officer, bent over and picked up a button. Cracking ice with his gloved hands, he pared it down to its original size and showed it to his superior.

Now that the snow had melted except for small patches where the sun couldn't reach, the two were methodically walking the meadow inside the yellow tape, able for the first time to get a really good look at the ground as it would have looked before the snow, near the time of the murders. Best calculations were that the shootings and the onset of snow were separated by less than four hours. Unfortunately, police boots had trodden the snow into mush all over and created soggy pits in the ground beneath. This was their best chance yet to look for that missing shell casing, the one that would have harbored the powder for the bullet that killed Stephanie. Until now they had only been able to clear and search a circle within a ten-foot radius of the spot where Gisele's body lay. If they could find that second shell casing, it would tell them where the shooter stood when he or she shot Stephanie.

"Zoltan was messing around, just about this exact spot, yesterday," Kronenberg said, taking the button from Seifert.

"Do you think he planted it? To throw suspicion on someone else?"

"Nope. Look again. Look where you found it. It was frozen solid in ice under undisturbed snow." He pointed to the spot now disturbed by Seifert's glove, some five feet from the bunker door and close to the rock wall. "And look at this. Here's a print that was made after the snow. It's a shoeprint. Woman's shoe. But it was made after the snow fell. See? See the difference?"

Seifert bent over and examined the shoeprint.

"Make a cast of this. It won't tell us anything about the shoe itself because melting has erased all the details that may have been there to begin with, but we may be able to get a shoe size, at least." Kronenberg slipped the button into his pocket. He turned and gazed out at the mountains to the south. "And call the handsome Milo. Tell him to pay us a little visit."

"Wouldn't it be easier for us to go down to town? He's probably at the post office."

"Why do I suspect you really want to go to LaMotte and get a nice lunch?" Kronenberg chided him. "Got cabin fever, huh? Stuck up here for a week?"

Seifert muttered a disclaimer.

"No. I want to talk to Milo on our turf. Let him worry while he's making his way up here."

TWENTY

In the early afternoon, we got a call from Juergen. His father had died. He had already talked to Kronenberg and agreed to return to LaMotte the next day, by which time, he thought, he would've relegated funeral and other duties to the appropriate people and wouldn't be required in Zurich again until the actual funeral. He sounded exhausted and depressed. He asked me if Odile had shown up—I said she had—and told me to keep her on for at least the next three days. "I have business to take care of here," he told me. "I need to meet with the lawyers Father appointed to execute his estate, and I have to take care of a hundred things at his offices and at home. You understand."

"Of course."

"And Dotsy? Thank you for suggesting that my father should never know about Stephanie. It was better this way."

I found Lettie, Patrick, and Brian in the living room and relayed the grim news. Erin and Babs walked in, Erin folding her legs beneath her in the large leather chair and Babs positioning herself attractively on one end of the sofa, her slim legs slanted just so. Chet's head peeked around the corner. I motioned for him to join us.

Chet slouched on the other end of the sofa and stared fixedly at the chunky, white candles on the glass-topped coffee table while I repeated the gist of Juergen's phone call.

Brian leaned back in his chair, looked at the ceiling. "Meeting with lawyers and taking care of business? I'd give a pretty penny to be a fly on those walls."

"Brian," I scolded gently, "he's lost his father. Cut him some slack. That's the thing about a death in the family. The lawyers and the bean counters won't let you grieve until the *important* things are taken care of."

"Well. That's that," Babs said.

"We've been talking about the dust-up between Kronenberg and Zoltan," Lettie said.

Neither Chet nor either of the Toomeys knew about this, so Patrick filled them in.

Erin said, "It doesn't surprise me. Zoltan gives me the creeps. I've been wondering why Kronenberg wasn't looking at him. He's a more logical suspect than any of us. Always slinking around, leering at Gisele."

"What about Stephanie? Did he get along with Stephanie?" Lettie asked.

"Based on what I noticed in the days before the rest of you got here, I'd say Zoltan caught hell from her as often as the rest of us did."

Chet's head shot up, as if he was considering some sort of defense of his late wife, then he returned his gaze to the candles on the coffee table.

"I'd say right now, Zoltan tops my list," Patrick said. "That sort usually solves problems with guns."

"That sort?" Lettie squeaked. "You're stereotyping, Patrick! I'm surprised at you. Just because he does manual labor . . ."

Patrick slunk lower in his seat. "You're right. Sorry. But there's actually a more likely suspect. What about Gisele's boyfriend, Milo?"

We exchanged all the information we had about Milo. I wondered if Odile was listening from around a corner and considered calling her in. She could tell us more about Milo than the scant facts that he worked at the post office and he argued with Gisele on the day of the murders. A second thought told me we should leave Odile out of it.

"I've said all along it was someone from outside this house," I said, trying not to look smug.

"Hell hath no fury like a—well, in this case—a man scorned," Patrick said.

Erin's little round face reddened.

"This Milo," Chet said, stretching out his legs and resting his coffee mug on his belt buckle, "is an unknown quantity. Young man. Probably hot-tempered. Most young men are. Plenty of motive if he'd just found out she and Juergen were fooling around."

"Why Chet, I think that's most unfair!" Babs cooed. "If he had any thoughts of killing her, he'd hardly let himself get caught hitting her."

"But he didn't know he was being watched."

"He didn't know Zoltan was lurking," I said.

"Since we seem to be trashing everyone who isn't here," Brian said, "what about Juergen?"

I opened my mouth to issue Brian a second warning, but he gave me no chance.

"I don't suppose there's any harm in telling all of you, now, that Juergen and the Merz family enterprises are in deep doo-doo. Their import-export business has gone bankrupt, reorganized, and reopened. Stephanie and Juergen are equal shareholders, and there's never been any love lost between those two. Right, Dad?"

Chet looked as if he hated making any comment about that brother-sister relationship, but all eyes were on him and silence reigned. "Right. No love lost between those two." He cleared his throat. "And Stephanie knew Juergen was making a play for Gisele, but she saw it the other way around. As far as she was concerned, Gisele was a gold-digger making a play for Juergen."

"Think, Chet!" I stopped myself and forced my voice down about fifty decibels. "What you're saying gives Stephanie a motive for killing Gisele, or Gisele a motive for killing Stephanie, but it gives Juergen no motive for killing either of them." I paused to give everyone time to sort that out. "I'm not sure I've mentioned this before, but the night of the murders, Juergen was searching frantically for Gisele. Running upstairs and down. He came into our room and asked if we'd seen her, and I know he went next door, too."

Babs nodded her assent.

I said, "I'd swear on a stack of Bibles the man who barged into my room had no thought of killing Gisele!"

"Come on, Mom! A guy barges into your room about midnight, wants to know where somebody is. You don't know where she is. He looks at you like he's about to panic. What's the difference in how he looks if he's thinking, 'Oh my God, I'm afraid something horrible has happened to her!'?" Brian made a face of wide-eyed terror. "Or if he's thinking, 'Oh my God, when I find that bitch I'm going to kill her!' " He made the same face again.

Kronenberg summoned me back to the van. He had taken to calling the house phone when he wanted any of us because whoever answered would either be the person he wanted or would be able to tell him where that person was. He kept all our cell phone numbers in his note pad but seldom dialed them.

I caught Patrick as he walked by the phone and confiscated his jacket in lieu of returning to my bedroom for my own. Nearly sixty-five degrees outside, I hardly needed anything more than my cotton shirt.

Forgetting to knock on the van door, I walked in and caught Kronenberg playing a card game on his computer and Officer

Seifert flipping rubber bands at a two-way radio. They snapped to and tried to look busy.

Thumbing through a few note pages, Kronenberg said, "You told me Herr Merz picked you up in the golf cart when your taxi cab brought you and your luggage up from LaMotte. Yes?" I nodded and he went on. "Did you see anyone on your ride to the house?"

"I saw Gisele. In fact, Juergen stopped the cart and let her hop on the back. She rode to the house with us. I remember it clearly, because I didn't know about the bunker yet and when we came over the hill"—I pointed west but, in this case, only at the rear wall of the van—"it seemed to me Gisele had popped up out of nowhere. It was really quite shocking."

Kronenberg stared straight into my eyes. I heard Seifert's pen scratching. Kronenberg said, "Had Gisele been inside the bunker?"

"I assume so. I didn't actually see her walk out the door, but it was like—one second the meadow was empty and the next second, there she was. I remember she was carrying a coil of rope over her shoulder. I remember thinking how very attractive she was."

"How did Herr Merz and Gisele act toward each other? Did they seem . . . friendly? Formal? How?"

"Friendly. Rather flirty, even." I wished I could take that last part back. It was an assumption on my part and it might mislead him.

"Flirty," he repeated. "Tell me about that."

"I shouldn't have said that. I only meant they were teasing each other. About whether Gisele was overworked. Nothing more than that."

"Did you see anyone else?"

"No."

"Are you certain?"

"Absolutely."

"Tell me about François Bolduc."

"Who?"

"François Bolduc," Kronenberg repeated, pronouncing each syllable distinctly.

"I don't know anyone by that name."

"Has your son Brian ever mentioned a François Bolduc? Think carefully, Mrs. Lamb."

"I don't think so. No. That's an unusual name. It sounds French, doesn't it? I'm sure I'd remember it."

Kronenberg glanced pointedly at Seifert. "Thank you, Mrs. Lamb. You may go."

"Brian, who is François Bolduc?" I barged into the bathroom where my son was shaving.

"What?" His razor hand froze.

"Kronenberg asked me if I'd ever heard that name. Asked me if I'd ever heard you use that name."

"Shit! I knew it!" He threw his razor into the basin and grabbed a towel. Wiping the foam from his face, he turned from the mirror to me. "Bolduc is the guy I was talking to in the bar that night when I ran into Dad."

"Your spy."

"Shit! I meant to call him and I forgot. I promised him I'd keep his name out of anything that came up, but Kronenberg had me by the balls. Either I had to tell him who I was talking to in the bar, or he'd assume I wasn't even *in* the bar. If Kronenberg's already talked to him, there goes my alibi. There goes Dad's alibi, too."

"You told Kronenberg about the meeting so you could help your father establish an alibi."

"*And* because you told me to. Remember?"

"You did the right thing. Now the problem becomes: How do

you make François Bolduc tell Kronenberg the truth?"

"And how do you propose I do that?"

"Tell him this has nothing to do with corporate raiding or whatever you call it. Tell him it has to do with murder. Tell him the truth is in no way a reflection on him. It doesn't matter why you two met at the bar. Only *that* you met at the bar. Tell him his alternative is to risk having to testify under oath, in court."

TWENTY-ONE

"Have you talked to Juergen?" Babs Toomey stood at the threshold of my bedroom, a double armload of clean, folded laundry reaching to her chin. This reminded me I was fast running out of clean clothes myself. I mentally scanned the various floors of Chateau Merz for a recollection of a laundry room and decided it would probably be on the bottom floor near the pool.

Juergen had returned an hour ago, located Chet, and immediately steered him up the stairs to the top floor. The door to Chet's room had been closed ever since. The quick glimpse I got when I met Juergen at the kitchen door showed me an exhausted man. He plainly did not intend to talk to any of us until he had talked to Chet. That made me think the current conference behind closed doors had to do with money. Specifically, with his father's will.

"No, I haven't. He and Chet are still in Chet's bedroom."

I turned back to the window. They were rolling up the crime-scene tape. Kronenberg stood on the little rise that obscured my view of the bunker door, directing the shutdown of on-site operations. A couple of men moved wooden blocks away from the van's tires and maneuvered a big-wheeled vehicle into position to hook up and haul away the van. Odile told me she overheard the men talking and learned they weren't actually leaving but moving to more comfortable accommodations in the LaMotte police station. With the snow now melted and all residents of the house thoroughly grilled, Kronenberg felt they could back off a bit, but he would never stop. Not until they arrested the killer. I watched the junior officer named Seifert moseying around the formerly taped-off area, pausing now and again to run a hand across the grass.

"May I come in for a minute?"

I jumped. I hadn't realized Babs was still standing in the doorway. "Please. Have a seat."

She sat on Lettie's bed, laying her bundle of clothes beside her. "It's a bit late, I know, but I want to apologize for the way I behaved toward you the other day when . . . when Patrick and Erin told us about their little problem."

Little problem? I'd like to have taken issue with her characterization of Erin's shadowy past as a "little problem," but something told me to concentrate on the first part of that sentence. Babs was trying to apologize. "It was a stressful time for all of us."

"And it still is." Babs's gaze wandered to her stack of laundry and to the boot leather-stained white sock on top. She tucked it into the middle of the stack. "Oh, what's a mother to do? You want to see your child happy, but you can't write the script, can you?"

"No." I sat on the side of my own bed, facing her.

"Patrick is such a wonderful boy. So good for Erin. They're both intellectual types, they both love the outdoors, they love animals, and they . . . they have fun together." Babs looked at me as if for confirmation, but I kept my face blank. "I've had time to think, the last few days. To think about it from Patrick's viewpoint. And yours. And Chet's. I realize now that calling off the wedding, or at least postponing it, was the right thing to do."

Postponing it? The wedding was not postponed. It was called off!

"When we finally get to go home—if we ever get to go home—and Erin and Patrick sort out the legalities of their situation, they will still have the problem of trust to work through. Patrick, quite understandably, has issues with that right now. But I do hope it works out for them. I want that so much, but what's a mother to do? You can't write the script for them, can you?"

"Indeed not." My head spun with things I felt I shouldn't say. That she obviously hadn't dealt yet with the seriousness of the trust issue. That Patrick's Catholicism was about more than Church rules. That Erin and Patrick might never marry and it might be for the best if they didn't. The nasty taste of saccharine swirling around my mouth, I said, "They're adults. We have to trust them to do the right thing."

"I'd better get going," she said, reaching for her stack of clean clothes. "But I wish I knew what was going on upstairs," she leaned forward and touched my knee with her hand, whispering. "Don't you? I wonder if Juergen is telling Chet about the will. I wonder how much money they're talking about."

Babs waited for me to hazard a guess at the net worth of the Merz family, but I just looked at her.

"Millions, I'm sure," she said.

"I imagine so."

"And Juergen! That little daredevil! He's never had to work, you know. Not until his father got too old to run things. I wonder if he misses his old life. Climbing Mt. Everest, racing motorcycles, setting world records—I found a scrapbook downstairs the other day. You would not believe some of the things he's done!"

"Setting world records? What world records?"

"I'm not real sure. I didn't read that closely," Babs said, as if caught in the act of exaggerating. "But he's tried everything—except marriage."

★ ★ ★ ★ ★

I slipped on my new jacket, intending to go out and look at the meadow now that the police had left, then noticed the bare metal shank dangling from the spot where a button should have been. I had no memory of having lost one, but past experience with this sort of button told me they tended to eat through the thread quickly. I knew I had an extra button somewhere but, for now, I put it back on its hanger and donned my black cardigan.

Chet caught up with me on my way up the hill. As I watched him approach, it seemed to me I had never, in all our years together, seen quite that look on his face. I couldn't read it. His lips tight, his eyes crinkling at the corners, it seemed halfway between the face of a scared rabbit and the cat that ate the canary. Rather like the old joke about the man who fell out of an airplane, but he was wearing a parachute, but the parachute didn't open—etc.

We stopped and looked toward the bunker, identifiable only by the small keypad and the thin dark line that marked the edges of the door. The granite-grey paint on the door handle had worn down, exposing the shiny metal beneath. A large mud puddle remained where the door to the van had been.

"Can we go in now?" Chet nodded toward the bunker. "Now that they're gone?"

"I suppose so."

"Do you know the combination?"

"Erin does," I said, recalling the morning she had opened the door, seen Stephanie's bloodied body, and fainted. "But I don't. Ask Juergen."

"Walk with me?"

We ambled across the meadow, picking our way around mushy spots. Chet slipped an arm over my shoulder. I moved away, using a sprinkle of new-looking goat droppings as an excuse for altering my path. "You and Juergen talked a long time. Is he all right?"

"All right? I guess so," he said, as if he hadn't thought about it. "Seems old man Merz left money to Juergen and Stephanie, in nearly equal proportions, except the family home in Zurich goes to Juergen alone. The businesses and other holdings are now divided between them, fifty-one percent to Juergen, forty-nine percent to Stephanie."

"Now what? I mean since Stephanie is dead, what happens?"

"Merz willed it to both of them, *per stirpes,* which is legalese for if one of them dies before the old man, *his or her* heirs become the beneficiaries. If the will had been worded differently, the old man's estate would have been redistributed to the remaining heir. In other words, Juergen would have gotten everything."

"Did Stephanie have a will?"

"Yep. We both made wills a few months ago, leaving our stuff to each other."

"A few months ago?"

"January second. That was one of our New Year's resolutions."

"Your will leaves nothing to the kids?"

Chet stopped walking and turned around, squinting east toward the looming Matterhorn. I think he was embarrassed. "Just a temporary will. I meant to change it."

I looked at the lying son of a bitch. He probably hadn't even thought about the kids. Probably didn't remember what he'd told the lawyer. Probably only did it to get Stephanie off his back. I thanked God he hadn't died before Stephanie. Poor Brian would have found himself working at Lamb's Farm Equipment with Stephanie as his boss. I shuddered to think of all five kids saying, "We get *nothing?*" I watched his face carefully as I said, "So you get half of the Merz fortune."

"Right." Chet tightened his lips and inhaled. He raised a

hand to his nose, as if he were about to sneeze—an obvious ruse to hide the grin threatening to pop out. "Except the house in Zurich."

"So you and Juergen are now co-owners of the various Merz enterprises?"

"Juergen says he'll buy me out if he can raise the money."

"You're rich." I found a nice boulder and sat.

Chet stuck one foot on the rock and leaned an elbow on his bent leg. "Yeah. I'm rich." He finally let himself smile. "So to hell with it all! I'm officially retired as of right now."

"What about Lamb's Farm Equipment?"

"To hell with it. Who cares?"

"You're going to let it go down the tubes? What about Brian?" I jumped up and put distance between Chet and me.

"I'll take care of Brian, of course." Chet was obviously making it up as he went. Brian hadn't crossed his mind until I mentioned him.

But perhaps I was being unfair. Chet had found out about his good fortune only this morning, and he hadn't had time to think about a lot of things. The name Bolduc flashed across my mind. François Bolduc, Chet's and Brian's shadowy alibi for the time of the murders. Uh-oh. "Chet? Listen to me. Before you go off dancing around the house, you'd better go to your room and think about how this affects Detective Kronenberg's view of who did and didn't have a motive for killing Stephanie."

"They know who did it. Gisele's boyfriend did it."

"Don't get too cocky. No one's been arrested yet."

A grapevine in the Alps, I learned, worked as efficiently as any we had back home in the mountains of western Virginia, and our new cook, Odile, was well-connected. She let Lettie and me cut up vegetables while she filled us in on the local gossip. I got the impression she was lonely, holed up in the kitchen all day, and eager to talk. She no longer seemed to consider me a suspect in the double murder, a change I attributed to her getting to know me better and seeing what an honest and respectable person I was. She told us Milo, Gisele's boyfriend, had been seen going into Gisele's parents' house every day since the murders and had been seen drunk more than once. She told us Gisele's parents had retained a lawyer.

She told us about the tapes.

How the police had let this information leak out I couldn't imagine, but they had questioned quite a number of folks in the village. My opinion of the quality of Kronenberg's work rose several notches as Odile ticked off the names of locals she personally knew had been questioned. She turned down the heat under a pot on the stove and took a seat at the butcher-block table. "*Ja!* Herr Merz gave three videotapes to the police. This house has a security system." She waved one pointer finger around in a big circle. "Three cameras and they were turned on the night of the . . . you know. This is how they know exactly when Herr Lamb came back to the house. They know that you"—she pointed to both Lettie and me—"did not leave your room all night except to go to the bathroom."

"They watched us going to the bathroom?" Lettie slapped her paring knife down on the table. "That's an invasion of privacy!"

I put my hand on hers. "Don't get your knickers in a twist. She said three cameras. I doubt that any of them are inside our bathroom."

"Let's go look."

"Later, Lettie. I want to hear the rest of this."

Odile's head had been swiveling from one face to another, apparently confused, but with my encouragement she went on. "The door to Herr Merz's bedroom was open all night. He got up several times, they said, and looked out the window in the hall but he did not leave the upstairs the whole night. The door to Herr and Frau Lamb's bedroom was closed all night. Herr Lamb came in at two in the morning, but *he did not go upstairs!*" Odile smacked her hand on the table. "*Ja!* You tell me why not! Why did he not go to his room?"

"He told me he didn't want to wake Stephanie—Frau Lamb—up. Because he'd been drinking."

"*Ja.* Maybe. Or maybe he knew she was not there."

I walked Lettie around the house until we located all three cameras and I convinced her none of them would have seen us inside the bathroom.

I said, "If what Odile told us is a hundred percent correct— and these things do tend to get warped if they pass through several people—the tapes show two things. One, Juergen couldn't have committed the murders because we all *know* where he was from eleven-thirty until he went to bed, and if he didn't leave the house after that, he couldn't have done it. But two, he knew something bad was about to happen."

"I see. Why else would he have kept jumping up and going to the window?"

"And why was he in a panic when he couldn't find Gisele?"

"Maybe because she'd promised to sleep with him?"

"That's what I think," I said, "and I wonder if he knew about her fight with Milo."

TWENTY-TWO

"This must be Milo," Sergeant Seifert said, leaning back in his chair and craning his neck to see around the corner. Two local cops had the skinny young man by the arms, seemingly not to keep him from fleeing but to keep him from falling down. He wobbled and his head nodded while the two cops checked in at the front desk.

Kronenberg and Seifert had taken over a small room next to the reception area in the LaMotte police station, a room with exterior walls of bare logs and with ruffled curtains on the windows. On one of the interior walls, a large whiteboard bore a messy diagram with names, circles, and arrows in three colors of dry erase marker.

"Finally! Tell them to bring him in."

Milo was brought in and seated, or rather dropped, into the lone empty chair. Limp, dark hair falling over a finely chiseled face, he would have been handsome but for the dark circles under his bloodshot eyes. His hair needed washing.

"We've been looking for you for two days," Kronenberg began, tapping the butt of his two-way radio against the table. "Where have you been?"

"Around. Drunk, actually. I didn't know you were looking for me."

"Or anything else much, right? You haven't been showing up for work."

Milo muttered agreement, sat up straighter.

181

Kronenberg slowly worked his way around to the critical question, coming at it like a lion stalking its prey into a corner. "Where were you between eleven-thirty last Sunday night and two A.M. Monday morning?"

"Eleven-thirty?" Milo studied the floor. "I might have still been in the Black Sheep at that point. But from midnight on, I know exactly where I was. Here. In the nice little cell they have in the back."

The book backed him up. Police, called to the Black Sheep Bar by its bartender, had picked up the completely paralytic Milo and booked him in at twelve-eighteen A.M. After breakfast Monday morning he had been released, no charges filed.

Kronenberg had already talked to the concierge on duty at the hotel where Brian said he had spent that night. He did recall Brian's asking how he might get to Chateau Merz the next day and remembered showing him the house's approximate location on an area map. The time, he thought, was around one A.M. The hotel registry showed a Brian Lamb had been their guest that Sunday night. But no one from Ukraine had been there for ages.

Minutes after Milo left, Kronenberg was delighted to receive a call from another man he'd been trying to reach for days, François Bolduc. Responding to Kronenberg's voice-mail message, Bolduc said he'd left his cell phone in his car and flown to Paris for a couple of days. Only just got back. Brian Lamb? Never heard of him. You have the wrong person. Sorry.

"So Brian lied to us again?" Seifert asked when Kronenberg hung up.

"Not necessarily. He told us he'd promised to keep Bolduc's name out of the sensitive investigation he'd asked him to conduct. It might be Bolduc who's lying." Kronenberg exhaled noisily through his teeth. He put his feet on the table and leaned back in his swivel chair, his hands behind his head. His gaze darted from one name to another on the whiteboard diagram. Words like *motive* and *opportunity* were written in green across black arrows. "If Juergen Merz killed his sister for money, he'd have definitely told his father she was dead. Give him a chance to change his will. I doubt if old man Merz would've cared to have Chet Lamb inheriting half his money. They didn't even know each other."

"Do you think Juergen already knew the terms of the will?"

"I *know* he did. He told me all the details the first day I questioned him."

"Why do you think the will was worded that way to begin with?"

"Think, Seifert. If it was worded so that if one child died, the other would get the whole thing, it would give both of them a strong motive to bump the other one off. This way, there's no motive."

"Surely their father didn't really think one of them would bump the other one off!"

"Juergen and Stephanie had never gotten along. Why not?"

"But brother and sister!"

Kronenberg clucked his tongue and gave his junior officer a paternalistic look.

"As it stands, Juergen's inheritance wasn't affected by Stephanie's murder," Seifert said. "And as for Gisele's murder . . ."

"No motive there either."

"Sir? What about the timing on Brian Lamb? We know he was in the hotel at or around one, but we don't know that he went to his room. Who's to say he didn't talk to the concierge to establish an alibi and then pop out another door, dash up to Chateau Merz, and kill Stephanie?"

"Who just happened to be hanging out in the bunker in the wee morning hours?"

"Why *was* she there at that time of night? For that matter, why was Gisele out wandering around the field at that time of night?"

"That's a question we must ask ourselves no matter who the killer was. I think one or the other of them was there at the killer's request."

"But not both of them?"

"Can't see how. Three's a crowd."

"What about the others in the house? The tapes don't show any of them leaving the house after they went to bed, but the tapes also don't show any of them *not* leaving the house. If you see what I mean."

"Very good, Seifert. You're right. The cameras only show us three narrow views."

"So no one is eliminated."

"By the tapes? Only Juergen."

"What did you mean when you asked Milo where he was between eleven-thirty and two? Didn't you mean, between eleven-thirty and four?"

"No. I've been thinking about that. By the time they did the autopsy, there was no way to make a good estimate about time of death. We knew that. Body cooling rate was no help. Both were cold. We've been saying eleven-thirty to four because the last call Stephanie made on her cell phone was at eleven-thirty, and because we know it started snowing at four. And Gisele's body was covered with snow. Therefore, according to the Law of Superposition, her body was there before the snow was."

Seifert grinned at Kronenberg's faux-scholarly tone.

"But *how long* before? That's what I've been thinking about. If the snow started falling on a warm body, it would have melted—at least the first snow that fell on it would have melted. So the snow on top of the body would have been much thinner than the snow on the ground."

"So the snow fell on a cold body?"

"Or at least a body that had been cooling for some time. So Gisele must have been killed at least an hour or so before four. Two o'clock or earlier, I think."

"That would tend to exonerate Brian Lamb. He'd hardly have had enough time."

"I agree."

"Makes Chet Lamb our best possibility."

"Makes Chet Lamb our *only* possibility. I've been telling you that all along." Kronenberg stood up, grabbed a red marker, and circled the name "Chet" on the whiteboard, tracing around it again and again. "Chet Lamb. *Motive.* Wife was ruining his business. Wife was on his back constantly. But if she's dead, he inherits millions. *Means.* Gun is right there in the bunker. He could've gone out earlier that day and made sure it was loaded. *Opportunity.* Seen on tape entering the house at two-eighteen, very close to the time of the murders."

"And killed Gisele because . . . ?"

"Because, for whatever reason, Gisele was out wandering the meadow, probably thinking about that fight with Milo. Chet spots her, knows she saw everything, has to kill her, too."

Seifert stared at the whiteboard and, after a long pause, nodded.

Kronenberg slapped his marker on the table. "We have enough for an arrest. Let's do it."

TWENTY-THREE

Marco called me back. "I have a little idea about the Ag and the Au on the notepad. You told me Stephanie also wrote Jo burg or Jo bury on the paper and we thought that might mean Johannesburg. With Johannesburg and the words gold and silver, I searched those three terms in our police data bank and came up with something very interesting." He paused too long for a mere breath. He was prolonging the suspense.

"Tell me!"

"Gold is being smuggled out of South Africa in large amounts. Here's what they are doing. When workers in the gold mines manage to smuggle out a small amount of gold, they save it until they have enough to melt it down into gold bars. Then they dip the gold bar in melted silver so it looks like a silver bar. Now it can be exported and imported into another country, like Switzerland, with only a small fraction of the customs fees and no questions asked about where the gold came from."

"Wow. It makes sense."

"And also, there is no record of gold missing from the mines, because it has been sneaked out a little at a time."

"Any connection to Russia or Ukraine?"

"The Russian mafia is behind this. They have numbered Swiss bank accounts. Ukraine? Well, there is not much difference, is there? The same gangsters are there as well. Did you go to the air strip as I suggested?"

"Yes, and I have a name. Anton Spektor. He owns the glider

and the launch plane. Mean anything to you?"

"No, but I will check." He asked me how to spell the name. "Have you seen the red Italian shoes again?"

I laughed. "No, but we have plenty of other stuff going on." I told him about Juergen's father, about how Chet stood to inherit millions, and about François Bolduc, Brian's absent alibi. I repeated the gossip Odile had passed along to Lettie and me—about Milo and about the videotapes.

"I am coming there. I will take a few days off."

"Don't do that, Marco. If I need you, I'll call."

"You need me. If the Russian mafia is involved, I do not want you there alone."

"I'm not alone, and I have no reason to think the Russian mafia is connected to the murders. The murders, I'm sure, were a local thing."

"You don't know that."

He argued with me for a few more minutes, then promised he'd wait a while before heading to Switzerland if I promised to call him every day.

The village grapevine crackled with the news. I was standing at the refrigerator, pouring myself a glass of orange juice when the phone on the wall rang and Odile answered it. The ensuing conversation was in German, but I could tell by her voice and by the volume of the caller's voice punching through the back of the receiver that something big was up. I caught a few words: Herr Lamb, *polizei, haus.* Odile glanced at me and turned her back, frowning.

I dawdled, slowly left the kitchen sipping my orange juice, and then returned when I heard the click of a replaced receiver. I acted as if I had forgotten something. "What was that about, Odile? It sounded like someone was in trouble."

"*Ja.* Someone is in trouble for sure. Herr Lamb."

"Herr Lamb? Do you mean Chet or Brian or Patrick?"

"Chet. Chester. Your ex-husband. They are coming to arrest him. The police are on their way right now."

I heard a thunk in the stairwell behind me. A thunk, a series of scrambling noises, and the crackle of an opening door. I dashed out the kitchen door and saw Chet high-tailing it up the slope toward the bunker. Into my head flashed the worst possible, but likely, scenario. Chet holes up in the bunker, armed to the teeth with weapons and ammo from World War II. Kronenberg and his posse arrive, also armed to the teeth. They demand he come out. He's in there with . . .

I worked out more details as I ran after him.

Chet's in there surrounded by granite, God knows how many feet thick. He's in there with enough stored food to last weeks and enough wine to fortify his nerves to the point of stupid. My mind's eye saw military helicopters careening over the ridges. I saw international news people with cameras. I saw what was left of my family, torn to shreds.

But Chet didn't run into the bunker. He ran past it, up and over the ridge to the north. Hoping I'd downed enough orange juice to keep my blood sugar up for a long chase, I followed, but Chet was faster than I was. He steadily put more ground between us as he skittered down the next slope, over glacier-smoothed boulders, and up another ridge.

I barely made it to the top of the next ridge, puffing, my leg muscles burning, threatening to seize up. I had to stop. *Damn him.* Fleeing from the police would make things a hundred times worse. Eventually they would catch him. Kronenberg had his passport.

I caught a glimpse of Chet's plaid shirt. He was heading for the river valley below and to the north of the meadow from which the paragliders launched themselves. Below and north of the high plateau where Anton Spektor's glider and plane probably still sat idle. If only I could get up there. If only that mechanic would be there. I might be able to talk him into flying me over the valley. I could promise him payment as soon as I got back to my credit cards. But the plane couldn't land in the valley. Bad idea. Even if I found Chet, I couldn't stop him. Glider probably wouldn't work either, I thought. But I didn't know for sure. Plus, what were the odds I'd find the mechanic and talk him into such a harebrained-sounding plan? Even without the language barrier, I didn't think I could pull it off.

My gaze swerved from the plateau down to the meadow. There, I saw three or four brightly colored gliders laid out on the grass and perhaps a half-dozen people standing around. I didn't stop to think because I knew my fear of heights would talk me out of it. I stumbled down the hill, fell over an exposed root, clambered to my feet, and stumbled the last few yards to the level of the meadow. I approached the strangers, shouting as I ran, "Does anyone speak English?"

One girl grabbed the silken canopy to which she was tethered and backed up, wide-eyed with fear. *Who is this crazy woman?*

"Please! I have to go down there! Quickly!"

"I speak English," a young man in baggy cargo shorts said.

How to explain? *My husband is* . . . No. That would sound like I was chasing a wayward spouse. *My ex-husband is* . . . That sounded worse. Sudden inspiration. "Were any of you here a few days ago when my son Patrick wanted to try this?"

Luck!

The kid who spoke English pointed to another young man and said, "That guy. Patrick. You took him up."

"Ah, yes." The second kid spoke English, too, but with an accent. "Patrick. He loved it. He wants to take lessons." He looked around as if expecting to see Patrick behind me.

We were wasting time.

"I am Patrick's mother, and I want to try it too. Can one of you take me?"

Incredulous looks all around. I could practically hear them thinking, *This old woman? Are you kidding me?*

"I know it sounds stupid, but for reasons of my own, I really need to do this. Please. I'll pay you anything you ask."

It seemed to take forever, but the same kid who took Patrick up stepped forward and began giving me instructions. And more instructions. I tried my best to listen, but the ringing in my ears blocked out his voice. I heard "run" and then I heard, "run like hell." I hoped that was the main thing I had to remember. I could do that.

I must be crazy! This is not going to work. Should I warn him we're looking for a man somewhere in the valley? Better not. I'll spring that on him after we're aloft. Oh, God. Aloft. I clamped my jaws together to still my chattering teeth.

Someone handed me a helmet and a pair of protective glasses. My jumping partner strapped me into a harness and clipped a big pack to his own back. He hitched up an incredible number of lines, draped some over his shoulders, and grabbed some with his hands. A few feet behind him lay a broad expanse of red and white cloth, billowing in the breeze even as it lay on the ground.

Turning me toward the precipice over which we were shortly to plunge, my partner clicked some things behind me, linking us together. Point of no return.

"When I say go, *go!*"

I ran like hell, but it was tough, trying to run without tangling my legs up with his. Then, no more than a foot from the edge, I tripped. Expecting to fall to my death, amazingly, I didn't fall at all. I rose. We were off!

Once in the air, too late to change my mind, I started enjoying it. The valley far below looked like a toy town with patchwork fields and dark green woodlands. Orange-roofed houses and thin grey roads. Sunlight glinting off ripples on the river winding through the U-shaped valley. Wind in my hair. My own feet dangling beneath me.

Find Chet! You're not doing this for fun. Looking down, I despaired of ever spotting him from this height. Even the cars looked tiny from here, and Chet was wearing a plaid shirt and jeans—hardly the outfit I'd have chosen for easy recognition. A blaze-orange jumpsuit would have been nice.

Since I hadn't told my partner why I wanted to do this, I figured I'd better play it casual. I turned and looked at him, smiled, and said, "Can you make us turn?"

He obliged. With a shift of his body and hands, he started us turning to the left. Swinging out, it was easier to see what was below me on the left side. I figured once Chet got to the valley floor, he'd probably follow the river, so I pointed to the right. "Let's go that way. Follow the river."

After a couple of minutes following the river and seeing nothing of note, I realized we were traveling upstream, toward the Matterhorn and toward LaMotte. Chet would be running *away from* LaMotte. I held out my left hand. "Can we go back that way?" In a wide arc, we swerved around and a fresh wind lifted us up, rather alarmingly. The rooftops below started shrinking. *Oh dear.* I pointed down. Lower.

Over my shoulder, I heard, "I can't turn this thing just any way! We have to ride the wind!"

"Sorry! This is such fun!"

Below us, a road paralleled the river's path. Traffic on the grey ribbon of asphalt was sparse. Patches of woodland and grassy fields spread out on either side. We dipped lower.

I saw him. Or at least I saw a man in a reddish shirt and bluish trousers scurrying along the road. He paused, turned, and stuck out his thumb to an oncoming vehicle. It had to be Chet.

I turned again, this time with a look of distress on my face, and put my hand over my mouth.

My pilot took the hint. He pointed. "Down?"

"Yes. Please."

We circled around and banked into the wind above what may have been a soccer field. Dropping lower, he shouted across my shoulder, "Don't drag your feet. Let me do the work."

I must have dragged my feet because the next moment we were tumbling together, completely covered by miles and miles of red nylon. Figuring I'd caused this kid enough trouble, I decided to assume a fetal position and let him figure out how to extract us. As soon as I saw daylight and felt the cleats behind me click open, I looked for Chet. And there he was, still standing by the road, about a quarter-mile away, looking at us and at our deflated sail, his arms hanging limply at his sides.

"I'm ever so grateful," I said to my young companion, "I want to give you something but I have no money with me. Can you tell me . . ."

"No, no!" He cut me off, waving his hands in front of him. I think his only wish at that point was to get away from me.

"I'm awfully sorry," I said, then decided anything I did to prolong this would only make it worse. I hobbled away, keeping my eye on Chet as I approached the road, thinking, *Don't you dare run!* He didn't.

Leading him by the elbow, until we were a safe distance from the road, I said, "You won't get away, Chet. You have to see this through."

"I can't go to jail, Dotsy."

"Let's figure out what to do next." For the next half hour, we talked about Chet's total situation: The evidence the police had against him and why they thought they had enough to arrest him. What this could do to our children and grandchildren. What we might do to prove to the police they had the wrong man. Chet had a disgustingly negative attitude. Throughout our discussion I kept accentuating the positive, trying to convince him his situation wasn't hopeless, and reminding him that he was a millionaire now, but he'd never see a penny of his inheritance if he ran away.

My legs were bleeding. Chet searched his pockets for something to clean me up but found nothing. The kid packed up his gear and left, heading toward a cluster of houses near the road.

"Let's walk over there," I said, pointing to the same cluster of houses, "and see if we can call a taxi."

"To take us where?"

"Into LaMotte. You have your wallet with you? Good. We can pay the cabbie and then we can pay a visit to the Black Sheep."

Chet shook his head. "We've been over all that. The bartender doesn't remember me."

"I have a couple of ideas, Chet. Will you trust me? Turn yourself in to the police. I'll get you out. I promise."

He just looked at me.

"Trust me?" I gave him my sternest look.

He stood there for what seemed like an hour, shoulders drooping, eyes cast down, but finally he nodded. No more than a slight dip of the head but it would have to do.

TWENTY-FOUR

I caught my breath as our little electric cab rolled by the La-Motte train station, praying that Chet wouldn't jump out and make a run for it. I had the driver take us past the police station first, so I could see what we were dealing with in terms of what was where. If the police station had been across the street from the Black Sheep, for instance, it would have been too risky for us to walk in the front door of the bar, but it wasn't.

Just as I thought, the tables in the Black Sheep weren't all visible from the long bar. An L on one end held several tables and ended in a hall leading back to the restrooms. The place was nearly empty at this time in the afternoon. The bartender looked up and nodded at us when we entered, but not as if he recognized either of us. In fact, it wasn't the same bartender as the one I had talked to that night when Lettie and I were there.

"Where did you sit that night?" I asked.

"I told you, I don't remember much about that night."

"You may not remember the name of the man you were talking to or how many drinks you had, but you can remember where you sat. You've only been in here once. Only one table in this room, and only one chair at that table should feel right. *Which one, Chet?* You sat here for hours, facing one of these walls. Do any of the pictures on the walls look familiar? You got up at least once and went to the bathroom. Where did you get up *from?* Which way did you have to walk to get to the bathroom? Did you go to the bar and order drinks or did the man you were talking to get the drinks? Or did someone bring them to your table? What feels right?"

"I was sitting in here." Chet shambled over to a table within the L and stopped. He walked around the table, put his hands on the back of the chair facing a row of downhill racing photos. "I was sitting here."

"And from the bar, the bartender wouldn't have been able to see you."

Chet turned and looked. "No."

"Which explains why he didn't remember you. Now, think again. Your glass is empty. What happens next?"

"I turn around and catch the eye of a girl. I hold up two fingers."

"A girl. Good. And she brought you and your friend two more."

"She must have."

"We need to find that girl."

"Let's talk to the bartender."

I thought about it. The longer the police had to keep looking for Chet the greater the chance they'd run into us, and they'd never believe Chet was just about to turn himself in. By this time Odile would have told them about Chet running and me chasing after him. "Let's go to the police station," I said as gently as I could.

"I can do it. I don't want you to go with me."

I understood how he felt, but wasn't sure I could trust him to do it alone. Ah well, I'd already done all I could do. I'd brought him this far and given him hope. If he fled now, I wouldn't try to stop him. "Give me some money before you leave."

He raised an eyebrow.

"You have a wallet and I don't. I may need some money before I go back to the house, and I'd like your driver's license, too. You won't need it where you're going."

Chet pulled the laminated card and a few variously colored Swiss francs from his wallet, handed them to me, sort of saluted, and walked out. I stepped into the main room and seated myself at the bar. While the bartender was pouring me a Coke, I asked him, "Do you have any way of checking who was waiting tables on the night of—let's see—it would have been last Sunday. I was talking to our waitress that night about a restaurant she recommended in St. Moritz. I wrote down the name but I lost the little slip of paper and we're going there tomorrow."

"I can check the time cards, but I can't give out any home addresses or phone numbers." He toweled the bar in front of me and deposited my glass of Coke.

"I understand. But she might be coming in today, mightn't she? And if so, I could stop back by."

He couldn't have heard my last few words because he had already disappeared through the doorway behind the bar. He came out a minute later and said, "Kelly Wheeler. She won't be in tonight because she works at the Edelweiss Restaurant on Saturday evenings."

Perfect. I thought I had seen a sign for that restaurant but I was wrong. I couldn't find it. After wandering a few narrow streets, I dropped in at the post office and asked directions. Once seated in the sleek, modern Edelweiss, I ordered a salad and asked for Kelley Wheeler. Not really dinner hour yet, most of the tables were already full. Kelly turned out to be an American college student taking a semester abroad. When she brought my salad, I introduced myself and asked her to have a seat, but she told me they weren't allowed to sit with customers.

"You're from Virginia?" she said, taking my menu. "Wait. Is this about the bunker murders at the Chateau Merz?"

"Are we that well known?" I shouldn't have been surprised, but I was. "Yes. I'm staying there." Without revealing my relationship to the victims, I asked, "Have the police talked to you? I'm not asking you to tell me what you told them, but I need to know if they've talked to you."

"No. They came in and talked to Hans but not to me."

"I wonder why they didn't," I said. "You were working at the Black Sheep that night, weren't you? That was last Sunday night."

Kelly scratched her chin against the menu she held to her chest. "Yeah. I was." She paused for a minute. "They probably didn't talk to me because my name wasn't on the work sheet for that night. They probably tried to talk to Ursula because her name was on the sheet, but she's been out all week. They called me at the last minute."

"Wouldn't Hans"—I assumed that was the bartender—"have told them about the substitution?"

"He probably wouldn't remember. When they get busy, he pays no attention to us."

I dug into my pants pocket and pulled out Chet's driver's license. "Take a real good look at this man. Might he have been there, possibly sitting at a table in the section near the bathrooms?"

She looked at the photo, then the name. "Lamb. Your husband?"

"No."

She squinted, wrinkled her nose, twisted her mouth to one side. "Yes! Absolutely! He and another guy—blond hair, hefty guy. This guy"—she touched Chet's photo with her pinkie finger—"was drinking scotch and sodas and the other guy was drinking beer. The blond guy left and this guy went on drinking until he was so wasted he couldn't walk straight."

"That sounds like him."

"I was worried about him, even. Oh my God! I can't believe it. This is the same man. I was worried about him, so I told Hans I was leaving for a minute because I wanted to make sure this guy didn't pass out in the street, you know. Hans paid no attention so I'm sure he wouldn't remember it."

At this point, Kelly apparently forgot the rules and sat in the chair opposite me.

"I followed him down the street and he turned on Wilhelmstrasse, then he turned back because he was obviously lost and he walked past me, so I asked him if I could help him, and he said he was looking for the elevator." She laughed. "I said, 'the elevator?' like—I figured he was delusional or something, but then I remembered about the elevator they have that goes up to the houses"—she pointed up—"where the Chateau Merz is. We make deliveries there sometimes. We send someone with the food to this door where we ring a buzzer and they let us in so we can leave the food in the tunnel."

"That's right. I've picked up food there myself."

Kelly looked over her shoulder as if to check whether she was being watched by the headwaiter. "I led him around and down Dorfstrasse, but when we got there, there was already a couple with a key to the tunnel. They said they were staying at one of the houses up above, but not Chateau Merz. I'd remember if they said Chateau Merz. They told me which one, but I forget what they said. Anyway, I sort of whispered to the woman and told her what the problem was, and she said they would make sure he got home. So I left him at the door to the tunnel and that's the last I saw of him."

I prodded her for anything else she could recall about this couple or the house where they were staying, but to no avail. Nevertheless, it was enough. There weren't more than three or four other houses that had access to the elevator, so I shouldn't have too much trouble finding the couple who could tell police exactly where Chet was, and in what state, late that Sunday night.

★ ★ ★ ★ ★

Back at the house, I found Odile in the kitchen and Juergen in his little office on the stairwell landing. Simultaneously typing on his computer and talking on the phone, he didn't hear or see me until I stepped around the side of his desk. He held up one finger and quickly ended his phone conversation. "What's happening?" He slid his chair back and steered me to the living room. On our way down the stairs, I learned that Juergen already knew about Chet's arrest. Somehow he'd heard that Chet turned himself in. I was relieved to know Chet hadn't chickened out.

Through the sliding glass doors to the porch, I saw Brian, one foot on the porch railing, also talking on the phone. I filled Juergen in on the afternoon's events and then asked him to help me locate the couple who helped Chet find his way home early that Monday morning. He returned to his office for his little black book where he kept a list of neighbors and their phone numbers. Four houses in addition to Chateau Merz had access to the elevator, he told me. He went down the list, phoning each one. No answer at the first one. Voice mail picked up at the second. On the third, he talked to someone, then rang off.

"*Ja*, that was old Herr Eggenberger. He and his wife are both nearly deaf. I don't think he understood what I was saying."

Calling the fourth house, he talked to a domestic who promised to deliver Juergen's message.

"Now what?" I said.

Juergen looked at his watch with the dancing dials. "We have time to run over to the Eggenbergers before dinner. I told Odile we'd eat about eight."

"Do you think they're the ones we're looking for?"

"I don't know, but they're home, so we might as well talk to them."

We tramped eastward, passing the elevator hut in the wood,

then climbed over a split-rail fence and up a steep slope. Juergen slowed his pace to let me catch up. He wasn't even breathing hard. "Are you certain about Chet? That he didn't do it?" he asked.

"As sure as I can be. I was married to him long enough to know he's no killer."

"I must say, you're kinder than a lot of ex-wives would be." He stopped walking and pointed to a house with dark timber siding, then altered his path in its direction.

"So who's our best bet now, Juergen? Chet didn't do it. Who did?"

"Until today, I'd have said Milo, Gisele's would-be lover."

"Until today? Why until today?"

"Because I got a call from a friend in town today, about noon. Milo has a perfect alibi." Laughing, he laid his hand on my shoulder. "He was in jail at the time of the murders."

"In jail? What for?"

"Drunk in public."

"So that must have done it for the police. With Milo out of the picture, they figured it had to be Chet."

"Kronenberg has been itching to arrest Chet from the very beginning. I thought, when I turned in those tapes, they would clear things up. Chet said he had come in straight from the elevator about two A.M., and I figured the tapes would back him up."

"Don't they?"

"They show him coming in about the time he said he did, but they don't show where else he might have gone, either before he came in, or after. Kronenberg says he could have come in and slipped out again."

"How do you know all this? You and Odile both seem to know everything at the same time the police do."

"We have our ways." He picked a purple columbine and

inserted it into a buttonhole of my cardigan. He stepped back and gazed out toward peaks to the south. "We used to communicate by yodeling from one peak to another. Our voices would carry for miles. Now we use the telephone and email, but we're just as terrible gossips as we've always been."

I was itching to ask him if he and Gisele had been lovers. There was plenty pointing to it. Zoltan's statement to the police that he'd seen them kissing. The flirtatious way I'd seen them interacting. The tapes showing Juergen going to the window at intervals, all that night. His anxiety when he couldn't find her at bedtime. Milo's anger at Gisele.

But I couldn't think of a way to ask.

After several knocks separated by long pauses, Frau Eggenberger opened the door. Her crinkled blue eyes lit up when she saw Juergen. Shuffling along in quilted bedroom slippers, she led us down a hall and onto a side porch with a breathtaking view of the Matterhorn. Herr Eggenberger started to stand up, but Juergen begged him to remain seated. He asked them to speak in English in deference to the language-challenged American, me.

For the next few minutes, both Eggenbergers assured us their hearts went out to us in this terrible time. I wondered how they felt about extending sympathy to Juergen and me since, as far as they knew, either of us might be the killer. I got the impression they had known Juergen since he'd been a child, and they might believe they knew him well enough to trust it wasn't he. But they didn't know me from Lady Gaga.

Juergen brought up the reason for our visit. "We are looking for someone who rode up in the elevator Sunday night with . . . with another American guest of mine."

Herr Eggenberger looked at his wife. "Gordon and Daphne. Didn't they say something about a man in the elevator?"

"*Ja.* Yes, I remember!" Frau Eggenberger leaned forward, one hand quivering eagerly. "Gordon and Daphne are friends of ours from London. They've been staying with us for the last two weeks. They told us . . ."

Herr Eggenberger interrupted her. "They told us they had to help a man find his way home. He was drunk." He glanced at his wife as if she might object to this characterization of a friend of ours. "A girl brought him to the tunnel entrance and asked them to look after him. Make sure he made it to where he was going."

"That's our Chet," I said.

"They said they followed him until they got close to your house, Juergen, and then they watched him until they thought he had gone inside."

Juergen looked at me and nodded. "Are they here now? Can we talk to them?"

"I'm afraid you have missed them. They left yesterday for Vienna."

Rats. The old joke came back to me again: *A man falls out of a plane, but he's wearing a parachute, but the parachute fails to open, but beneath him is a nice soft haystack, but in the haystack is a pitchfork—tines up, etc.* "Might you possibly have a number where they could be reached?"

Frau Eggenberger pushed herself up from her chair. "I do. I have the number of their hotel in Vienna. Excuse me while I go and get it."

—but he missed the pitchfork.

Chet had well and truly missed the pitchfork. As soon as Juergen and I got back to the house, I called the number for the hotel in Vienna and talked to the English couple. They remembered Chet, said the time of their encounter was about two A.M., and promised to call Detective Kronenberg at their earliest convenience.

We were seven for dinner. Babs had usurped Stephanie's old spot at the end of the table opposite Juergen, an act that might have raised everyone's hackles except for the fact that it eliminated the awful emptiness in that chair. Lettie had enjoyed her day wandering the streets of LaMotte, reading gravestones in a little churchyard there. Patrick had spent most of his day visiting a few friends who were still in residence at the hostel where his and Erin's former wedding guests had stayed. Babs and Erin told us they'd done the touristy train ride up another mountain for a better view of the Matterhorn. I told them the whole story of Chet's day on the lam and his subsequent incarceration. Brian and Patrick, at first deeply concerned, lightened up when I told them about my paragliding insanity in pursuit of their father. Juergen described our visit with the Eggenbergers and the phone call from Vienna that would, hopefully, get poor Chet released.

I secretly hoped the English couple would wait a bit before making that call. A night in jail wouldn't hurt Chet and it might do him some good.

TWENTY-FIVE

Sunday, April 18—a day I will never forget.

I lay in bed an extra long time that morning, longing for my pillow back home. The one that smelled like me. I could hear Lettie, snoring softly with her mouth open. The comforter on my bed wasn't wide enough and it slid off sideways, the sudden chill waking me and forcing me to drag it off the floor several times every night. I lay there and rehashed my last dream, in which I'd been serving a dinner to many people at several tables and thoroughly botching the job. Putting gravy on their ice cream, forgetting people until they shrank to skeletons, bashing soft-shelled crabs trying to crawl off the plates. Another one of my frustration dreams. I tend to have them when life deals me more than I can handle. They've happened before.

Chateau Merz had no cuckoo clocks. I don't know why that thought flitted through my mind at that moment. Probably because I wished I could find out what time it was without actually opening my eyes. The house was so chopped up, multi-leveled with narrow halls and angled stairs, that kitchen smells didn't travel as far as my room. I could see light through my closed eyelids, but I couldn't tell if coffee was brewing yet or not. I wondered if Chet had come in during the night.

When would Kronenberg let us leave? He couldn't keep us here forever. Reminding myself to call Marco sometime today, I realized I wanted, more than anything, to talk to Jeffrey and Charlie. For Charlie, in Virginia, it was six hours earlier, wee hours of the morning. Jeffrey's dance troupe was on a U.S. tour and probably somewhere in the Mountain Time Zone by now. Maybe one o'clock. So Jeffrey might still be up from last night. I could try—how silly. I'd probably scare him to death, calling him at one in the morning.

I heard Lettie slip out of bed.

I needed to do laundry. I opened my eyes and greeted the new day the way a child greets the start of the third hymn. I threw on a pair of jeans and the same shirt I wore yesterday, gathered my dirty clothes into my arms, and headed for the laundry room on the bottom level. "Dotsy, where are you?" Lettie called from somewhere. I let her find me. Wide-eyed and flushed, she grabbed my arm and said, "Detective Kronenberg wants to talk to you. He's in the kitchen."

"What time is it?"

"Nine-thirty."

"What's he doing here so early?"

"He wants to talk to you."

My heart did a flip. "Is Chet here? Did they release him yet?"

"No. I asked Kronenberg about that but he avoided the question." She looked at my double armload of clothes. "I'll take those down to the laundry room for you. You go talk to Kronenberg."

I hadn't even brushed my teeth yet.

Kronenberg let me grab a glass of orange juice and a piece of toast before leading me to the dining room, where we automatically took the same seats we'd adopted in our earlier sessions. His junior officer, Seifert, whispered something to him, eyeing me none too subtly as he did so. Kronenberg mumbled something back and Seifert left the room.

"I need to ask you a few more questions about Sunday evening. Let's start with the time after dinner, about ten o'clock, when you decided to go for a walk."

My heart started pounding. We'd been over this. He already had detailed notes on my every move between dinner and the next morning. What was he looking for? I exhaled slowly.

"It was turning cold at that time. What did you wear when you went out?"

What did I wear? This sounded really ominous. I had to think about it. "I changed out of my traveling clothes before dinner and freshened up. I wore my pink cashmere sweater and black slacks and my black slides. Gold hoop earrings."

"Slides?"

"Shoes."

"No jacket or coat?"

"Oh. When I went outside, I put on my new tweed jacket."

"May I see this jacket?"

What the hell? I slipped across the hall to my room and yanked the jacket off its hanger. I handed to him. "I seem to have lost one of the buttons."

"When did you lose it?"

"I don't know. I noticed it the other day, but since it's warmed up, I haven't needed to wear it." So this was something to do with my missing button. What? Had it been found in a place where it shouldn't be? In the bunker, maybe? I flashed on a mental image of that next morning, dashing into the bunker with Erin, finding Stephanie's body. That was the first and only time I'd ever been there, and I certainly hadn't been wearing my new jacket. I'd run out the kitchen door in my robe and slippers.

"When you came back from your walk, did you take off your jacket or did you continue wearing it while you"—he consulted his notes—"while you visited with Babs and Juergen in the living room?"

"I'm sure I must have taken it off. It would have been too

warm in the living room with my cashmere sweater."

"But you don't actually remember taking it off."

"I'm sure I must have."

Seifert returned and pulled out a chair for himself. Kronenberg handed him my jacket, somewhat furtively, I thought. He asked the younger man, "What time did Lettie Osgood and Patrick arrive?"

More note flipping. "About eleven, sir."

"And after they did arrive, Herr Merz asked you to go to the kitchen and brew coffee."

"He told me to check and see if Gisele was in the kitchen. If she was, I was to tell her to make a pot. If not, he asked me if I would do it."

"And about that time he got a phone call?"

"Yes. From Stephanie. Something about wine."

"When you went to the kitchen, were you wearing your jacket?"

"No! Why would I put on a jacket to go to the kitchen?"

I shouted this. Frustrated, angry, I failed to use my indoor voice. This brought Brian up the stairs from below and Patrick in from the hallway. They converged on the scene like barroom bouncers on a table of drunks. Brian held his arms clear of his sides the way he does when he's ready for action.

Kronenberg and Seifert didn't appear to be armed, and I prayed they weren't. I caught the look Kronenberg sent his partner as he threw up his hands, recoiling. "We mustn't impose on these good people any more, Seifert. We can handle the rest of this interview at the station."

Both policemen stood and quickly gathered their belongings.

Brian, still at threat level orange, said, "You're taking my mother with you?"

"I need to ask her a few more questions."

"Does she need a lawyer?" Patrick's gaze darted from me to

Kronenberg and back.

"Not at this point."

I didn't like the sound of that. "If I think I need a lawyer, Patrick, you can be sure I'll ask for one." I gave both my sons my best mother-is-in-control look, now praying only that no fists would fly before we left this house.

They had brought the LaMotte police vehicle with the huge tires. I hadn't seen it since that first morning when the local police had driven it across new snow up from the western road. They put me in the back seat with a partition between me and the two of them in the front. How had it come to this? A half-hour ago, I was innocently taking my clothes to the laundry room.

Brian, Patrick, and Juergen beat us to the police station. Having taken the elevator down, they sat in a row on a bench outside, saying nothing but presenting a unified front. Kronenberg took me to an interview room that didn't look much like the ones I'd seen on TV. The standard recording device, a phone, and a box of tissues sat on a Formica-topped table but the chairs were oak spindle-backs and the window was trimmed with cotton eyelet tie-backs. I felt as if the last suspect interviewed here might have been the Big Bad Wolf. But my mood darkened when I glimpsed an official-looking form on the file cabinet behind Kronenberg's seat. He punched a button on the recorder and spoke the date, time, and persons present into its plastic face.

"You didn't like Stephanie Lamb, did you?"

"She wasn't my best friend, but I didn't hate her, either."

"There's a lot of room between best friend and hate. Tell me more."

With the recorder running Kronenberg sat, arms folded, while I endeavored to describe my feelings toward the woman who, some five years before, had wrecked my plans for the rest of my life. I tried to sound sincere without sounding vengeful. "I've gotten past that now. I've made a new life for myself in teaching. I love teaching. I have my five children, my grandchildren, and a nice circle of friends back home." I waited for Kronenberg to relieve me of the burden of this monologue.

He merely nodded and said, "Continue."

"I don't know what else to say." I paused, then softened my voice. "When Patrick and Erin told me about their plans to get married here, I assumed we'd all be staying at hotels of our own choosing, but then they told me about Juergen's chalet and how much it meant to them for us to all be together. Of all my children, Patrick is the one who's had the most trouble accepting the divorce." *Why am I telling this to policemen? They have no right to know these things.* I felt as if I were walking naked through Times Square. "For Patrick's sake I said okay. So I came here determined that we *would* all get along—and we did. Until . . ."

"Yes," Kronenberg muttered. He consulted his notes. "Let's go back to the evening of the murders. You all had dinner together. Did you say, when Stephanie Lamb walked past you, 'Someone is walking on my grave'?"

"I don't recall saying anything of the kind."

"What did you mean by that?"

I made note of the fact that my denial was ignored and figured he had certain knowledge I *had* made that statement. Someone at our table that evening was trying to frame me. Who? Hurriedly replaying what little I remembered about the dinner conversation—Stephanie called to the phone, strange reactions from Babs, from Erin, and from Juergen when Gisele had announced, "Telephone, Steph."

"Grave. I remember now. I did say, 'Someone's walking on my grave,' but it had nothing to do with Stephanie. I said it when I shivered. A cold breeze must have blown through just then. It's an old country saying in America. When you shiver for no apparent reason, you say, 'Someone's walking on my grave.' "

Kronenberg said nothing. He flipped through a few note pages, raised his eyebrows at something he'd written, and then looked up at me. "Why did you bring me the notes from the telephone notepad in the kitchen? It seems like such a strange thing to do. You wanted to make sure I saw what was on that pad, didn't you? Why?"

"I simply thought the last words Stephanie ever wrote in her life might be of interest to you. I wondered myself whose phone number she'd written down."

"The Cook County, Illinois, Bureau of Vital Records. And you must have made a copy of the note before you handed it to me because you called it yourself later that same day. At eleven forty-one, our time."

How could he possibly know that? I'd got a recording when I called, so either the Bureau's answering machine keeps the numbers of after-hours calls or Kronenberg had gotten access to my cell phone records. "If you know this, you must also know what the Cook County Bureau of Records had to tell us. Erin had a problem with her marital status that did, indeed, call a halt to the wedding. Somehow, Stephanie must have suspected this and called Cook County. Erin has even told me Stephanie confronted her that evening. It was to Erin that Stephanie said, 'If you don't tell him, I will!' Do you remember? I told you about that the first time you talked to me, but at the time I guessed she'd been talking to Gisele, not Erin. I was wrong."

Kronenberg slouched nonchalantly and threw one arm over the chair's spindle back. "It's taken me a long time to straighten out this mess, Mrs. Lamb, but I've finally done it. Every resident of the house had a motive for killing either Stephanie or Gisele, and the other could have been killed because she witnessed the murder. So I've been following a hundred false leads, examining videotapes that, I now realize, mean nothing. Searching for a bullet casing I'll never find because the killer has long since disposed of it. Here's how it happened."

He leaned forward and squared his forearms on the table. He glanced toward Seifert and then toward the top of the file cabinet. "You probably came here with the intention of killing Stephanie Lamb. All this one-big-happy-family thing was an act. As soon as you arrived, you started asking Juergen questions about the bunker. What did they keep inside? What sorts of weapons? After dinner, you took a walk, alone, to check out the situation. You walked around the house, walked to the bunker, noticed the bunker door could only be opened by the keypad and you didn't know the combination.

"About eleven-thirty, you hear Juergen talking to Stephanie on his mobile phone and they're discussing wine. Aha! Stephanie must be in the bunker right now because that's where they store the wine. And then, as luck would have it, Juergen asks you to go to the kitchen, which gives you an excuse to leave the room."

Kronenberg paused, pressing his laced hands to his chin. "I doubt you really meant to do it that night. Not so soon after arriving. Looks too suspicious. But there it was, your perfect chance. Stephanie is in the bunker with a huge stash of weapons, and all you have to do is run up there and do it. You don't even have to make up an excuse to get her up there alone. She's already there. No one can question why she was in the bunker at that time of night because she's just explained it to her brother while everyone in the living room was listening. Perfect.

"You run to the kitchen, tell Gisele to make a pot of coffee, dash out the side door, up to the bunker. Was the bunker door standing open? I'll bet it was. You probably had to talk to Stephanie for a few minutes while you located a suitable weapon . . ."

"Stop! None of this ever happened!"

"While discussing the merits of Italian wine, you spotted a handy Glock, already loaded, on the shelf with a number of other guns, grabbed it, grabbed Stephanie. But Stephanie surprises you. *She doesn't want to be killed!* You struggle. Stephanie heads for the door. You grab her, she grabs your jacket. One of the buttons pops off. Flies out the door."

He signaled to Seifert, standing near the window, his head framed by eyelet curtains. "Where's that evidence bag with the button?" Seifert pulled a file drawer open, drew out a plastic bag, and handed it to Kronenberg. "We found this less than a meter away from the door to the bunker." He let me take the bag into my own hands.

It definitely was my missing button. No doubt about it. Like the buttons still on the jacket, it had a metal shank on the back, and the front was covered with the same tweed material as the jacket itself. "It's my button all right, but I don't think it went missing until a couple of days ago."

"Are you sure? Can you prove that?"

"I don't know. I'll have to think about it."

"You can't prove it, Mrs. Lamb, because it didn't go missing *a couple of days ago*," he said, his voice heavy with sarcasm. "We found this button frozen solid in ice. Ice from the snow that fell about four o'clock that morning, then partially melted and froze again. There's no way this button was put there *after* the snow."

I knew something was wrong with this picture, but I was damned if I could see what.

Kronenberg returned to his fantasy. "As I was saying, the button flies off but you don't notice because you have more important things on your mind. You grab Stephanie around the neck, put the Glock to her head, and shoot. She falls."

I swallowed hard to keep from throwing up.

"You wipe your prints off the gun, press Stephanie's hand around it, fire again so gunpowder residue will be found on her hand. You fire out the open bunker door and, talk about rotten luck, Gisele is outside. She's curious about why you went running out the kitchen door like that and has decided to check it out. Your second shot hits Gisele squarely in the heart. Without so much as a sound, she falls to the ground, dead. You look at the floor and see two shell casings. You pick up one of the shell casings, leaving one behind so it will look like suicide. You probably didn't think it would make any difference which one you picked up. You didn't know the clip had been loaded with bullets from two different boxes. Same caliber, different brands. You go back to the house and casually take the coffee upstairs. No one suspects a thing.

"I imagine you thought about it a long time that night. Juergen came to your room looking for Gisele. That must have caused you a moment of panic, what? I imagine you lay awake for a long time that night, thinking. 'Where is Gisele? Could she have seen?' "

"Oh good Lord! Stop! This never happened!"

"When Gisele's body is found the next morning, you have to come up with an explanation for that, don't you? So you make up an overheard argument between Gisele and Stephanie. When I take over the case, you tell me you heard Stephanie yell something like, 'I know what you're up to.' Now it makes more sense that Stephanie would have shot Gisele, panicked when she saw what she'd done, and killed herself."

"But Patrick also heard the argument. I didn't know what Stephanie had said, because it was in German. Patrick translated it for me and told me not to worry about it because it was not our problem. Ask him!"

"Patrick is your son," Kronenberg muttered tonelessly. He glanced toward Seifert, then toward the top of the file cabinet.

I knew it was a signal for Seifert to pick up the arrest warrant already filled out with my name on it. I said, "What do you suppose I did about all the blood that must have been on me? I saw Stephanie's body that morning. Whoever put that gun to her head must have caught some of the spray."

Kronenberg's eyes gleamed as if to say, "I see. We're playing hardball now." He drummed his fingers on the desk, and said, "Your tweed jacket will be tested when we take it to cantonal headquarters. I'm sure you've cleaned off the visible stains, but our lab can find blood spatter your eyes can't see."

Seifert moved around behind me, placing himself between the door and me as Kronenberg stood and droned, "Dorothy Lamb, I have here a warrant for your arrest . . ." I didn't hear the rest because, attempting to stand, I sank to the floor.

Twenty-Six

As jail cells go, this one wasn't bad. The little window had a couple of iron bars, but the eyelet tie-back curtains softened the effect. The bed was reasonably comfortable, the sheets were clean, and the tile floor gleamed. It smelled of lemon soap. I got the feeling this cell was not intended for hardened criminals but rather for the occasional disorderly visitors who, police hoped, wouldn't go home and tell bad tales about their experience in the LaMotte lock-up.

I had nothing to read, nothing to occupy my mind but the mess I was in. I had always thought I could handle jail better than most because solitude doesn't bother me. In fact I enjoy it. Throughout most of my adult life I've longed for a place to get away from, *Mom, where's my book bag? Dotsy, what's for dinner? Can we count on you to be cookie chairman again this year?* A cave on a mountain top, that's what I'd like. Or a jail cell. Meals delivered through a slot in the door by someone who didn't want to hang around and talk. Always sounded good to me.

But as soon as that door clanged shut, as soon as I heard the key turn in the lock, I panicked. *I can't get out!* If I call out that I'm having a panic attack, that I'm on fire, that I'm having a heart attack, that the room is full of bees and I'm allergic, it will do no good. *I can't get out!* I resorted to deep breathing in a lotus position on the floor (fortunately spotless) and closed my eyes until my heart rate tapered off.

Brian arrived after I'd been there an hour or so. They let him come into the cell with me and locked the door behind him. "I've retained a lawyer for you. That is, if you approve of her. Juergen says she's good. She'll be coming by to see you shortly, but in the meantime don't say anything to the police. You know how that goes."

I offered him a seat on my bed, but he preferred to stand.

"Where's Patrick? And Juergen?" I'd seen the three of them on a bench outside the building when we first pulled up.

"Juergen is trying to arrange bail for you, but apparently we have to wait until the judge or whoever *sets* bail. He can't pay it until they know how much it is."

"And Patrick?"

"I had to get rid of him. He was going ape shit."

"How did you get rid of him?" My voice carried no real alarm, in spite of the ominous sound of that statement because I knew Brian would never hurt his brother.

"I told him Dad needed him back at the house." He paused and looked at me, blinking back a tear in each eye. He pulled me to him and held me close. "And Dad probably does, in fact. They released him here at the same time they were talking to you up at the house. We passed him coming out of the elevator hut as we were going down."

"Did you tell your dad what was happening?"

"I told him Kronenberg had taken you down in the police car. He's had time to think about it now, so what do you think, Mom? Is Dad feeling guilty because you busted your buns to track him down and get him released? He can't do anything to help you, you know. Or is he sitting up there drinking scotch and thanking his lucky stars he's not where you are?"

"You mustn't be so hard on him. Think what he's been through during the last week."

"Oh yes! The poor man inherited millions of dollars. I'd like to go through that myself."

"He's lost his wife, been arrested, and—I wouldn't be surprised—discovered his son has hired a spy without mentioning it to him."

"Do you think he knows?"

"Probably. Kronenberg knows, and they probably talked about it when Chet turned himself in."

I told Brian about the interview, about the jacket button, and about Kronenberg's theory. I had to explain why I'd asked Juergen so many questions about the bunker, because Brian hadn't come to the house until the next morning. My curiosity, I told him, came from my interest in World War II and not from any clandestine plans for the bunker's use.

He listened, then exhaled disgustedly. "I'll give the man credit for one thing. He's got a vivid imagination. Seriously, Mom, Kronenberg is on the spot. He has to solve these murders. It's all over the news and he hasn't the *foggiest* notion who did it. It must've blown his mind when that English couple called and alibied Dad. He thought his work was done until they dropped that bombshell on him. Now what?"

"I had high hopes for Gisele's boyfriend Milo," I said, "then it turns out he was in jail that night."

"But he was there earlier in the day. I'll bet he knows something we don't. He works at the post office, doesn't he?"

I nodded.

"I think I'll have a little talk with him."

"Careful, Brian. We don't want Kronenberg thinking you're trying to horn in on his territory."

"I'll be careful." He seated himself beside me on my tiny cot and lay an arm across my shoulders. "Have you thought about Zoltan? Has anyone? Talk about a suspicious character."

"What motive would he have?"

"Maybe he tried to assault Gisele—sexually. Maybe she told Stephanie about it. Zoltan might have felt he had to kill them both to keep his job."

"Or avoid going to jail."

"You see? Motives are a dime a dozen."

"And he was caught red-handed inside the crime scene tape, sneaking in when he didn't think the police would be looking," I said.

"What?"

"Patrick heard it all. He was inside the van when Kronenberg and Seifert hauled Zoltan in."

"Holy crap! And, being a handyman and all, he could have moseyed around the place anytime, day or night, and if anyone asked, he could always say, 'Just looking for something I lost,' or something like that."

I put my hand on Brian's knee. "We have to solve this, Brian. You and me. Kronenberg has a perfectly logical scenario of how I committed these murders. It's wrong, but it makes perfect sense. He has my jacket, he has my jacket button. Someone has given him a statement, out of context, that I made at dinner— *someone is walking on my grave.* He thinks I was referring to Stephanie, but I wasn't. I just had a chill. He finds something ominous in the fact that I made a copy of Stephanie's phone pad notes before I turned them over to him, and he thinks I made up the argument Patrick and I overheard." I squeezed Brian's knee and stood up. "And Lord knows I had motive. Actually I didn't, but anyone outside our family would think I did."

"Anyone who *knows* you would know you didn't."

"Now. Back to that phone pad note. I think it's the key to everything, Brian. While everyone is focusing on us, we're forgetting about Johannesburg, and gold and silver, and gliders doing reconnaissance over our house at all hours, and Anton Spektor, who may or may not wear red Italian shoes."

Brian gave me his best incredulous look.

I laughed. "How long will they let you stay with me? Let's put our heads together."

My next visitor was Lettie. She brought me a bundle of fresh clothes in a plastic bag. "I did your laundry for you." She dropped the bag and looked at me, tears already streaming down her face. I hugged her to me and let her cry until my shoulder was wet.

"I'm okay, Lettie. Really I am. They're quite nice here and look! As jail cells go, this is great. Nice and clean. Plus, they seem to be lenient about visitors."

"You're not okay. You're charged with two counts of murder."

"Have you seen Patrick?"

"I had to slip him a mickey."

"You what?"

"He was so upset, he was shaking. You know how he gets. He was talking crazy, and I got concerned. I didn't know what he might do, so I gave him a caffeine-free Coke with two sleeping pills in it."

"Lettie! That's dangerous!"

"No it isn't. I've done it myself plenty of times."

"No you haven't! When did you ever put two sleeping pills in a caffeine-free Coke and drink it?" That stumped her. I asked her about Chet and told her all I could remember about the interview leading up to my arrest.

"By the way," she said when my tale was done, "where is your pink cashmere sweater?"

"In the dresser. Second drawer from the top."

"No, it isn't. Right before I left the house, Kronenberg came in with a warrant that gave him permission to take several things and the first thing on the list was your pink cashmere sweater. I looked in all the dresser drawers, but it wasn't there. They turned our room upside-down looking for it. You should see the mess! But it isn't there. Could it have gotten mixed up with your laundry? Maybe slipped down behind the washer?"

"I'd never put cashmere in the washer."

"Well, where is it? Kronenberg looked at me like he thinks I hid it."

"I'll have to think about it, but if I figure it out I don't think I'll like the answer."

The young man who had locked me in here and who had brought each of my visitors clanked in with one more—my lawyer. She introduced herself and nodded to Lettie in a dismissive sort of way. Lettie took the hint and left.

First, the lawyer explained why I'd have to stay here a while: I was charged with two counts of murder, I was not a Swiss citizen, and if I left the country they'd have a devil of a time extraditing me back. "Juergen Merz is working to get you released on bail, but if we can arrange it at all, trust me, it won't be low. It will be astronomical. But Herr Merz can afford it, can't he?"

"Let's talk about the charges," I said.

For the next hour, we went over everything I could think of to tell her and everything she could think of to ask. Meanwhile, my dinner arrived on a tray with regular silverware and—I had to laugh—a linen napkin. My lawyer seemed like a nice enough woman, about forty, small and trim. Her English was flawless and Juergen knew her. I decided if she was willing to take my case, I was willing to let her. She lectured me on the three legs in a murder case—means, motive, and opportunity—and the fact that the police had all three, in spades. The hard evidence was thin, she said, and mostly circumstantial. The button, my jacket (yet to be tested for blood spatter) and now, my missing pink cashmere sweater. She hadn't heard about that yet. When I told her what Lettie had just told me, she looked at me hard and then wrote some notes. The police might or might not have found my hair or fingerprints inside the bunker, but if so, they meant nothing since everyone knew I was the first on the scene that morning.

"Means, motive, opportunity, and a button. That's not enough, Mrs. Lamb. Now tell me: When they test the jacket and the sweater, *will they find blood?*"

With a long night looming ahead of me and nothing to read, not even a crossword puzzle for diversion, I started to prepare for bed, wondering if a nightgown was standard attire in jail or if one was expected to sleep in one's street clothes. Lettie had brought me a gown, but what if they came in during the night? Someone needed to write a book on jail cell etiquette. I brushed my teeth at the tiny sink beside the toilet and checked my blood sugar level.

I heard a commotion.

Within a minute, I discerned the hubbub was in two or more languages and a good bit of Italian was mixed in. Not just any Italian but the booming voice of Marco Quattrocchi. I couldn't make out what the argument was about, but I assumed it was about me and the fact that I was here. The shouts continued for a good five minutes, and once or twice I thought I heard something hit a wall. Then, approaching footsteps and the clank of a key in the lock.

Marco stood there in his black Carabinieri uniform. Epaulets on his shoulders, a red stripe down each leg, and a white bandolier across his chest. I had never seen him in uniform outside of Florence, and even then only when on duty. He had obviously donned full dress for its impact and, on me at least, it was working. I wouldn't mess with him, and I doubted anyone else would either.

He stepped across the room and took me in his arms. I didn't want to cry. I tried to hold it back but after one long, strong, kiss, I couldn't help it. He held me until I got myself under control. He removed his uniform jacket with all its clinking hardware, folded it lengthwise and laid it across the tiny sink. We both sat crosswise on the cot and leaned back against the wall, my feet sticking out straight, his dangling near the floor. For the fourth time I recited the evidence against me, the ordeal I'd been through, and the reasons I felt my only hope was to find the real killer. "This is a double murder, Marco. Kronenberg has to get a conviction, and I won't be leaving this cell until he has someone to take my place."

"There is another possibility. Can we prove you could *not* have done it? You did that for your ex-husband. Can we do it for you?" I heard no rancor in his voice, but it occurred to me I had never heard him refer to Chet by name. "What about those videotapes? Your lawyer will be allowed to view them if she asks. What do they show?"

"I don't know."

"What about Lettie? Can she swear you didn't leave your room in the middle of the night?"

"Probably not. She was exhausted from her long trip and couldn't wait to go to bed. She probably conked out as soon as her head hit the pillow."

I thought I heard someone coming. Marco sat up straight and shifted forward until his shoes touched the floor. I moved away from him, but heard nothing more. False alarm.

"I have learned a little about Anton Spektor," he said. "Interpol has him on their radar screen. He is suspected of being affiliated with the Russian mafia, but he is currently listed as residing in Berne. He owns a flat there. He has a pilot's license and a Swiss driver's license. I found a single engine Cessna airplane and a glider registered to him."

"Good for you!"

"It is not much, really. But here is something more interesting. Do you remember what I told you about the gold being smuggled out of South Africa disguised as bars of silver? I have looked into this. Shipments of silver have been imported from South Africa into Switzerland by MWU. This company was owned by the Merz family but it went bankrupt. It opened up again after a reorganization, and now it is not clear who owns it."

"I don't understand."

"The owner of record is old Heinrich Merz, but the money it took to set the company back on its feet came from . . . well, it is not clear where it came from."

I thought about the money Brian told me was missing from Lamb's Farm Equipment and shuddered. It was too coincidental not to suspect that Stephanie had funneled it into MWU. And why hadn't Juergen, acting on behalf of his father, simply ponied up the money from the family coffers? They had millions, some of which Chet had now inherited. I asked Marco about this.

Marco stood up, walked to the bars that separated me from the free world, and peered down the hall outside. "I think the money came from the Russian mafia," he said. "When they destroy a company, it is with the idea of taking it over. If the former owners try to save their company by pouring in more money, the mafia does it all again. They pay crooked cops to raid the place, file big lawsuits, make false charges, confiscate records. Or, if all else fails, they simply arrange for the owners or members of their families to disappear.

"The silver was imported in five kilogram bars by MWU and then transported to a precious metals company in Zurich. But the Zurich company's paperwork and the paperwork MWU presented to customs officials in Geneva do not match." Marco turned to me. "There are a few bars missing."

"What? How do you know that?"

"At least on one shipment, they do not match. The weights

223

do not match. MWU imported some one hundred kilograms of silver from Johannesburg and one day later, they sold about eighty kilograms to the Zurich metals company. It looks as if twenty kilograms went missing overnight."

"I don't get it. Who makes the money here? They import silver but it's really gold. They sell it to the metals company in Zurich, but for how much money? Do they sell it like silver or like gold?"

"Dotsy, *mio angelo.* You really have no head for business!"

"I have a good head for business!" I put on a fake scowl. "I do my own taxes."

Marco stepped forward and kissed me again. "Let me explain. MWU pays customs on the shipment as if it is silver. Not very much. They sell it to the Zurich company as if it is silver. About fifty thousand Euros, I would guess. But under the table, the Zurich company gives MWU enough to make the transaction a good deal for both parties. And the money changing hands all along the chain may or may not be dirty money that the Russian mafia needs to get laundered."

"You say twenty kilos is missing? Assuming it's gold, not silver, how much would that be worth?"

"Do the math. Gold is about thirteen hundred Euros an ounce. Thirty-two troy ounces in a kilo."

I scratched invisible numbers in the air with one finger and made cash register sounds. "Eight hundred thirty-two thousand Euros. More than a million in U.S. dollars. See? I do have a head for business."

In the few minutes we had before the guard tramped down the hall and started clearing his throat pointedly, but not actually telling Marco he had to leave, we talked about my predicament. "Someone in the house is working against me, Marco. My pink cashmere sweater is missing. Kronenberg is going to assume it was covered in blood and I've disposed of it, but I'm sure it was in my dresser as late as yesterday. Today, it's gone."

TWENTY-SEVEN

My little barred window was open and the fresh air smelled good. They turned out the lights at eleven, and by that time the smell of lemon floor cleaner was getting to me. Too chilly though. I climbed twice from my little cot to add more cover, using the face towel the jail issued me plus two T-shirts and a pair of slacks from the bag Lettie brought. Then the street noise kept me awake. Partiers, tacking from one bar to another up and down the main drag, yelled nonsense in several languages while dogs from all corners of town barked in protest. I could have reached the window and closed it if the cot hadn't been bolted to the floor. At some point exhaustion took over and I slept.

I awoke with the key to my own freedom! Why hadn't I thought of it before? It's funny how the sleeping brain works. Swept clean of all the cares and demands of the day, it roams around through waving fields of unrealized possibilities. Granted, most of them are stupid, but if you can hold on to the rare good one until you wake up, it's amazing how often it turns out to be the very thing.

I could hardly contain myself while I washed up at my tiny sink and ate the breakfast a new policeman brought me on a tray. I went over and over it in my mind. Making sure I was right. I slipped into the only corner of my cell that couldn't be seen from the corridor outside and changed clothes. *Now, how do I call a meeting?* Weren't you supposed to draw your tin cup across the bars and yell?

But soon the same policeman who brought my breakfast came back. "They want you in the interview room." He unlocked me and led me down the corridor and around to the same room as yesterday. I passed Marco, now wearing civilian clothes, in the reception area near the front desk. He waved at me but didn't follow. Inside the interview room my lawyer sat on the near side of the table opposite Detective Kronenberg and Officer Seifert. My escort dragged in a fourth chair for me.

Kronenberg said, "Captain Marco Quattrocchi has suggested we visit a small landing strip that lies some one or two kilometers west of the Chateau Merz. He tells us you have been there yourself and have raised questions about the plane and the glider hangared there."

"Yes, but before we talk about that, I need to clear up something else."

My lawyer extended an arm toward me much like a mother, slamming on brakes, throws out an arm to keep a child from falling forward. She leaned toward me and asked for a synopsis of what I intended to clear up. I explained as succinctly as I could.

"I need to see my jacket," I announced. "And that button."

Kronenberg's head jerked. He looked at Seifert. "Haven't we sent it on to cantonal headquarters?"

Seifert said he'd check and left the room.

"I don't understand. This is highly irregular, Mrs. Lamb."

"We have a right to see any and all evidence," my lawyer said.

I hadn't caught her name yesterday, so I asked her now. She told me her name was Something Gaudin, I didn't catch the first name and, at the moment, couldn't be distracted by such trivia.

Seifert returned carrying a large brown paper bag. "They

hadn't sent it yet," he said.

"Get the button. And we'll need fresh evidence bags as well," Kronenberg pulled a Swiss Army knife from his pocket. "I hope you are not playing with us, Mrs. Lamb. This is highly unusual. We have strict rules about the chain of possession of all evidence. This jacket has been entered, dated, and signed into evidence, and when we take it out, we must do it all again."

"I'm not playing with you."

Kronenberg extracted my tweed jacket and plopped it on the table. Beside it, Seifert dropped the clear plastic bag containing my button.

I spread the jacket on the table so the metal shank, still dangling where a button used to be, was front and center. "Can we take the button out of its bag, too?"

Kronenberg sighed but did as I asked.

I placed the button face down, on the jacket. Just as I recalled from my brief look yesterday, the shank was still firmly attached to the button back. "Can any of you explain to me how a button can have two shanks?"

Attorney Gaudin gasped, threw both hands to her mouth, then laughed. "Oh my God!" She grabbed up both items and put them down quickly, still laughing.

It took the men a minute to get it. Seifert and Kronenberg lapsed into German as they talked it over, man to man. Seifert pointed to the back of the button and brought the shank on the jacket up alongside it. Soon, both agreed and admitted—the button they found frozen in ice near the bunker door had not been ripped from that jacket.

"May I suggest you go to my room at Chateau Merz and locate the little envelope that came with the jacket? It should have a sample of thread and an extra button, but I'll bet the button is missing."

★ ★ ★ ★ ★

I waved to Marco through the window when I returned to the front desk. He'd gone outside and taken up his vigil on the wooden bench. I didn't demand my jacket and button back, because I thought I'd let the police keep them a couple of days. They might make use of them in a training class as an example of why evidence should be carefully examined. But Kronenberg insisted. Along with my watch, purse, and jewelry, he pressed the former evidence into my hands.

I didn't want to go back to Chateau Merz just yet. Patrick had to be dealt with first, then Chet, and I needed some down time to gather my thoughts before tackling either. I wondered if Patrick had slept off the sedatives Lettie so recklessly slipped him the night before.

Marco met me outside the police station and we walked through the town, arm in arm. The day promised to be lovely, with bright blue skies and the slightest nip in the air. Marco told me he was staying at the hotel on the far end of the street. We passed the little Catholic church where Patrick and Erin would have been married, and I recalled Lettie telling me about her visit to the cemetery. Diverting our path, we walked through, reading epitaphs and enjoying the flowers planted in each tiny plot. A few of the epitaphs were in English but most were in German, French, or Italian. Marco translated these for me. I had to laugh at one that touted the mountain-climbing successes of the occupant, who nevertheless did fall off the Matterhorn on his last climb. We found a bench and sat.

"Now that I'm in the clear, we still have to find out who did it." I laid my blue plastic bag of clothes on the bench beside me. "Do you think Kronenberg will let me go home now?"

"No, I do not. You are not in the clear, Dotsy. All Kronenberg knows now is that your button was deliberately planted, probably by someone who intended to throw suspicion on you.

229

It has nothing to do with whether you actually did it. You are still under suspicion as much as anyone else in that house."

It seemed the sky had suddenly darkened. "What do I have to do, for heaven's sake? Can he keep us all here until the case is solved? What if it's never solved?"

"I suppose there is a limit. He has to let you go sometime. And if Kronenberg checks out the leads I have given him, he should be able to solve it fairly soon. It has to be connected to the gold smuggling operation." Marco planted his hands on his knees and squinted out toward snow-capped peaks in the distance. He chewed on one side of his mustache. "*Has* to be!"

"One problem. Who swiped my pink cashmere sweater? Obviously someone inside the house did, and I don't think Anton Spektor or any other members of the Russian mafia could be wandering through without someone noticing."

"And who, other than Kronenberg and his assistant, knew the sweater was about to be taken in as evidence?" Marco said.

I thought about it. "This is probably way off the mark, but Odile, our cook, seems to know everything the police know. Might she have a friend at the station?"

"Talk to her. Find out."

"From the very beginning I've bounced back and forth between insider and outsider. Were the murders done by someone staying at the house or by someone else? It's almost unbelievable, but I still don't know."

"Why were Gisele and Stephanie up there at that time of night anyway?" Marco asked, using their names as familiarly as if he had known them. "Exactly when did the murders take place?"

"Between eleven-thirty and four A.M., they say. I know Stephanie was in the bunker at eleven-thirty, pulling wine for the house. No one saw either of them after that."

Marco stood and stretched. Holding out a hand to me, he

pulled me up and we resumed our graveyard tour. "Tell me about Juergen."

"He's rich, of course. He's spent most of his adult life as an adventurer, climbing mountains and things like that. I think he chafes a bit at being forced to stick close to home since his father got too old to oversee the family businesses himself. His family is important to him. You should have seen how Stephanie's death and his father's death told on his face. He loves astronomy. He keeps a telescope at the chalet."

"Astronomy?" Marco put an arm around my shoulder.

"It's logical, I think. An adventurer who hates being tied down. Climb mountains. Reach for the stars! If you can't reach the stars, stand on a mountain top and look at them. Maybe that's why he's never married."

"What was his relationship with Stephanie?"

"Funny you should ask. Odile told me they fought like cats and dogs when they were children."

"That means nothing. Most brothers and sisters fight."

"Plus, Stephanie was a woman who got her own way and stuck her nose in other people's business. She was about to tell Patrick about Erin's previous marriage—although I'm grateful to her for that. Funny, I wonder how she did find out. And why she apparently waited until she got to Switzerland to call the Cook County Vital Records place."

"And you suspect Juergen and Gisele were having an affair?"

I didn't recall telling him that, but supposed I must have. "Gisele had a boyfriend here in town. A guy named Milo. By the way, Brian told me yesterday that he was going to pay Milo a visit. I wonder if he did."

"Go on. What about this Milo?"

"I've never met him. But I got the feeling that first night, Juergen was so upset, looking for Gisele. I sort of thought she and he intended to spend the night together. Later on, I found out about Milo and heard she and he had a fight in the meadow near the bunker that afternoon."

"Do you think Juergen is gay?"

Marco's question startled me. "I've never thought about it. I don't think so."

"It might explain why he's never married."

"Oh come on, Marco. Lots of people don't get married for lots of reasons."

We had circled the main part of LaMotte and come back around to the intersection of the main street and the one leading to the tunnel. I said, "Do you want to come up to the house?"

"Not yet. There will be enough going on when you walk in. They do not know you are out of jail. It would not be a good time for me to meet your ex-husband." He kissed me on the cheek. "Tell Patrick I'm here and I'd like to talk to him. He can come to my hotel."

TWENTY-EIGHT

I called the house and told Odile I was on my way up so she could buzz me in at the tunnel entrance. Stepping out into the sweet pine-scented air above, I indulged in a little Julie Andrews euphoria and hoped no one was watching. As I approached the house I looked to the meadow beyond it and spotted Chet plodding toward me from the direction of the bunker. He quickened his steps when he saw me, then grabbed me, and folded me in a hug. I couldn't help comparing his embrace to that of Marco's of a few minutes earlier. Marco's won. By comparison, Chet's felt sterile. Cold. Perfunctory.

"Where have you been?" he asked, now holding me at arm's length. "We've been expecting you for more than an hour."

"How did you know I was out?"

"Odile told us."

"Ah, yes. The mountain grapevine."

"So you outfoxed them, eh? Something about the buttons on your jacket."

"Later. Where's Patrick?"

"At the house, I think. He was in his room a little while ago."

Over Chet's shoulder I spotted Juergen just emerging from the bunker. "Have you and Juergen been in the bunker?"

"He was showing me some old artillery. He has short-wave radio and gas masks from the forties." His arm still around my shoulders, he steered me toward the house.

"What was it like yesterday, when everyone heard I'd been arrested?"

"Patrick and Brian and Juergen came running in, and Patrick was having a fit. Brian was trying to calm him down and he took him off—somewhere. I don't know. Juergen told me they'd arrested you. Odile got all flustered and ran to the phone. I asked him to tell me more, but that's all he knew at that point. And listen, Dotsy. I have never felt so helpless in my life. After all you did for me, risking your neck to bring me back. If you hadn't done that, they'd have launched a manhunt and I'd probably have been killed! And here I was, listening to Juergen telling me about how they'd arrested you, and there wasn't a damned thing I could do to help you."

You could have done what Juergen and Brian did do. Hire me a lawyer. I said, "Odile ran straight to the phone, did she? Did you overhear anything?"

Chet stopped dead in his tracks, as if he hadn't expected the question, and tilted his head to one side. "No. She was talking in German."

"Then what?"

He paused a moment. "I went up to my room. I wanted to think, you know."

Yeah, right. You probably wanted to take a nap. "Where was everyone else? How did they find out?"

We had reached the porch steps. Chet looked at me questioningly. I waited for him to think about it, because I needed to know who knew Kronenberg was coming for my pink cashmere sweater, *how* they knew and *when* they found out.

"Babs was in her room. Lettie was somewhere, because she came running to the kitchen when she heard Patrick. I don't know where Erin was." He nudged me up a couple of steps. "Oh, yeah. I remember looking out my window when I got to my room and I saw Zoltan coming toward the house. Then I heard the kitchen door, so I guess he came in that way. Now there's a weirdo for you."

I found Odile in the kitchen, pounding chicken breasts into thin slabs. She seemed startled to see me, her smile of welcome delayed a second too long. "Something smells good," I said. "But after my last twenty-four hours, anything other than a jail cell would smell good."

"The food was not good?" She pronounced it "goot."

I let the small talk work its way around to the LaMotte police station and how much she knew about it. As she finally told me, after much beating about the bush, her sister's daughter worked in the front office and sometimes, yes—she didn't mind telling me because there was nothing wrong with it—her niece did call her up from work just to chat.

Certain that Odile's quick phone call had been to the police station, I tried to drag out more details about what her niece had told her about my arrest. Had the niece overheard any of the interview? Had Kronenberg or Seifert walked into the front room and talked about it? Specifically, had they said anything about a pink sweater? Of course. Someone had to type up the search warrant that listed the sweater among other items. Would that job have fallen to Odile's niece? What other items were on the list? I made a mental note to ask Lettie. If she got so much as a glimpse of that warrant, her photographic memory would have recorded it all, right down to the creases in the paper. She'd probably be able to write it out, even if it was in German.

Patrick began weeping when he saw me, and I was glad Chet wasn't there. He had never had much patience with Patrick's tendency to go soft. I wondered what had happened to that burst of aggressive dynamism he'd shown when he found out about Erin and called off the wedding. When I told him about the extra button shank and the scene in the interview room, he perked up, let out a whoop, and pumped the air. "Go, Mom!"

"Marco is in town," I said. "He wants to see you." I told him where Marco was staying. "Patrick, have you heard anyone mention a pink sweater?"

His head jerked back. "Pink sweater? No."

"Were you here when Kronenberg and Seifert came up yesterday afternoon with a search warrant?"

He shook his head. "I was outside. Brian told me to take a walk because I was hyperventilating, sort of. When I came back they had left, but Lettie told me about it and showed me the mess they made of your room. I don't recall her mentioning anything about a sweater, though."

Patrick walked to his bedroom window. Since the shifting of rooms following Erin and Patrick's breakup, he'd been sleeping in the room next door to Lettie and me. Our windows looked out at the meadow, now erupting in yellow bloom, but the bunker door was hidden from our view behind a grassy mound. "The police are here," he said. "They're talking to Zoltan."

I joined him at the window. Zoltan, Kronenberg, and Seifert stood outside the tool shed at the edge of the meadow, Zoltan fiddling with a leaf-blower and Kronenberg gesturing westward with one arm. "I wonder what they're talking about." Zoltan seemed upset, shrugging his shoulders, swinging the leaf-blower this way and that. Could Zoltan have been the one who planted my button outside the bunker? "Patrick, when you were in the van that day and they were questioning Zoltan, did you hear them say anything about a button?"

"A button? No, not that I recall."

"Did they bring in anything else when they brought him in?"

"Not that I remember. They each had him by one arm, and they sort of threw him down in the chair and Kronenberg started firing questions at him."

I remember what Kronenberg had told me: the button had been there before the snow. It was frozen in ice as it would have been if it was lying under the snow, the snow partially melted then refroze, encasing the button. Zoltan's trespass inside the taped-off area was much later, after the snow and ice had mostly melted. Since then, the weather had been mild.

A few minutes later, the policemen left Zoltan to his work and disappeared down the path that led west. I thought they might be heading for the road if they had come up here in a vehicle, or they might be heading for the landing strip, as Marco had strongly suggested. To solve their case, Marco told them, they had to follow the gold. And the landing strip with its glider seemed the only connection between Chateau Merz and the shady Anton Spektor. Why was the glider buzzing our house at odd hours? To see who was here? To see if someone in particular was here? Or were they really interested in the bunker? What could they see of it from the air but a rock wall? Was something they wanted inside the bunker, and were they buzzing the place looking for a chance to sneak in unobserved? They'd have to know the keypad combination or else have an accomplice who would let them in.

Brian and Babs appeared from around the corner of the house and climbed the outside stairs to the deck. I heard a sliding glass door in the living room below open, then close.

The gold! What if the missing gold was in the bunker?

Patrick said something to me, but I shushed him. I had to hold on to that thought. Okay. Suppose the smugglers were using the bunker to stash their gold until they could move it along to their buyers. Suppose some of it got mislaid—left behind when they moved the rest along. That would explain why they were keeping the house under surveillance. They were looking for a chance to pick it up. Using a glider because it made no noise. Wouldn't draw attention to itself even passing low over the house, whereas an airplane would. A plane or a helicopter flying so low would sound like an invading army inside the house. If this were all true, someone at Chateau Merz would have to be in on it. Working with them. That meant Juergen, Gisele, or Zoltan, probably. Stephanie? All the American guests seemed highly unlikely. We'd have had to be in on this longer than any of us had been here. Not likely at all.

"Mom? Where are you?" Patrick was pushing my shoulder to bring me back to the real world. "I've been talking to you for the past five minutes and you haven't heard a word I've said."

Babs Toomey's eyes were red, as if she'd been crying. I found her and Brian in the living room, having an early shooter. I passed on Brian's offer to fix me one, and sat down. Babs's shoes were wet from hiking through dew-heavy grass.

"We're talking about how much longer we'll have to stay here," Brian said. "Babs has big trouble with her job."

"I told them yesterday I would be flying back, probably today, and they promised not to fire me. I really thought the whole thing would be over . . . oh, I'm sorry, Dotsy. I don't mean I was glad they arrested you or I thought you really did it . . . of course, I knew you couldn't have done it. I . . ." Babs was getting herself in a hopeless tangle.

"It's okay, Babs. I hadn't even thought how this would be affecting your job back home." Unlike the rest of us who had salaried jobs or owned our own companies, Babs made hourly wages at an insurance company where she hadn't worked for very long. They might well replace her.

Brian said, "She called them again a few minutes ago and they told her not to bother coming back to work."

The talk around the dinner table that night centered on one topic: When can we go home? Juergen said he hadn't heard anything and didn't know what the standard procedure in a case like this would be. Obviously police couldn't keep us here forever, but the case hadn't been solved, and once we left the country extraditing any one of us back would be a lengthy and uncertain process.

Brian said he intended to take a swim after dinner, Erin and Chet wanted to watch a tennis match on TV. Juergen said he would set up his telescope on the ridge north of the house and invited me to join him. Poor Babs. I recalled how eager she'd been to hang around Juergen and his telescope on the last occasion and thought it insensitive of Juergen to invite only me. Babs had lost her job today, and this was one more blow. One more rejection.

Rather brightly, she swallowed a sip of Riesling, glanced at her watch, and said, "What time is it at home now? Oh, good. I still have time to make a few calls."

Juergen told me to wait at least fifteen minutes for my eyes to adjust to the dark. Meanwhile, I helped him set up by staying out of his way. Against the background of stars, Juergen and his telescope appeared like black paper silhouettes in a Victorian picture.

"Thanks for hiring that lawyer for me, Juergen. If she sends you a bill, I'll gladly reimburse you."

"Anallese? Right. She's a very capable woman. I've known her since we were children." He handed me a star chart to hold. "If she sends a bill, she'll send it to Brian. He's the one who actually retained her."

"I guess you've heard about the jacket button and why they had to let me go."

I thought I heard him chuckle. "Odile had to explain it to me a couple of times, but I finally got it."

"Odile seems to know a good bit about what goes on at the

239

police station."

"I told you, didn't I? Now that we don't have to yodel our messages from one mountain to another, news travels even faster by telephone."

"Odile has a niece who works at the police station. Did you know that?"

"Aha! That explains how she knew about the button before we told her."

"And my pink sweater. The police came here yesterday with a search warrant and turned my room upside-down looking for the pink sweater I told them I was wearing on the night of the murders. I know it was in my dresser drawer the day before, but when the police came in with their warrant, it was gone."

"Are you sure you haven't mislaid it? Taken it down to the laundry room or something?"

"I'm positive."

Juergen opened a folding canvas chair and sat. My dark-adjusted eyes now saw his outline more clearly against the glow from the house lights. "Odile is incapable of keeping her mouth shut. She very well may have told several people about the sweater, whoever was here at the time." His fancy wristwatch danced and glowed like a digital light show. "Watch out for Babs, Dotsy."

"Babs? Why?" The simplicity of this statement and the gravity in his tone startled me.

"I don't know anything for sure, but I did notice she was act-ing strangely when Brian and Patrick and I got back to the house. She was watching us all like a hawk. I've seen her and Odile talking . . . whispering, you know . . . more than once."

Babs. Babs? I tried imagining that Babs was behind all this. She did have a compelling reason to wish Stephanie dead and she, as well as anyone else, could have slipped out that night and run up to the bunker. That very night, Stephanie had told

Erin she was going to tell all about Erin's marital problem and she could have done it at any time. If Erin or her mother intended to do anything about it, they would have had to act quickly. But the big picture with gliders and spies and gold, if indeed these were part of the picture, was beyond anything I could imagine Babs being involved in. They didn't fit.

"Chet said you took him to the bunker today."

"Right. We're allowed to go in now. The police have done everything they need to do."

"You have equipment from World War II in there?"

"Do you want to see it? I'll take you there tomorrow."

"Thanks. I'd love to."

He called me over to the telescope to see Jupiter. Focusing in on the dancing circle in the eyepiece, I saw the planet with its famous Red Spot. Awesome. Juergen explained how to locate Jupiter's four Galilean moons, but they moved out of the field of vision before I got the hang of it.

Backing away from the telescope so Juergen could refocus it, I noticed his watch again. "Your watch fascinates me, Juergen. Am I imagining things or does the face change colors? It's blue now with glowing dots, but earlier I noticed it was white."

"You like it?" He unbuckled it from his wrist and turned it over. On the opposite side was another face, white, and with more dials. The blue face side had constellations and a built-in compass that made one part rotate as he turned it.

"Oh, you Swiss. You do love your timepieces, don't you? By the way, why are there no cuckoo clocks in the house?"

"Because I don't like cuckoo clocks. They drive me crazy."

Juergen and I were lugging our star-gazing equipment back to the house when we passed Brian, heading for the elevator hut. "I'm going to the Black Sheep. See ya," he said, and kept walking. I helped Juergen stow the telescope in a hall closet and headed toward my room when I heard a sort of "psst" from the stairwell below. It was Brian again. Apparently he had followed us back and come in through the kitchen. I descended to the lower level and found him.

"I'm going to the Black Sheep to meet up with François Bolduc."

"Your spy?"

"Right. He came to town earlier today to talk to Kronenberg and come clean—almost clean."

"That's good!"

"Right. Now I've got an alibi just like everyone else. Would you like to come with me, Mom? I'm going to ask him about this other stuff—the landing strip and Anton Spektor and all that. You never know, do you? He's been looking into the Merz enterprises, so maybe he knows of a connection."

I checked my watch. "Sure, I'll go with you. Let's take the tunnel key."

François Bolduc turned out to be a slick, mustachioed chain-smoker who, in light of the relatively new local ban on smoking in bars and restaurants, preferred to conduct our meeting outside. Brian and I found him at a table on the Black Sheep's small patio.

Brian spent the first ten minutes assuring Bolduc that nothing he had told the police would come back to haunt him. They had both told Kronenberg their meeting on that fateful night involved only the farm equipment business and the possibility of expanding into Europe. Neither had mentioned the Merz family. The reason for Brian's original claim that he hadn't arrived in LaMotte until the next day, they both said, was simply because Brian wasn't ready to let his father know about his potential plans.

I said, "Mr. Bolduc, I have reason to suspect a man named

Anton Spektor is involved in the problems the Merz businesses, particularly MWU, have been suffering. Does that name ring a bell?"

He pulled his cigarette from his lips and stubbed it out in the ashtray. "No. Never heard of him."

I decided he was probably telling me the truth. I gave him a brief synopsis of what I knew and why I had mentioned that name, Brian butting in frequently to add or clarify something. Bolduc's eyes darted left and right as I talked, taking in every stroller past our patio, every window, every little electric car. "I know it sounds crazy but there simply can't be more than a couple of pairs of cordovan red shoes like these on the planet. I saw them in a store in Capri, on the feet of a man who followed me into a women's clothing store, and on feet dangling from the chair lift between the landing strip and the valley. It can't be coincidence. The ones I saw in Capri may still be there, but the pair I've seen twice while here *must be* the same."

"Red shoes? With patches in odd places? I've seen them, too," Bolduc said.

"Where?"

He went silent for an inexcusably long time, lit another cigarette, blew the smoke upward straight into his own eyes, blinked, rubbed his eyes, tapped his cigarette on the side of the ashtray. "Getting into a car in the parking lot at MWU enterprises."

Brian and I looked at each other, stunned.

"I don't know who he was, I don't know if he works there or if he was visiting, and I doubt I'd recognize him if I saw him again. But you're right, Mrs. Lamb. I'd recognize those shoes if I saw them again."

"When was this?"

Bolduc pulled a BlackBerry phone from his jacket and pushed a few spots with his thumb. "April fifth"—he pushed another spot—"at . . . just a minute . . . I must have it set to the wrong time zone. I was going to tell you exactly what time on the fifth, but I know it was around seven o'clock in the evening."

"I wish I knew when that gold shipment came in from South Africa," I hit the table with both fists. *I wish I knew!*"

Brian grabbed his beer glass to save it.

The phone in my purse rang. Startled, I fumbled to find it before it stopped ringing. It was Marco, calling from his hotel room less than a quarter mile away. "Marco!" I nodded to Brian as I said the name. "We're in town, not a stone's throw from you. Why don't you join us?" While saying this, I realized a potential problem. I was inviting an Italian Carabinieri captain, a military policeman, to meet François Bolduc, a corporate spy. Definite problem. Excusing myself from the table, I retreated to a row of bushes along the back of the patio. "Listen, Marco. The man Brian and I are talking to is the one I told you about— the one he hired to look into the Merz family business. So he's a spy, basically, and he might take exception to having a beer with law enforcement."

"I have nothing to do with business in Switzerland."

"I know that, but please don't show up in uniform. It's intimidating."

"I am wearing only my underwear right now. Would it be all right to come as I am?"

I returned to our table, still laughing from the phone call, as Bolduc was saying goodbye to Brian. I wondered if the call had scared him off or if he really did have to leave. After he had gone, Brian assured me his leaving had nothing to do with Marco's call.

Marco showed up in wrinkled trousers, T-shirt, and flip-flops. "You said no uniform. Is this casual enough? Where is our local spy?"

I introduced Marco and Brian.

Brian rose and shook hands with the man he'd heard me mention often. As he recapped our meeting with Bolduc, I interrupted him to say, "So! The red shoes pop up again, this time in the parking lot of MWU enterprises. Still think it's a co-incidence?"

"I never said that," Marco said, rolling his eyes.

"April fifth. That's when Bolduc saw the red shoes. When did that shipment of gold arrive?"

"April fifth. The gold passed through customs on April fifth." Marco's tone turned serious.

"How would they have transported it?"

"Who knows? By armored car, if everything was normal and legal, but since it was not legal, they might have used something less conspicuous. I do not know."

"Where was everyone on April fifth?" I said. "I was at home grading term papers on April fifth."

Brian said, "Stephanie was already here. She flew to Switzerland a week early to make wedding arrangements. Dad flew over that Friday. What day would that be?"

I pulled out my little datebook and rifled through to April. "The ninth. So he wouldn't have been here yet."

"Patrick and Babs and Erin flew over together, and I think they got here after Stephanie but before Dad."

"What about Juergen?"

"Don't know."

"He was here before I was," I said, "but I don't know how long he'd been here."

Marco paid the waitress for the beers he'd ordered. "Do not look at me. I was in Florence."

"What do we do next?" I asked.

"I have told Kronenberg he needs to check out the landing strip you told me about, and if he is any good, he will have done so already." Marco sipped his beer and wiped the foam off his mustache with his wrist. "With police computers at his disposal, he will already know more about Anton Spektor than you were able to dig up, and he will possibly have already talked to him and heard his story about why he has been spying on your house. I say 'his story,' because we must not assume he will tell Kronenberg the truth."

"It has to be the bunker," I said. "That must be what they're interested in, and for the past two weeks, the bunker has been off-limits to everyone but the police. We need to tell Kronenberg to search inside the bunker with a fine-tooth comb."

"I hardly think you would need a fine-tooth comb to spot a stack of gold bars." Marco chuckled. "I think they would catch your eye."

"Plus, they've already searched it," Brian said. "They've had it taped off for more than a week."

"Then we have to do it—and soon," I said. "Unless we're wrong on all counts, things will start unraveling fast now that Kronenberg is on to the guys in the glider."

TWENTY-NINE

The next morning, Lettie and I were on our second cup of coffee in the kitchen when Erin popped in and announced: "I have to go to the bunker. Last night, Juergen asked me to bring down some wine and some other booze—he wrote me a list. It was late when he thought of it and he had to leave early this morning and drive to Zurich."

"Oh! May I go, too?" The opportunity had fallen into my lap so easily. This would be better than going with Juergen because Juergen would've given me the guided tour and I'd have had to leave when he did. I'd have had no chance to snoop around on my own. Lettie said she wanted to come along, and a minute later the three of us were tramping through the morning dew. In my head, I prepared to be dazzled. Pictures I'd seen of the gold at Fort Knox flashed through, and I reminded myself I was only looking for a few bars. How large would they be?

Erin punched the entry numbers on the keypad and swung open the thick metal door. I looked around the meadow before entering, to see if anyone was watching us.

The room, about twenty by twenty feet square, was concrete on all sides, floor, and ceiling. One wall held nothing but a wine rack with hundreds of metal-wrapped bottle necks sticking out. Neat laminated labels—Chardonnay, Merlot, Sauvignon Blanc—tacked to the rack here and there, sectioned the whole into smaller units. Skis, ski poles, boots, and bicycles leaned against the opposite wall. More shelving held canned goods, liquor, and an incredible array of party paraphernalia. Punch bowls, pitchers, trays, and chafing dishes that looked as if they hadn't been used for some time. A waffle iron with a frayed cord, the likes of which I hadn't seen since my grandmother's estate sale.

"Where are the guns?" Lettie asked.

Erin headed straight for the wine rack, Juergen's list in her hand. I spotted a simple wooden door with a brass knob in the back wall and opened it. Beyond the door lay a bathroom with shower stall, sink, and exposed pipes that led to a cylindrical water tank in one corner. I flipped a light switch. It worked.

"Here they are!" Lettie said.

I backed out and turned. Guns and ammunition filled the whole wall adjacent to the exterior door. Long guns like rifles lay flat on shelves, handguns in a wooden box, lidded but unlocked. Boxes and boxes of ammunition, some so old their cardboard had yellowed, their labels faded. This was where Stephanie and Gisele's killer had stood and selected his or her weapon. I lifted the lid on the box of handguns and peered inside. An ominous empty space lay between two guns.

"Why don't they lock this stuff up?" Lettie stretched her arms toward the weapons cache. "This is so dangerous!"

"It *is* locked up, Lettie." Erin set a bottle of wine on the floor. "The bunker door is always locked. If they ever had to hole up in here, like in the event of an attack, they'd probably have to dash in quickly and they'd have nothing with them. That's why they use a keypad rather than a key. Imagine you and your family are running for your lives and you get this far, but no one has the key.

"And if you needed to defend yourselves, you certainly wouldn't want the guns locked up and the key back at the house, would you?" Erin had it all figured out.

I looked around again. In the corner between the guns and

the party supplies, a wooden table supported an ancient-looking metal box with dials, needles, and knobs. A short-wave radio from the forties, no doubt. This place gave me the shivers.

"Let's see what else is here," I said. Lettie followed me through the door into the bathroom. On the far wall of that room a smaller door, only about four feet high, lay between the shower stall and a chemical toilet. I heard Erin calling to us from the big front room.

"I'm going back to the house," she said. "Do you want me to leave the door open? If I close it, you can always open it from the inside."

"Leave it open!" Lettie called back.

I bent down and stepped through into a long hall hacked out of native rock. The musty smell of wet rock and mildew mingled with gloom and deep silence. "Can you find a light switch out there, Lettie?" I couldn't stand up all the way. The ceiling forced me to keep my head and shoulders painfully bent. I felt around on the wall near the little door—no switch. And Lettie was having no better luck in the other room. Even with the door open, it was too dark in here to see anything more than lumps along both walls. I had almost given up when a string brushed my face and made me jump, banging my head. A light cord. I pulled, and an overhead bulb lit up. Luckily I had banged my head against rock and not the bulb. It was screwed into a bare socket.

Now I saw long rows of boxes. Gas masks. The World War II equivalent of a hazmat suit stretched out on a bed of boxes like a headless corpse along one wall. I sat on the floor, and called to Lettie that I'd be in here a while because I wanted to look in all these boxes, but there was no room for two people.

"I'll wait outside, if you don't mind," Lettie said. "In the sunlight. This place is giving me the creeps."

Opening box after box, I found nothing but supplies: extra

light bulbs, batteries (years past their shelf date,) toilet paper, soap. No gold bars. By the time I had scooted myself the length of the hall and opened every single box, my legs had gone numb and my back ached. I had to scoot back to the doorway, unwilling to attempt standing until I could straighten all the way up.

"That's about it, Lettie. No gold." Holding onto the necks of wine bottles as I went, I wobbled out to the bunker door where Lettie stood, bathed in sunlight. "I guess it was a long shot, anyway." I turned, surveying the whole room one more time. "Now, if I wanted to hide gold bars, where would I hide them?"

Lettie stuck her head inside. "Where would you hide a tree?"

"In a forest."

"Where would you hide gold bars?"

"In a pile of gold things? Gold-colored boxes? Something that looks like gold bars? I don't see anything." My eyes found the yellowed boxes of bullets. They were about the right size and shape, but they looked nothing like gold bars. But could the bars be inside these boxes? With a sigh, I realized I would now have to open every damned one of those ammo boxes. *Wait a minute. I'm not looking for gold, I'm looking for silver. The gold bars had been silver-plated to get them through customs.* "Duh! Where would you hide silver bars?"

Lettie responded as expected, "In a pile of silver things."

My gaze swerved around the walls to the party paraphernalia on shelves near the canned goods. The silver punch bowl, the silver trays, the silver pitcher. Some now tarnished from long disuse, some still shiny. I ran to the wall and reached for the huge punch bowl. I couldn't lift it. The bowl sat on a shelf a little higher than my head, and, reaching up, I found I couldn't even budge it.

Lettie found a five-foot stepladder against one wall and dragged it over. From this higher vantage point I could peer into the bowl and see its contents. I began pulling items out and handing them down to Lettie. Two silver dippers, a silver bread basket, serving knives and forks, a silver cigarette box.

Three silver bars. Snatching one out, I almost dropped it because it was twice as heavy as I expected it to be. "God, it's heavy!" Some numbers and marks, all meaningless to me, had been impressed into the metal. The silver color seemed somewhat dulled by a light coating of tarnish. "I need a file or something." Lettie handed me one of the knives. Scraping one corner of the silver bar, I released the dazzle of pure gold hiding just beneath the surface.

Lettie's eyes were like saucers. "What do we do with these? Where do we take them?"

I thought about it for a minute. "Nowhere. Let's put this one back with the other two in the punch bowl, close the door, and call the police."

Lettie and I decided we dared not let the bunker go unwatched for even one minute. Someone could have been watching us from the house, from the tool shed, or, with binoculars, from any of several nearby peaks. She agreed to stay outside and watch the bunker's entrance while I ran inside the house to call the police. Odile greeted me, wiping her hands on her apron, and showed me the number for the LaMotte police station, written on a neatly laminated card and taped to the wall beside the phone. I started to dial, then reconsidered. If Odile heard what I was about to tell Kronenberg, it would be all over town within the hour. Praying I'd remembered to recharge my cell phone, I wrote down the number and headed for my bedroom. I found the phone still plugged into the wall, yanked it out, and took it to the porch.

Neither Kronenberg nor Seifert was there, but a female voice gave me Kronenberg's mobile number. I called it.

"Kronenberg."

"I've found the missing gold bars."

Kronenberg shouted something in German to someone nearby and began asking me for more details. As we talked, I could hear him panting. Running. "We will be there in thirty minutes. Wait for us and don't leave the bunker unattended until you see us."

Next I called Marco and found him in the hotel restaurant eating breakfast. While he was still on the phone I heard him ask for the check, rush out of the room, and through a revolving door. "Wait!" he said. "How do I get there?"

"Do you have a car?" I remembered he did have one. He had driven up from Florence. "Never mind. You'll never find it if you drive. You need to go to Dorfstrasse and locate the tunnel entrance." I explained how he could recognize it. "When you get there, push the button and I'll buzz you in. Take the elevator up and, when you leave the little hut, head west. There's a path. Follow it."

Thanks to the difficulties of maneuvering the big-wheeled police vehicle up what I had dubbed "Sheer Terror Canyon" and across the rocky terrain to the meadow, Marco arrived long before the police did. Meanwhile Erin, Patrick, and Brian had learned what was going on and had taken spectator positions on the porch.

Kronenberg already knew the entry combination to the bunker, and I told him where to find the gold bars. Marco, Lettie, and I waited outside. After the two policemen had been inside only a few minutes they stepped out. Kronenberg said, "There is no need to be careful about contaminating the scene. Too many people have been in and out in the last few weeks. Any fingerprints we find on the bars may possibly help us, but the serial numbers should tell us where they came from and when." He turned to Marco. "Captain Quattrocchi, you know more than I do about how this illegal importing works. Whom do I contact? What should I do next?"

"You need to call the Swiss Central Bureau of Interpol and you need to call the customs agents at the main airport in Geneva. The date you are interested in is five April."

"You already know these people, Captain. Would you do it for us?"

Marco beamed. I knew he was champing at the bit to take over, but he couldn't ask. It would have been presumptuous and insulting to Kronenberg. The fact that Kronenberg *had* asked, and had done so without a hint of rancor, raised my estimation of the big Swiss policeman. "I will be happy to do this, Detective Kronenberg. Is there a place where you and I can go to be more comfortable? This will take some time, and I may need you to help with translations."

I led Marco and Kronenberg to Juergen's little office behind the living room and left them alone. By this time the house was in full rubber-neck mode, everyone dying to know more. I found them in the living room pretending to read, write letters, or work Sudoku. Odile was pretending to dust the bookshelf. I told them everything I knew and, together, we waited.

An hour later, Marco and Kronenberg emerged and joined us. Kronenberg stood in front of the big glass doors exactly as he had done that morning when he'd told us both Stephanie and Gisele had been murdered. With the light behind him, his face was less clear to us than ours were to him.

We heard footsteps on the outside stairs and Juergen popped in, obviously taken aback by the large group assembled in his living room. "What is this?" he said.

Kronenberg explained.

Juergen's face reddened. "Gold bars? What are you telling me? Someone has been storing gold in my bunker? I cannot believe it. Who, besides me and a few others"—he looked at Erin—"know how to open the door? Certainly, none of us would have anything to do with such a thing!" His voice rose to a squeak and his face turned even redder. "Thank God my father can't hear this. I'm sorry he's dead, but at least he doesn't have to . . ." He stumbled to the ottoman, the only unoccupied seat in the room, and collapsed on it.

Kronenberg rocked up on his toes. "Do any of you know *anything* about these gold bars? Tell me now, because we *will* find out how they got here and we will eventually know if you have withheld any information."

"I've never even seen a gold bar," Babs said, smoothing the front of her blouse.

"They aren't gold," Lettie said. "They're silver."

"Wait a minute!" Rounding on Kronenberg with a vicious glare, Juergen said, "You said gold! Is it silver or gold?"

Kronenberg explained to Juergen, and then to all of us said, "I must ask you not to leave the premises until we sort this out. I have your passports and I will return them to you shortly but, for your own protection, I will have men watching the house, twenty-four-seven, as you Americans say."

"For our protection?" This came from Brian.

"Dotsy has told us about a glider making frequent passes over the house," Kronenberg said. "We have reason to believe a man named Anton Spektor, the owner of the glider, is involved in an international smuggling operation and if so, he probably knows the gold is in the bunker and he may have been looking for a chance to go in and get it. Now that we've taken down the crime scene tape, he's likely to make the attempt."

"This is making no sense to me," Patrick said.

Kronenberg turned to Marco and nodded.

"Interpol is working on it. Switzerland's Central Bureau, a part of Interpol, is able to contact law enforcement in South Africa and any other countries that may be affected. Detective Kronenberg and I have called and told them everything we know. They, and the Swiss customs agents in Geneva, are talking to each other right now. We believe the gold, disguised as silver, was brought here by air from South Africa and cleared customs in Geneva early this month. The customs officials will have records, and Swiss law enforcement will be able to sort this out. I am sure."

THIRTY

Awkward! I never dreamed Marco and Chet would occupy the same room at the same time, but here we were and with orders from the police to stay on the premises. Marco could have left, but he showed no inclination to do so. He and Chet shook hands and made the proper noises when I introduced them. Seeing both men together, I could only think how very handsome Marco was and how much I enjoyed his presence. Chet toddled off to his room and the young ones took to the porch. Lettie, Marco, Babs, and I sat in the living room, dissecting theories about how this could have happened.

Marco suggested one or more of the smugglers, knowing somehow that their missing gold was in the bunker, dropped by in the early morning hours. Gisele and Stephanie, hearing noises, rushed outside and encountered the smugglers in the act of breaking in.

"Wouldn't the smugglers have brought their own weapons?" I asked. "The gun they used was already in the bunker."

Babs said she didn't think two women would have dashed out like that. They'd have roused one or more of the men in the house. "And where's the connection between these guys and the bunker? You've told us about the connection between the smugglers and MWU, owned by the Merz family, but how did gold that was supposed to go to MWU in Zurich, end up in the bunker here?"

That was the smartest thing I'd ever heard Babs Toomey say.

How *did* it end up here? "Let's not forget the notes Stephanie left on the phone pad early that evening," I said.

Babs winced, probably because those notes contained the Cook County Vital Records number—the start of all her troubles.

"Her note had a reference to Johannesburg and to gold and silver. Stephanie knew what was going on. That's probably why she was killed."

Lettie, meanwhile, had been fiddling with her phone. "No wonder I missed that call . . . I have the wrong time zone. Hey, Marco, do cell phones automatically change time zones when you do?"

"Some do and some do not." He took her phone and pressed a few things. "You have the correct time."

"The gun, people, the gun!" Babs leaned forward until she nearly fell out of her chair. "These murders must have been done by someone who knew what was in the bunker."

My three companions went on for some time, playing armchair detective, but I was lost in thoughts about Lettie and her phone—and time zones.

Kronenberg barged in shortly after dinner. Once again, we gathered in the living room.

"Anton Spektor and his partners are in our custody. We caught them at the Geneva airport." Kronenberg could scarcely keep the grin off his face. "In a spectacularly stupid move, they tried to clear security in the very airport where they'd been the main topic of conversation all afternoon." He held up his palm as if reading from it. "Ah, yes. Anton Spektor. Have you enjoyed your stay in Switzerland? Anton Spektor! Guards!"

We all indulged in a refreshing laugh.

"One of his companions, by the way, was wearing a most unusual pair of shoes. Red leather shoes with strange patches sewn in odd places." Kronenberg looked at me and nodded.

Marco, sitting next to me on the sofa, gave me a hug and kissed me on the forehead.

"Go, Mom!" Patrick and Brian yelled this, or something like it, simultaneously.

"Now for the bad part," Kronenberg said, his tone suddenly serious. "Spektor and his cronies have alibis for the night of the murders. They all spent the night at a hotel in Geneva and they stayed in the bar until after two, drinking and talking so loudly the bartender says he will never forget them. Security cameras have them on tape, wobbling to their rooms at approximately the same time the murders here were taking place."

Chet spoke up. "Are you saying we're back to square one?"

"I'm saying that, unless they had allies here, in LaMotte, the smugglers did not kill Stephanie and Gisele."

"While I'm basking in the glow of your congratulations," I said, "let me ruin it by asking if you've double-checked the time on Stephanie's phone. She had a BlackBerry, and on those phones you can manually change the time."

The room went dead quiet.

"Explain, that, please," Kronenberg said, his hands flying out as if to silence the group that needed no silencing.

"We've been assuming all along that Stephanie and Gisele were killed after eleven-thirty, because that's what her phone says was the time she made her last call. The problem all along has been explaining who could have done it or how they could have done it, between eleven-thirty and the time the snow started. But what if they were killed before eleven-thirty? What if the time on Stephanie's phone was wrong?"

Inadvertently, I had just convicted Juergen Merz. We all heard him "talking" to Stephanie at eleven-thirty. They were talking about wine, supposedly, and Juergen had even mouthed *Stephanie* while he was "on the phone." If she was already dead, he was talking to no one. I hadn't heard his phone ring. He'd pulled it out of his pocket and we'd all assumed it was on vibrate, with the ring tone silenced.

All these thoughts rushed through my head and, I suppose, every head in the room, in less time than it takes to explain it.

Juergen jumped to his feet. *"Das ist verrückt! Ich will nicht hier sitzen . . ."*

Kronenberg, too, fell back on his native German, attempting to calm Juergen and make him sit down. Marco's hand found mine and our fingers laced. Seifert appeared from somewhere behind me and stepped around the sofa, his gaze darting from Juergen to Kronenberg, his hands poised to grab.

Juergen turned to me, his face purple with anger and fear, and pronounced a long, scathing condemnation of me in German. I was grateful not to know what he said.

We all sat, afraid to move, long after Kronenberg and Seifert ushered Juergen out of the room. When Kronenberg did return, he issued his orders to us in measured English. "We are going to the station in LaMotte. The guard we have already placed will remain overnight, so there's no need to be afraid. We've removed the gold from the bunker and the smugglers are in custody. But who knows if we have got them all?

"Herr Merz will be helping us with our inquiries for a while. He is not under arrest. Yet. Before we go, does anyone else have something to tell me? Anything at all that will help us wrap this up so you good people can go home?"

"Yea!" Lettie yelled, then slapped her hand over her mouth.

"He's lawyered up," Brian announced early the next day. "Odile's hotline is burning up the wires this morning."

We all sat on the porch, as if the air in the living room had become stale. A minute earlier, Babs had popped out and announced that Chet had found her a job as bookkeeper at a John

Deere dealership near where she lived. For the first time in weeks, we were turning our eyes toward home. Erin announced the arrival of a new baby giraffe at her zoo. "One hundred pounds and six feet long. Mother and baby are doing well," she said. The sun was shining and the coffee was good.

I heard Marco's voice. After spending the night at his hotel in town, he had apparently found his own way back to Chateau Merz. I fetched him a chair from a closet inside and unfolded it for him. He kissed me on the lips in full view of my sons and ex-husband. It felt comfortable.

"I have been already to the police station this morning and I have the latest news," he said. We gave him our full attention. "Juergen's lawyer had to drive in from Zurich and he did not get here until this morning. Of course, he told Juergen to say nothing until they had time to plan out their defense, but earlier in the evening, Juergen was rambling on and saying plenty. They also called in Zoltan. Someone drove up the mountain to his little hut and picked him up. When Zoltan realized how much trouble his employer was in, he forgot loyalty and started talking to save himself. Naturally, he did not want to be charged as an accessory."

Odile brought Marco a cup of coffee, which he accepted with a smile.

"Tell us!" Lettie bounced in her deck chair and tapped her little feet.

"Where should I begin?"

"At the beginning."

Marco set his coffee on the porch rail and leaned back, folding his arms across his chest. "Here is what we now believe happened. Some of the details are probably wrong but, in time, it will all work itself out. Juergen knew about the smuggled gold. He hated it. These men had ruined his family's largest business and they had picked on the Merz family because it was being run by an old man who was no longer able to play their game. They drove the company into bankruptcy and took control. That is when old man Merz called Juergen in from the Himalayas or wherever he was at the time, and told him to take over. Juergen tried, but failed. He was unable to prevent the smuggling so he decided to turn them in to the authorities. But first he needed hard evidence, so he stole three gold bars, covered with silver, after the shipment had passed through customs and hid them in the bunker here."

"Who says he was planning to turn them in?" Brian asked. "How do they know he didn't plan to keep it for himself?"

"Three gold bars are not worth enough for Juergen to put himself at risk. The Merz family is still rich, you know. But it may be that Juergen's real plan was to use the bars for blackmail. If so, he was playing a very dangerous game. I cannot imagine he would win. They would have killed him. We can only hope these things will be revealed in the trial that is sure to come.

"Sometime shortly before the murders, Stephanie discovered the gold hidden in a box in a back room of the bunker, took them out, and hid them in a new spot—inside a silver punch bowl where she thought they would be safe."

In my mind's eye I saw the boxes of supplies lined up along the wall in the bunker's back hall. I looked at Lettie and found her already looking at me, nodding.

Marco continued. "Juergen found out that Stephanie knew, and he tried to explain it to her. To get her on his side. But Stephanie was not cooperating. She threatened to hand over the gold to the police immediately, and that would have gotten him killed. Gotten both of them killed, in fact, and quickly, before either of them could testify about the smuggling operation." Marco looked at me and added, in a sort of parenthesis, "I am making some of this up, of course. I do not really know what he had in mind, but I have been in this business for a long time

261

and I know how these things usually work."

Lettie piped up. "So, that's who Stephanie was talking to when you heard her say, 'I know what you're up to.' "

"No," I said. "Stephanie was talking to a woman. I think it was Gisele, and Stephanie was accusing her of making a play for Juergen."

"That's my Stephie, all right," Chet said. "Straightening everybody out. Me, Juergen, Erin, and Gisele—we all caught the sharp side of her tongue."

Patrick shot his father a disapproving scowl.

"Juergen's plan was to kill Stephanie in order to save himself. He lured her to the bunker that evening and shot her with a gun that was always kept in the bunker. Then, to make it look like suicide, he wrapped the gun in Stephanie's hand and fired again, through the open door. He had no idea Gisele was in the meadow outside. But, as luck would have it, she was, and the second bullet hit her squarely in the chest. Juergen picked up a shell casing so it would look as if the gun had not been fully loaded to begin with and had been fired only once."

"He should have picked up the casing from the second bullet," I said.

"He probably had no reason to think it made any difference which one he picked up. He probably did not realize the clip held bullets from two different boxes."

"Now you've really got me confused!" Erin said.

Marco grinned and went on. "After he picked up the extra shell casing, he grabbed her mobile phone and set the time *forward* an hour or so, then called his own number. He had all this planned out ahead of time. He probably planned to spend the night with Gisele so as to give himself an alibi for the whole night, but bedtime rolls around and he cannot find her! He panics. He runs all over the house looking for her and, when he cannot find her, he turns on the house security cameras, knowing that one of the cameras is directed down the hall toward his own bedroom. Kronenberg told me this morning that this part had always bothered him. The security cameras were not often turned on to record. Why that night, of all nights? And was it not convenient that the camera on the top floor hall could see straight into Juergen's room and that he left his door open all night?"

"Too coincidental," Babs said.

"Gisele had a boyfriend named Milo. Milo has admitted to the police that he and Gisele fought that day. He found out that Juergen was trying to seduce her. Gisele's head must have been turned by the thought of all that money. Milo is poor. Juergen is rich. He came up here that afternoon and they fought. He called her a whore. Then he went to town, to the Black Sheep Bar and got drunk. The police put him in jail for the night to sober up."

"We still have one big problem," I said. "We have no explanation for how my jacket button wound up just outside the bunker door. I swear I didn't go up there that night, and I'm certain the button didn't go missing until later. It wasn't off my jacket, anyway. It was the extra button that came with the jacket when I bought it."

"I was getting to that. Juergen needed a backup plan. In case he forgot something or the forensic people were able to determine it was not suicide but murder, he needed someone else they could pin it on. And that person, Dotsy, was you." Marco's eyes beamed sympathy at mine. "He could have taken the button from your room any time you were not there. He probably dropped it in a likely spot outside the bunker that night, knowing that the police would find it but, unless they suspected murder, they would not think it was important. He did not know it would snow that night. The button was covered with several inches of snow and he could not find it without a good deal of searching. With the crime scene tape all around the bunker entrance that was impossible.

"This is where Zoltan comes in. The police brought him in last night and questioned him. At first he would not say anything, but when they convinced him that his employer was headed for a conviction for a double murder, he decided to save his own skin. He told them he got a call from Juergen the day he was driving to Zurich to visit his father in the hospital. The snow had mostly melted by this time, and Juergen did not think the police were watching the bunker as closely as they did at first. By this time, the police had decided Chet was the killer and Juergen did not want anything to confuse the issue. Since they thought Chet was the one, he wanted *everything* to point to Chet. So he told Zoltan to find the button and get rid of it."

I glanced at Chet. Sitting forward in his chair, his elbows on his knees, his mouth quivered in an unsuccessful effort to hide a grin.

"But before Zoltan could pick it up, Kronenberg and Seifert ran out and grabbed him. Seifert found the button later and had to crack the ice off it before they could see what it was. But they did not worry about it too much until their case against Chet fell apart."

"Thanks to Dotsy," Chet said.

"Thanks to Dotsy," Marco repeated. "Then they did think about the button and about how and when it came to be there. They decided it could only have fallen there on the night of the murder and probably as a result of a fight between Dotsy and Stephanie. Dotsy, remember, was the logical one to suspect to begin with. Stephanie had stolen her husband."

"Oh, this is just too bad!" Lettie said. "It's making me sick to my stomach."

I said, "Gisele. She was just an innocent bystander?"

"Collateral damage, they call it," Brian said, his voice heavy with irony.

I recalled that morning and how Juergen had hovered over Gisele's body. His keening whine had been sincere. He hadn't known until that moment that he had killed her, too. Had he had feelings for her, or was she simply his employee and his alibi? The full impact hit me suddenly, like a fist. *How evil! How cold!* He had meant to use Gisele for his own purpose and instead he had killed her.

THIRTY-ONE

Kronenberg came, bearing our passports. "I know this has been hard on all of you, and I apologize for the time you have had to spend away from your jobs and families. It couldn't be helped."

I had already called my school and told them not to expect me before next Monday. It gave me a couple of days to spend in Florence with Marco. Chet had arranged for Stephanie's body to be cremated, but hadn't decided whether to carry her ashes back to Virginia or put them in the Merz family's space in a Zurich cemetery. He knew he'd have to come back to Switzerland, probably a number of times, until the inheritance was worked out. Given the fact that if Juergen was found guilty of killing his sister, it might have ramifications for his own inheritance, Chet might end up filthy rich. But, as Brian pointed out, Juergen didn't kill his father. I asked if anyone knew whether the rule that says you can't benefit from a death you caused also applied in Switzerland. At lunch that day, we had bandied this about but had come to no conclusion. We all agreed that I'd never see my pink cashmere sweater again.

Kronenberg said, "If you would like me to make flight arrangements for all of you, I will be happy to do so. You've all been put through hell. I can explain this to the airlines and get you on the earliest flight possible. They always have a certain number of seats set aside for hardship cases. I assume you will all want to fly from Geneva?"

"Oh, no!" Lettie cried, taking a step backward. "Not me! I

can't leave from Geneva . . . that is, I don't *want* to leave just yet. I want to go to Florence with Marco and Dotsy. Spend a few days seeing things I didn't get to see the last time we were there."

This, of course, came as a complete surprise to Marco and me. We hadn't invited her, and frankly, we wanted to be alone.

"You can't leave from Geneva? Why not?" Babs asked.

"Because they told me not to ever come back."

"Aha! The airport fiasco! I forgot all about that." Patrick laughed.

I remembered that evening when Lettie arrived at Chateau Merz. I went to the kitchen to make coffee and when I returned, everyone had been laughing at some story Lettie had told. Something about an airport adventure. "I forgot to ask you about that, Lettie," I said. "What happened at the airport?"

Lettie blushed, looking around at Babs, Erin, and Patrick, all of whom were laughing. "I don't want to talk about it," she said, glancing quickly toward Detective Kronenberg.

"Whatever it is, Lettie, it will go no farther than this room," Kronenberg said. "I promise."

"You know how uptight everyone is these days about airport security," she said. "Don't get me wrong. We're all uptight for good reason. I have no problem with all the new security measures, and I completely agree that when you're standing in the line waiting to go through the metal detector you should not make jokes."

"Uh-oh," I whispered under my breath.

"The woman standing in front of me said that her feet were killing her because they had confiscated her gel insoles in Washington, and I . . . well, I suppose I was trying to sound like the young people do today. I hate to sound like I'm behind the times, you know. So I said, 'bummer!' The security guards were French, I think."

"And?"

"They thought I said 'Bomber' and they evacuated the whole terminal!"

ABOUT THE AUTHOR

Maria Hudgins, a former high school science teacher, lives in Hampton, Virginia, with her two Bichons, Holly and Hamilton. Her previous novels in the Dotsy Lamb Travel Mystery series are: *Death of an Obnoxious Tourist, Death of a Lovable Geek,* and *Death on the Aegean Queen.*